Nick Malone wasn't happy.

He didn't know anything about this woman to whom his child had suddenly become so attached.

Yet he, too, despite himself, was drawn to Cari Hallen.

There was a quiet innocence about little Danny's new nurse. A deep compassion. But it was the sadness in her blue eyes that tugged at Nick.

His gaze moved to Cari's white uniform, which did little to hide the outline of her full breasts or the fact that her legs were long and shapely.

Nick's body began to react, and he abruptly tore his gaze away. Damn! He didn't need this!

His sole concern was that his son could get hurt.

Nick Malone might have millions.

But he couldn't afford for his son to get hurt. No way...

Dear Reader,

It's February and so we couldn't resist giving you a story with a tie-in to Valentine's Day; look for Natalie Bishop's *Valentine's Child*. It's a secret baby story with a difference!

Still on the subject of babies, this month our THAT'S MY BABY! title is by relative newcomer Martha Hix. She gives us a heroine who 'inherits' her baby sister and a smooth lawyer who'll look after both of them. Then, the other child orientated novel this month is a real tearjerker; the young son of the hero has had a heart transplant and he's already been abandoned by his mother so his dad's *very* protective...too protective...?

Substitute Bride by Trisha Alexander is a classic story of twins and substitution, but is the hero marrying the right or the wrong twin? Time will tell. Laurie Paige gives us a dramatic, romantic tale of passion, love and blackmail in *The Ready-Made Family*, and finally there's a story of a woman who's always known she loves Travis McCallister, but who's always had her advances rebuffed...until now.

Enjoy them all and come back to us next month for more great books.

The Editors

Nothing Short
of a Miracle

PATRICIA THAYER

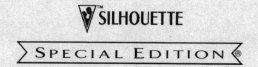

SILHOUETTE

SPECIAL EDITION ®

Silhouette, Silhouette Special Edition and Colophon are registered trademarks of Harlequin Books S.A., used under licence.

*First published in Great Britain 1998
Silhouette Books, Eton House, 18-24 Paradise Road,
Richmond, Surrey TW9 1SR*

© Patricia Wright 1997

ISBN 0 373 24116 X

23-9802

*Printed and bound in Great Britain
by Mackays of Chatham PLC, Chatham*

Dedication:

My thanks to Tara Gavin and Karen Taylor Richman for having
faith in me to tell this story. And for agreeing it's a story that
needed to be told. Also to all the little Angels out there who will
never know what hope and joy they bring to others.

Acknowledgement:

To Sharon Frizsche, Nurse Co-ordinator of Cardiac Transplant,
Lorna Linda University Medical Centre, thank you for answering
all my questions. And to Susanne Fitzpatrick for making me realize
the importance of the Organ Donor Programme. Any mistakes in
this story are mine, not theirs.

PATRICIA THAYER

was born and raised in Indiana and now resides in
Southern California. She's been happily married for the
past twenty-five years and has three sons, and she adores
the attention she gets from being the only female in the
house. Besides writing, she enjoys research, especially
when it means she has to travel! Pat also loves long walks,
hand holding and quiet talks with her best friend, her
husband, Steve.

Prologue

We need a miracle.

The doctor's words echoed in Nicholas Malone's head as he paced the small area outside his two-year-old son's room in the cardiac care unit. Neither the Malone millions nor all the heart specialists in the world would prevent Danny's life from slowly slipping away.

"C'mon, Nick. Sit down," Larry Keaton said from his seat against the wall. "You've been at this all night."

"Dammit! I can't." Emotions clogged Nick's throat as he turned to his business associate and friend since college. "My son is dying...."

Larry got up and walked toward Nick. "You don't know that. There's still a chance that they'll find a donor."

"It's been four months already." He pushed past his friend and walked over to the large windows.

Larry followed. "But Danny's on the top of the list now. As soon as they find someone compatible—"

Nick spun around. "We're nearly out of time, Larry. Do

you know what it's like every time I go into my son's room? You should see that look he gives me." He clenched his fists, wanting his anger to hide his fears. "I feel so damn helpless."

Larry patted his back. "I know, pal. I know."

Nick turned away and stared out the window. It was all a blur. He hadn't been able to focus on much of anything since the doctors announced Danny's already defective heart had worsened. In layman's terms, without a new heart his son would die.

It hadn't seemed that long since Nick had gone through this with his own father. Daniel Thorton Malone had died only two years ago, just before he was able to see his first grandchild. But his heart condition had never interfered with his life-style. In fact, under medication and a cardiologist's care, Thor Malone had been able to function pretty normally for most of his sixty-five years.

"You think I should call Tory?" Larry asked.

Nick glared over his shoulder. Just the mention of his ex-wife's name made him livid. "The last thing Danny needs now is a mother who never wanted an imperfect child. Besides, you already contacted her when he was transferred up here three weeks ago."

Larry looked awkward. "Well, it's different now."

"And how's that? Tory's suddenly developed maternal feelings?"

"C'mon, Nick. I know she's never been perfect mother material, but she's torn up about what's happening to Danny."

"Was that why she took off for Europe six months ago without so much as a goodbye to her son?"

"She's home now."

"And that's where she can stay. I don't want her here. I'm the one who's raised Danny. I've been the one by his bedside during all his hospital stays. And, God forbid—" he nearly choked on the words "—if the worst happens,

I'll know I've done everything I could for my son. That includes getting down on my knees and praying for a miracle.''

The discussion ended when the doctor came rushing into the waiting area and announced with a big smile, ''We've found a heart....''

Chapter One

Cari Hallen stared at the calendar on the receptionist's desk. She clutched her hands against her stomach as the familiar ache brought tears to her eyes. Would the twenty-fifth of every month always cause her such pain? Such bad memories? Would a time come when she could make it through any day without the cold emptiness and guilt eating her alive?

"Ms. Hallen...Ms. Hallen?"

Cari glanced at the secretary. "Yes."

The young woman smiled. "Mrs. Linley will see you now."

Cari nodded, wondering for the hundredth time if this was an insane idea. She already had a job, a very rewarding one at a reputable hospital outside Seattle. But she had known for a long time that she couldn't stay, not with all the...memories.

Cari managed to curb her fears and followed the secretary into the personnel office. Behind the desk sat a woman in her mid-fifties. Her hair was a gray and brunette mix, cut short in a no-nonsense style. She had rich blue eyes with tiny lines etched deep in the skin surrounding them, a sure sign that she smiled a lot.

The tall, willowy woman stood and extended a hand. "Hello, Mrs. Hallen." There came the expected grin. "I'm Bess Linley."

Fighting the impulse to wipe the moisture from her palm, Cari exchanged a handshake. "Hello."

"Please, have a seat," the interviewer said as she slipped on her glasses and began to go over the file. Cari took a chair in front of the desk, anxiously perching on the edge of the seat.

"I talked to Marge Brunner this morning," Bess said, looking up. "She gave you a glowing report. Said you were one of the best nurse practitioners at St. Margaret's." The woman leaned back in her chair. "But I'm a little curious as to why, after having been employed at the hospital for so long, you want to leave."

Cari's heart skipped a beat. She was under the impression her friend and supervisor had helped pave her way. "Didn't Marge explain?"

"She did, some. But if you don't mind, I'd like to hear it from you."

Cari drew a deep breath and released it, yet it didn't calm her speeding pulse. "It has nothing to do with the hospital. I've worked at St. Margaret's since graduating from nursing school. I love it and I have friends there." She swallowed, trying to relieve the tightness in her throat. "A little over two years ago, my husband and daughter were killed in an auto accident. I was on duty in the emergency room when they were brought in." The tears welled in her eyes, but they couldn't blur the image of Tim's and Angel's limp bodies being wheeled in on the gurneys.

"I'm sorry," Bess Lindley murmured.

Cari saw the honest compassion on the other woman's face and nodded. "Thank you. Marge and the grief support group she runs have helped me a lot, but I feel the best thing to do is to try and get on with my life someplace else. When I heard about your new cardiac wing, it sounded like a good idea."

As the director looked down at the file once again, Cari held her breath, uncertain if she was hoping to get the job or to get turned down.

"Are you sure Santa Cruz, California, is the place you want to be? What about the rest of your family?"

Cari shook her head. "I have no one else."

Bess sat in her chair and studied Cari. "So you want to find a place with no memories. A place to start over."

"Yes."

The older woman leaned forward in her chair. "Right now all we have available is a part-time position, but in another month or so the cardiac unit will be completely operational and we'll need to fully staff it." She smiled. "How would you feel about working in our new cardiac pediatrics ward?"

"Are you offering me a job?"

Bess nodded. "According to Marge you have a great rapport with kids. So how about it?"

"Oh my." Insecurity hit. Did she really want this? Did she want to be a stranger in a new place…a new job? But it was the only way. Wasn't it? "I'll have to give notice at St. M's and to my landlord. I could be here, say, in… three weeks."

"Perfect."

"Thank you, Mrs. Linley."

"Since we'll be working together, why don't you call me Bess? We're like family here at Riverhaven." She stood. "Cari, we also take care of our own, so if you ever need to talk, I'm always here. We may be a smaller hospital than you're used to, but we have a wonderful support-group system. Maybe after you get settled, I can give you some information.''

"Thank you. I'd like that.'' Leaving the security of Marge and her support group had been Cari's hardest decision.

"I think you'll like working here, too. In fact,'' Bess said, checking her watch, "if you have time, I'll show you the new wing.'' She came around the desk and opened her door. "I should be there anyway for the Malone dedication.''

"Dedication?'' Cari followed Bess out the door, still somewhat apprehensive about the decision she'd just made.

"The Malone family has been very generous in helping to raise money for the new cardiac wing. It's named after Daniel Malone, who died of heart disease almost five years ago. Nicholas Malone and his son, Danny, will be doing the dedication. In about ten minutes to be exact. We'll have to hurry.''

They continued down the long corridor. Although Bess was older, she moved at a fast pace. Cari had no trouble keeping up. Not after doing a job where she had to be quick on her feet. She'd spent years chasing down crash carts when every wasted second could cost a life.

"You should see little Danny, he's a real cutie.'' They stepped into the elevator and Bess pushed the button for the fourth floor. "Of course his daddy, Nick Malone, isn't bad, either.''

Cari wasn't listening to Bess's description of the hospital's handsome benefactor. Men hadn't interested her much lately. Not that she was still actively mourning Tim's death, but she'd never been the type of woman who thought much about sex. Even her marriage to Tim had resembled more of a deeply felt friendship than the he-can't-keep-his-hands-off-me stuff that her fellow nurses always talked about. And since she'd worked the night shift at the hospital and Tim worked days, there hadn't been a whole lot of time to think about lovemaking. It wasn't a top priority, especially with a baby to take care of. Cari smiled sadly to herself as her thoughts turned to her sweet baby girl. Her little Angel.

The elevator bell chimed and Cari returned to reality as the doors opened to a crowd of people. She stepped out, but didn't get far. There were several newspeople and photographers blocking the way. Bess managed to push through and Cari followed closely behind so as not to get lost in the chaos.

Whoever this Mr. Malone was, he sure drew a lot of attention, Cari thought as they found an open area. There was a row of chairs against the wall, all empty except for two. A little boy, about four, sat quietly at the end of the row. He was dressed in a navy suit and a white shirt with a burgundy-colored tie. He had a round face and his dark hair was perfectly groomed along with the rest of him. He looked more like a miniature adult than a child.

Next to him was a woman in her early fifties. She was dressed in a plain charcoal suit and prim white blouse. Her brown-and-gray-streaked hair was pulled back in a tight bun, exposing an oval face, pale and contorted with pain.

Bess walked up to the pair. "Hello, Danny." She smiled and the boy nodded shyly. She turned to the woman with him. "Mrs. Foster, are you feeling all right?"

The woman only shook her head, then groaned.

Bess sat down in the chair next to her. "Do you want me to get Mr. Malone?"

"No," Mrs. Foster protested weakly as she clutched her stomach. "He has to do the ceremony."

Bess glanced around. "You look awful. Let me take you to see Dr. Mitchell. His office is just down the hall."

Mrs. Foster shook her head. "The boy. I can't leave Danny."

"You can't risk him catching what you may have, either. Cari will watch Danny. She's a nurse." Bess turned to Cari. "Would you mind?"

"Of course not," Cari agreed. "I'll sit with Danny until his dad comes."

Bess mouthed her thanks as she helped Mrs. Foster up. The stricken woman paused and gave careful instructions to the boy not to move until his father came back. Then Bess helped her to her feet and together they slowly walked off.

Cari smiled as she took one of the empty chairs a few seats from Danny, wondering if he would be frightened of her. "This sure is a big party."

The child looked up at her, his chocolate brown eyes large. "It's not a party. It's a ded-d-cation."

Cari felt a tightness in her chest. Angie would be about the same age if... She pushed away the memories. "That sure is a big word. Do you know what that means?"

The boy's head bobbed up and down. "The hospital is going to thank my dad for giving them money and a picture of my grandpa to hang on the wall."

So this darling child belonged to the generous Nicholas Malone. "Well, what your daddy did is a very nice thing."

The boy studied his shiny dress shoes for a moment, then raised his head and examined Cari closely. "Do you have a little boy?"

Cari froze at the child's innocent question, her words lodged in her throat. "No, but I had a little girl. She would be four years old—"

"I'm four," he said, excitement lighting up his eyes. "Is she here?"

Cari felt her pulse race. How could she explain to a boy Danny's age that her daughter was dead? That was a terrible thing to have to tell a child. The only other choice was to lie, and she knew she couldn't do that. She'd only have to answer more painful questions. Cari shut her eyes momentarily and prayed for guidance. "No, she's not here."

"Is she home with her daddy?"

Cari shook her head, feeling tears sting her eyes and wanting to scream at the same time. After all this time it was hard for her to admit it even to herself. "No..." She swallowed and tried again. "My Angel got hurt in an accident...and she and her daddy live in heaven now."

"Oh." That seemed to be the end of the child's questions, then suddenly he turned toward her in the chair. "Are you still sad?"

Cari nodded. "Sometimes."

They were silent for a while as more people walked past them, trying to get closer to the podium. Then the boy spoke once again. "My grandpa went to heaven a long time ago. It was before I was born. My dad named me after him. Grandma always says I look like him." He rolled his eyes. "She calls me Daniel."

"Well, you're very handsome, Daniel."

He wrinkled his nose at her as if he'd heard that too many times. Bess had been right—this little guy was adorable.

"Everybody else calls me Danny."

"Then I'll call you Danny. I'm Cari and I'm a nurse."

He studied her closely. "You're pretty, Cari. I'm glad you don't work for the newspaper. 'Cause I'm not supposed to talk to you if you're a 'porter."

Cari bit down on her lower lip to keep from smiling. "No, I'm not a reporter. I'll be working in the new wing your daddy helped build."

"Wow! I come here to see Dr. Matt. He's the best doctor in the whole world. Will you be here when I come in for my 'pointment?"

She had to meet this wonderful Dr. Matt. "Maybe."

The boy started to speak again when someone called his name. They both turned around to find a tall, intense, good-looking man walking toward them. Cari knew right away it was Nicholas Malone. He had broad shoulders that filled out his navy pinstripe suit, which obviously had been tailored just for him. His black wavy hair was cut and styled perfectly, similar to his son's. He moved with graceful but determined steps, as if he were on a mission. An *urgent* mission.

He knelt down in front of Danny, concern etched on his face. "Where's Mrs. Foster?"

"She went to see the doctor with Bess 'cause she's sick. She told me to sit here with Cari and be good. I was, Dad. I was only talking to Cari."

As Nick Malone turned to her, Cari got a good look at his cool gray eyes. His gaze locked with hers and held, wary and full of mistrust. She found herself having trouble breathing under his piercing scrutiny but was unable to break the powerful connection. There was something about the man that demanded her attention. And he sure got it.

"I gave strict orders to the media that my son is off limits. You'll have to attend the press conference to get any information."

Cari was taken aback by the man's suspicious tone. "I'm not a reporter, Mr. Malone. I'm a nurse." She got some small satisfaction as the man's expression grew confused.

"Yeah, Dad," Danny added. "It's neat. Cari's going to work here with Dr. Matt."

Before Cari could have the pleasure of hearing Mr. Malone's apology, he was approached and summoned to the podium.

"C'mon, Danny, it's time," he said to his son, his piercing gray eyes still riveted on Cari's.

Obediently, Danny slid off the chair and took his dad's hand. As father and son turned and walked away, the boy looked over his shoulder and grinned at her. Cari was waving when Bess came up beside her.

"Did you have any trouble with Danny?"

"No, he's a great kid."

"Did Nick Malone say anything? I bet he wasn't happy to find his son with a stranger."

Cari studied the man on the podium. "No, he wasn't."

"I should have warned you, they're a pretty private family. We had a rough time just convincing Mr. Malone to attend the dedication today. Of course, with all the publicity he's had in the past, he has good reason to be cautious."

"Then maybe the Malones should have made an anonymous donation."

"Probably wouldn't have done them any good. They're well-known in this area for their generosity, and most people would have figured it out, with Daniel Malone dying of a heart attack, and then all the hoopla about little Danny's condition."

"His condition?"

Bess studied her for a moment. "I guess there's no reason not to tell you since you'll be working in the cardiac wing. Danny had a heart transplant."

Nick Malone's gaze searched the restless crowd. Most of the room was filled with media people and he couldn't care less about their impatience. Two years of trying to protect his son from their insensitivity and cruelty had taught him not to trust the lot of them. No matter how attractive they were. His thoughts returned to the angelic-looking blonde who had managed to get close to Danny. He smiled wryly. He'd just bet she was a nurse.

Nick glanced down at his son seated close to his side. Only four years old, he'd been through so much in his short, fragile life: his health problems, his mother's desertion, the transplant operation. Even now, his healthy heart could be rejected by his small body at any time.

No! He wouldn't allow himself to think like that. Danny

had been in good health for the past year, and as long as they followed Matt Landers's instructions, everything would be fine, and Danny would lead a normal life. But nothing the renowned cardiologist said could stop a father's nightmares.

Harry Douglas, the hospital administrator, approached. "I think we should get started, Mr. Malone."

Nick nodded. "Good, I'd like to get my son home as soon as possible."

The older, white-haired man stepped to the microphone and introduced the guests. Applause erupted when Nick made his way to the microphone.

"I want to thank you all for coming. This is a wonderful day for the Malone family," he said. "To see our dream becoming a reality. There have been remarkable advances in heart research in the past decade. At Riverhaven we're striving to become one of the top pediatric cardiology units in the country. My family discovered firsthand how important the best medical care can be when my own son became sick." Nick found himself swallowing hard against his emotions. "With this new cardiac wing we want to give new hope to heart patients."

A reporter stood. "How is your son going to benefit from the wing? He's already received a heart transplant."

Nick stiffened. "My family didn't donate this wing just to help my son but to help a lot of children whose lives might be cut short because of heart problems. We worked hard to acquire the best medical staff possible."

A man jumped up in the crowd and shouted out, "Are you going to slaughter innocent animals for the sake of research?"

"No" was all Nick said, and no one questioned him further about it.

This time a female reporter called out, "Is it true that only the wealthy will be able to afford the services here at Riverhaven?"

Nick was angry now. "No one will be turned away." He motioned for Danny to come to the podium and lifted him in his arms. "You can't put a price on a life, especially a child's. We'll be setting up a fund to help those who can't afford it." He turned to his son and smiled. "Danny and I will expect a nice donation from all of you before you leave."

Another reporter started to speak, but Harry Douglas stopped him. "That's enough questions for now. We're here to honor the memory of Daniel Thorton Malone. And it gives me great pleasure to name the new wing the Malone Cardiac Wing." He walked to the wall and pulled away the sheet that covered the brass plaque. The crowd applauded politely and cameras flashed as Nick and Danny stood for pictures. Then just as quickly the reporters began to file out of the room to call their newspapers.

Cari and Bess stood out of the way as people rushed to the elevators. "That went pretty well," Bess began. "I expected more protest from the animal rights activists."

"Have they been causing problems?"

Bess shrugged. "When they heard about the research department, they picketed for a while during construction, but nothing more."

Cari glanced up as Danny and his father made their way across the room. She tensed. She didn't want a confrontation.

"Oh, look, Mr. Malone is coming this way. I'll introduce you."

Before Cari could stop her, Bess was leading her toward the Malone family. Although Nicholas Malone was smiling, she had no doubt that the last thing he wanted to do was meet the staff.

"Mr. Malone, I know you've already met Cari Hallen. She's going to be one of the nurses working in the wing."

Cari felt a warm sensation as he took her hand. His touch also seemed to affect her breathing. "Nice meeting you, Mr. Malone,'' she said, her voice a little husky. "That was a very eloquent speech.''

"Thank you, Ms. Hallen.'' His eyes continued to hold hers in an appraising stare. "I only spoke the truth.''

"See, Dad, I told you she was a nurse,'' Danny said. "I'm going to see Cari when I come in for my 'pointment with Dr. Matt.''

"We'll talk about it later, son. Right now we have to get Mrs. Foster home. She isn't feeling well. And we can tell Grandma how everything went.''

"Can we stop by McDonald's like you promised?''

His father frowned. "The drive-through window.''

Nick Malone turned back to Cari with a polite smile. She wondered if he had any idea the power that smile carried. "It was nice meeting you, Ms. Hallen.''

"Nice to meet you, too.''

Danny tugged on her hand. "Will you be here when I come to see the doctor?''

She knelt down beside him. "I'm not sure if I'll be working when you come in. But ask for me.''

That seemed to satisfy the younger Malone. She glanced at his father as she stood up. He didn't look happy.

Father and son walked to the elevator and pushed the button. It wasn't long before the doors opened and they stepped inside. Cari watched until they were gone. What had she done to make Nick Malone so distrustful of her?

"Don't take it personally,'' Bess said.

"What?''

"Nick Malone has a right to be suspicious. His family is wealthy, and since his son's illness, along with all the publicity…'' Bess shook her head. "Then his wife walked out on the both of them. But the man took over everything, from the family business to caring for his widowed mother, and then Danny nearly died.'' She glanced down at Cari. "It was a miracle that they found a donor in time.''

A donor. Cari felt as if the walls were closing in on her.

Sound roared in her ears and sweat slicked her palms. She closed her eyes on a wave of nausea. Why here? Why now? Her emotions were nearly shredded as it was. Why did the hellish memories have to come flooding back? Her small daughter hooked up to life-support. A machine forcing air into her tiny lungs as an IV fed nourishment through her body. She wanted to cover her ears as the doctor's words echoed through her head. The same words she'd heard too many times about her other patients. *Sorry, there's nothing more we can do.*

Cari took a steadying breath and opened her eyes. "I hope the Malones appreciate their miracle," she murmured.

"Oh, gosh, Cari. I'm sorry, I forgot. Your husband and daughter."

Cari drew a breath and swallowed the horrible ache in her throat. The dull, never-ending ache in her heart wouldn't go away. "No, I'm sorry. I'm not like this all the time."

Bess's arm went around Cari's shoulders. "You needn't explain. Losing your family is something you never get over. And the loss of a child is especially traumatic."

As a trained medical nurse, Cari knew that the doctors had done everything they could for both her husband and daughter, but it still didn't take away the pain...or the loneliness...or the yearning in her gut every time she saw a small child. "I guess seeing little Danny..." She tried to smile.

"I warned you he was a charmer."

Cari nodded. Seeing someone as healthy as Danny also made her realize that she had made the right decision two years ago to let them harvest her daughter's organs. And she'd made the right decision to relocate to northern California.

But something besides the beautiful scenery had drawn her here.

Fate? Maybe. Cari remembered the late hour when she had said her last goodbye to Angel. She should have gone home after they wheeled her daughter into surgery, but instead she'd hung around...

And discovered that Angel's tiny heart was being flown to San Francisco.

Chapter Two

Cari rushed through the doors of Riverhaven Hospital and headed straight for the elevators. She was late. Her first day on the job and she didn't make it on time. She jabbed her thumb against the button several times, then began to pace in front of the doors, willing them to open.

Damn that traffic jam. She glanced at her watch. She was supposed to have reported to the pediatric nurses' station thirty minutes ago. Cari drew a long breath and released it slowly. It seemed as if she had been racing through the past few weeks. Between working out her two weeks' notice at St. M.'s, surviving her fellow co-workers' goodbyes and packing everything that the moving van hadn't taken into her small car for the drive to Santa Cruz, she hadn't had a moment's rest.

Tired from her two-day trip, she'd gone in search of a place to live, only to find that an apartment in the quaint seaside town was way out of her price range. She'd ended up renting a small economical apartment in the agricultural community of Watsonville. It was all she needed for herself. But from now on, she'd have to allow herself more time for the twenty-mile drive to work.

When the bell chimed, Cari stepped into the elevator and punched the button for the fourth floor, praying she had an understanding supervisor.

Two days later, Danny Malone sat perched on the examination table in the doctor's office, his legs swinging. "Dr. Matt, am I better enough so I don't have to take my medicine anymore?"

Dr. Matthew Landers shared a glance with Nick Malone as he put his hand on the boy's shoulder. "We talked about this before, Danny," Matt said. "You will always have to take your medicine. It keeps your heart healthy."

"But my heart is working good."

Matt smiled. "Yeah, it is working good. And that's because you take your medicine."

Danny wrinkled his nose, as if he were thinking over the doctor's comment. Nick knew his son was doing just that. More and more in the past few months, Danny had been questioning every medical procedure. And the four-year-old wasn't easily pacified.

"Okay, I'll take my medicine, but do they have to stick that big needle in my leg?"

A sudden pain pierced Nick's heart. He knew the yearly biopsy had been painful for Danny. If he could take the test for him, he wouldn't hesitate. "Yes, son, they have to do that, too."

"Look at it this way, Danny," Dr. Landers said. "After it's all over, your dad will buy you anything you want. And what about all the attention you get from the pretty nurses? Wish I got half the notice that you do."

The boy's eyes lit up. "Can Cari be there for my test?"

Matt frowned. "Who's Cari?"

"She's a nurse," Danny informed him. "And she said she'd be working here when we were at the ded-d-cation."

Nick thought his son had forgotten all about the woman who had sat with him the day Mrs. Foster had gotten sick. Nick's own thoughts had drifted back more than once to the pretty blonde.

Dr. Landers picked up the phone. "If there's a Cari here, we'll find her," he told Danny. Then he spoke into the receiver. "Yes, is there a nurse on staff by the name of Cari? I don't know her last name." He listened intently. "There is? If she's not busy, do you think you could send her to my office? There's a patient who'd like to see her." He hung up the phone. "Well, you lucked out, kid. Cari Hallen is working today."

Cari had just come out of the supply room when Ruth, the nurse at the desk, called to her. "You've been summoned to Dr. Landers's office. You lucky girl. He's the most eligible bachelor in the hospital."

Cari frowned. Why would he want to see her? "Where's his office?"

Ruth pointed her in the direction and gave her a push. "Don't look like you're being sent off to a firing squad. He probably just wants to welcome you to the staff, but you can always hope for more." The young nurse wiggled her eyebrows.

Cari was smiling as she walked down the hall. She was used to nurses teasing about doctors. It happened in all hospitals, and she guessed Riverhaven wasn't any different. She automatically checked the front of her white uniform and adjusted her light blue cardigan. Years of working in her profession had taught her that periodic inspections were a necessity.

After finding the door with the correct nameplate, she walked into the waiting room and introduced herself to the cardio-thoratic surgeon's receptionist, who directed her down the hall to the second examination room. Cari knocked on the door and waited for a reply. When a baritone voice called out, she opened the door and found Danny Malone sitting on the table. When he spotted her, he climbed down and rushed to greet her.

"Cari!" He flung his arms around her.

"Hi, Danny." She was a little surprised by his enthusiastic greeting. "How are you?"

"I'm fine." He glanced up at his dad. "See, I told you she'd be here."

"Yes, you did." Nick turned toward her, his gray eyes once again wary. "Hello, Ms. Hallen."

She nodded and swallowed back her nervousness. "Mr. Malone. How is Mrs. Foster?"

"She's better. Thank you for asking."

Dr. Landers stepped forward. "Since no one is willing to introduce me, I guess I'll have to do it myself." He gave Cari a dynamite smile that was both charming and sexy. "Cari, I'm Matt Landers. Welcome to Riverhaven." He shook her hand. "I hope you'll like it here."

She returned his smile. "Thank you, Doctor. I've only been working a few days, but so far it's been great."

"Well, you're all Danny's talked about since he walked in here." The blond, brown-eyed doctor folded his arms across his chest and studied her. Cari felt a little self-conscious, but the handsome doctor's attention wasn't what disconcerted her. It was Nick Malone's cool gaze that was making her nervous.

Nick watched as his son asked dozens of questions of his new friend, noting the way Cari listened, her long, slender hands gently stroking Danny's shoulders. Ms. Hallen had a competent, interested demeanor that would be appealing to all ages.

In a way, Nick was jealous of the easy rapport the four-year-old had with the woman whose blue eyes shimmered like sapphires. But his son hadn't learned to be suspicious.

Danny had been protected from the outside world. Nick had made sure of that.

"Next week Dr. Matt is going to put a big needle in my leg and it hurts." Danny's eyes filled with tears.

Cari ran her thumb along Danny's soft cheek, her heart crying out to this brave little boy. "Oh, honey, sometimes these things can't be helped. They need to be done to keep you healthy. But I'm sure Dr. Landers will be as careful as he can not to hurt you too much."

"I won't be so scared if you're there. Could you be?" he pleaded.

"Oh, Danny...I don't know." Cari glanced up at the doctor, hoping for some guidance. "Maybe Dr. Matt has other nurses in mind. Ones who know the way he does things. I'm pretty new here at my job."

"Have you assisted on heart biopsies before?" Matt asked.

"Yes, with Dr. Clifton Bailey at St. Margaret's, near Seattle."

He pursed his lips. "I've heard of Bailey. He's a good man. I'd like to have you assist me on Danny's big day."

"Of course, Doctor. I'd be happy to."

Well, Nick wasn't happy. He didn't know anything about this woman to whom his child had suddenly become so attached. And since Danny had had so little contact with his own mother, Nick knew that any female attention would be eagerly welcomed by the boy. And despite himself, he, too, was drawn to her. There was a quiet innocence about her, but it was the sadness in her deep blue eyes that tugged at him.

His eyes moved to her nurse's uniform, which did little to hide the outline of her full breasts or the fact that her legs were long and slender. His body began to react and he tore his gaze away with a jerk. Damn! He didn't need this. His main concern was that his son might get hurt, and he couldn't allow that.

"It's time we go, son. Dr. Matt has other patients to see."

Danny nodded and looked up at the doctor. "Do all the kids you take care of have new hearts like me?"

"No, just my special ones." Matt bent down and tickled the boy. "That's why I'll be seeing you next week. Okay?"

Danny's look grew serious as he glanced at Cari. "Cari, please be here."

Cari didn't know what to say to the child. How could she promise him? She didn't even know her shift schedule. "I'll try—"

"We'll work it out, Danny," the doctor interrupted. "You just go home and try not to worry." The doctor leaned down and whispered, "And think about the nice surprise you're going to get from your dad."

"Thanks a lot," Nick said as he moved across the room and took his son's hand. "C'mon, Danny, let's get out of here before the doctor charges us extra for staying so long."

The boy giggled. "Bye, Dr. Matt. Bye, Cari."

"Bye, Danny," Cari said as the Malones walked out the door. Nick glanced over his shoulder. His eyes met hers, sending a jolt through her, letting her know that he found her attractive but sure as hell didn't like it. He turned away and followed his son out the door.

Cari released a breath, realizing only now that she had been holding it. Nick Malone had her more than just a little confused.

"I'll go ahead and ask your supervisor to schedule you that day," Matt Landers said, drawing her back to the present. "Danny's been a pretty brave little boy since his transplant two years ago, but biopsies can be scary, as you know. Your presence might make it easier for him."

Cari agreed the biopsy was a tough procedure even for

adults, but she couldn't dismiss the look on the boy's father's face. "I don't think Mr. Malone feels the same way."

"Nick Malone is just protective of his son, which is not uncommon with donor-recipient parents."

The doctor picked up the file and handed it to her. "Right now, my concern is for the patient. And you're good for Danny." He smiled. "I have a feeling you're very good with all kids, Ms. Hallen."

"It's Mrs. Hallen." She touched her bare ring finger.

He tossed her a teasing smile. "Darn. All the good ones are always taken."

Cari glanced away as she toyed with her ringless finger. The decision to remove it had come with her move to Santa Cruz. "I'm widowed. My husband and daughter died two years ago in a car accident."

"Oh, jeez, Cari. I'm sorry."

This had been the hardest part about changing jobs. People were curious, and she had to answer some painful questions.

"You know Danny more or less lost his mother when he was only a baby."

"She died?"

Matt Landers shook his head. "No, but she physically removed herself from his life about three years ago. The Malones have been divorced for two years, and Nick was awarded full custody of his son." He pointed to the file she held. "I'd like you to familiarize yourself with Danny's case."

"Of course, Doctor."

"If you don't need to get back to the floor, you can stay here and read the file, then just leave it with my receptionist."

Cari nodded. "I have time."

"Good. We'll discuss the procedure in a few days," he said, then was out the door.

Cari sat down at the desk and opened the thick manila folder.

It started with Daniel Nicholas Malone's birth on February 4. He was only a few hours old when the doctor's discovered he'd inherited the congenital heart defect, dilated cardiomyopathy.

The file showed page after page of procedures and medications, mapping out a trial and error period that had to have been pure agony for the Malone family. Especially little Danny. But nothing seemed to work. By his first birthday his condition had worsened, and there were more complications.

Cari turned the page. Several other specialists had been brought in for evaluations. She recognized the names of some of the most famous cardiologists in the country. One thing they all had in common was their diagnoses.

Danny Malone would not survive to his third birthday without a new heart.

He needed a donor.

Cari's hands trembled as she turned another page to find Danny's numerous hospital stays. Tears filled her eyes as she imagined how frightening it must have been for the toddler. Then thoughts turned to Danny's father. She knew how devastating it was to watch your child slipping away, to know there was nothing you could do about it. She had lived through the same hell...over and over again.

For weeks, little Danny Malone had lain in the San Francisco hospital until a compatible donor was finally located. Cari quickly scanned all the medical jargon until she found the date Danny had received his new heart. It glared at her as if it were surrounded by a flashing neon sign.

June 26.

Cari gasped as her own pulse pounded in her ears. Oh, God! Could it be...?

Her numb fingers trembled as she searched the pages

for Danny's blood type. *O positive*. The file dropped from her hands.

Angel and Danny shared the same blood type.

Cari jumped up. She wanted to scream as panic seized her; her stomach suddenly somersaulted. She glanced at the door and wanted to run as far away as she could get, but she couldn't. She had to finish her shift.

Drawing a deep breath, she paced the small room, trying desperately to calm herself. She had to do something. What? Think, she ordered herself, clutching the file to her chest, trying not to let unrealistic hope take hold.

Marge and her bereavement group had warned her it wasn't good to bottle up her emotions. The healing wasn't going to start until Cari faced her feelings. Instead, Cari had closed that part of her life as if it were a chapter in a book and buried herself in her work. She'd decided that she wasn't meant to have a family.

And it had been the one thing Cari had wanted her entire life. She had been orphaned at the age of eight, when her mother died of a rare blood disease. She had no idea where her father had gone, not that she even remembered the man ever being around. Since there were no other relatives to claim her, she was placed in the foster care program. Though she was eligible for adoption, no family seemed to want a skinny eight-year-old girl who was all legs. So she'd spent the next ten years moving from foster home to foster home. Some were better than others, but Cari had concentrated on simple survival. When she was eighteen she'd gotten a job and found a place to live. At night she started college, taking courses that led toward a nursing degree. Then she meet Tim Hallen. Within a month, he had told her he loved her and proposed marriage.

Cari's feelings were genuine for the generous man who'd given her all the love she could possibly want and the only home she had ever known. They had been happy, and then they were blessed with a baby, a wonderful healthy girl. The moment Tim held his tiny daughter in his arms, Angela Louise Hallen was christened with the nickname "little Angel." Life couldn't get any better.

Then, barely two years later, Cari's life was shattered. She could still picture her husband and little girl's limp bodies being wheeled into the emergency room. A capable team of doctors worked fervently on Tim, but it was in vain. He was already gone. Angel held on for a few days until the doctors announced there was nothing more they could do for her.

Cari had wanted to die along with her family. She remembered standing next to Angel's bed, squeezing her hand, trying to coax life into her tiny body. Praying. Making deals with God. *Please, just let my baby live.* Cari had asked for so little in her life. He'd already taken her mother and her husband, surely he could spare one small girl. Her little Angel. But the poor child's head injuries were too severe. Twenty hours later, Angela Hallen was pronounced brain-dead.

Throughout the seventy-two hours her daughter had been in intensive care, Cari had been visited several times by a psychiatric nurse, Marge Brunner, who counseled families of critical care patients. With the help of the counselor, she made the decision to donate her daughter's organs. Cari knew that Angel's life had to mean something...some part of her had to live on, even if it was in another child's body. Another child might possibly live because of her daughter.

Still, two years later, Cari hadn't been able to put closure to her decision. Not that she ever regretted it. Although she understood the confidentiality given to the patients and families of donor recipients, Cari couldn't stop wondering who had received Angel's heart.

Was it only the memories that had driven her from Seattle? Cari wanted to believe it was the scenic beach town that had drawn her to northern California. The sunnier weather. The new state-of-the-art cardiac facility at Riverhaven. She told herself she had several reasons to pull up stakes from her home of seven years and move to Santa Cruz.

But there was another reason. Two years ago on June 25, the day she gave consent to have her daughter taken off life support and her organs harvested, Cari also overheard the doctors say that Angel's heart was being transported to the Bay area.

And Danny Malone had received his new heart in a San Francisco hospital on June 26.

Sweet heaven, the pieces fit. She had been drawn to this town, to this little boy. A little boy who more than likely had Angel's heart.

Three nights later, Nick walked through the double oak doors of the Malone home, set his suitcase on the floor and his briefcase on the drop-leaf table in the hall. He knew he shouldn't leave it there, but he was anxious to see Danny. He was walking across the tiled floor toward the wide staircase when he spotted Marion Watts, the housekeeper and cook, coming through the dining room.

"Welcome back, Mr. Malone. Hope your trip was pleasant."

He smiled at the white-haired woman who'd been with the Malone family since he was a child no older than Danny. It still seemed strange that the same woman who had swatted his hands away from her homemade cookies was now calling him sir.

"Yes, as pleasant as business trips go. Has everything been calm here?"

The housekeeper quirked an eyebrow. "With Master Danny around?"

Nick sighed. "What did he do this time?"

She waved her hand in the air. "He still hasn't been able to outdo you, sir. But give him a few years..." Her smile disappeared. "I'm concerned about Mrs. Foster, though. She was not feeling well again. Her coloring was bad the last few days, and her stomach cramps started again. I convinced her to let John take her in to see the doctor."

Nick nodded, grateful the chauffeur was escorting her. He had known when he left on his trip that Mrs. Foster hadn't looked well. But she had assured him she was fine. He hoped she didn't have anything contagious, a germ she could pass on to his son. "Thanks for convincing her to go to the doctor. Where's Danny?"

"He's with your mother in the den. They're having tea and juice in front of the television."

Thank goodness for TV and video games, Nick thought. They had helped entertain the boy through some rough periods. "How's he handling the new medication?"

"Like a champ. You couldn't tell there were any changes at all, except that he didn't eat too well last night."

Nick's gaze shot to hers. "How about today?"

"He always eats his peanut-butter-and-jelly sand-wiches."

"What about vegetables?"

"We have to coax him just as we did you."

He ignored the glint in her eyes. "I think I'll go see them. When is dinner?"

"The roast will be on the table in thirty minutes."

"We'll be there," he said as he loosened his tie and headed for the den at the back of the house where his mother's rooms were located.

After years of battling arthritis, the beautiful, regal Eleanor Malone had finally resigned herself to the fact she needed a wheelchair.

Nick stood in the doorway and watched as Danny sat beside his grandmother. His son was pointing to the pop-ular purple dinosaur on television and was giggling. Nick glanced at his mother, who was smiling, too. What a delight Danny had been to Eleanor. Since Thor Malone's sudden death, Nick had been haunted by the fear he would lose his mother, also. When he and Tory broke up and Danny's condition worsened, Nick had decided to move home. The house was plenty big enough. His mother lived downstairs in a bedroom off the den. He and Danny lived upstairs in a private suite of rooms. But they liked being a family. His mother wasn't lonely, and Danny, with all his restrictions, had a companion. The situation was perfect for all of them.

Once again his son's laughter rippled through the air. Nick walked into the room. "Just what is all the noise about?" He bent down and placed a soft kiss on his mother's cheek.

"Dad!" Danny cried, and came out of his chair. To Nick, his son's laughter was the most heavenly sound. It chilled him to think that the day might come when he would never again hear it.

"I missed you," the boy said. "What did you bring me?"

Nick crossed his arms over his chest. "That's all I get? What did you bring me?"

"Well, you always bring me stuff," the boy said as he began checking his father's pockets for treasures.

"You're just like your father," Eleanor said as she watched her son and grandson. "He never failed to bring you something home."

At sixty-five, Eleanor Malone was still a classic beauty, her silver hair worn swept away from her face. She always dressed as if expecting the ladies to come for tea.

It wasn't long before Danny discovered the compact video game in his dad's coat pocket. "Neat!" Danny cried.

"Maybe after dinner I'll show you how to play—if you eat all your vegetables."

"Yuck." Danny wrinkled his nose. "I hate carrots."

"Well, how about broccoli, or cauliflower, or spinach? Are they more to your liking?"

The boy looked thoughtful for a minute. "Can I have corn on the cob?"

Nick was taken aback. "Sure. I didn't know you liked corn."

"Cari said that it tastes better because you get to eat it with your fingers."

"Cari?" Nick frowned as he looked at his mother. "When did you talk with her?"

"She called to talk with Daniel about his test on Friday," his mother stated. "She seemed very nice. They talked for a while on the phone."

Nick frowned. "That's strange."

"Why? She wanted to assure Daniel she'd be assisting on Friday for his test. I think it was nice of her."

"Yeah, nice," he said distractedly, remembering how often the shapely Cari Hallen had come to mind this past week. "Remember, Mother, the Malone family helped build an entire wing at Riverhaven. Why shouldn't the staff be nice to us?"

She waved her hand in the air. "You are much too suspicious, son."

"Yeah, Dad," Danny said. "Cari's really nice. She used to have a little girl, but she died with her daddy. Now they live in heaven. But it makes Cari sad."

His mother gasped. "How terrible."

My God! She had lost her entire family. Nick felt a familiar dull pain in his midsection, recalling the sadness in her eyes during Danny's last doctor's visit.

"I'm going to be really good for my test 'cause I like Cari."

Marion came to the door and Nick welcomed the change of subject. "Looks like it's time for supper."

"No, sir," Marion began. "John just called. It seems that Mrs. Foster just went in for surgery."

"Surgery?" Nick was shocked. "What happened?"

"From what John said, her appendix nearly ruptured. The doctor said she was lucky she made it in."

"Dad, can we go see Mrs. Foster at the hospital?" Danny pleaded. "We can take her some candy so she'll feel better."

"Son, I don't think Mrs. Foster is up to eating anything right now." Nick looked at Marion. "Have you called her daughter in Los Angeles?"

"I'll do that now, sir." The housekeeper left the room.

"Oh dear, Nick." His mother sighed. "That poor woman."

Nick patted his mother's hand reassuringly. "As soon as I change, I'll go to the hospital to see how she's doing and talk to the doctor handling her case. Will you be all right while I'm gone?"

Eleanor nodded, and he turned to Danny and gave him a hug. "You be good for Grandmother, son."

"I will, but who'll give me my medicine?"

"I'll be home later. If not, Marion can give it to you."

"What about tomorrow? You'll be at work." The child's eyes lit up. "Maybe Cari can come here and stay with me."

Nick stepped off the elevator at the third floor and headed for the nurses' station.

"I'm looking for Claire Foster's room," he said to the dark-haired nurse who was on the phone. She put her finger to her lips in a shushing gesture.

"Look," he began, refusing to be silenced. "I was told downstairs that Mrs. Foster was sent here after surgery. If you can't help me, maybe I can see her doctor."

The woman covered the mouthpiece and glared at him. "If you'll wait a moment, sir, I'll be right with you."

Nick didn't want to wait, but he nodded anyway, then walked away so he wouldn't tear the phone out of the woman's hand and throw it across the corridor. He rubbed his hands over his face and took a seat on the sofa in the small waiting area. He was exhausted.

The merger he'd been working on for the past three days was no closer to being a reality than it had been six months ago, when negotiations started. Now they were back to square one. And without the purchase of Micrographics, he could kiss Malone Industries' new software program goodbye. He couldn't let all the hard work of rebuilding the family business go down the tubes. It was imperative they continue negotiations. And worst of all, to repair the damage, he would probably have to spend more time away from home…and Danny.

He glanced toward the desk. First he had to find out about Mrs. Foster. There was no way he could fly to New York without someone capable and experienced looking after his son.

He could send Larry Keaton. Nick shook his head. He doubted Micrographics would take kindly to having his vice president of marketing addressing their board of directors.

"Mr. Malone."

Nick raised his head to find Cari Hallen. Her fair hair lay softly around her shoulders and a warm smile lit her pretty face. His body swiftly let him know that he appreciated what he saw.

"What are you doing here?" he asked.

"I'm on duty."

"I thought you worked in the new wing."

"Since it's not completely operational, I'm filling in wherever I'm needed until I reach full-time status. How's Danny?"

"He's fine. He's not looking forward to the biopsy, but he knows it has to be done."

"Well, let me know if there's anything I can do."

He was having trouble listening to her words; all he

could seem to focus on was her sparkling blue eyes. They were captivating, almost as if she had cast a spell on him. He shook his head to come out of the trance and stood up.

"Do you know anything about Claire Foster's condition?" he asked.

"She's out of recovery and in her room. She's doing well, but it was rough going earlier." She frowned. "We're lucky John brought her in when he did."

"I've been out of town the past few days." He stood up. "I had no idea…" Maybe he should have, he thought. "When I left, she was recovering from a stomach virus. Claire's been a practical nurse for twenty years, but she doesn't always take such good care of herself. Maybe I should have insisted she go back to the doctor."

Cari reached out and placed her hand on his arm. "No one is blaming you, Mr. Malone. Sometimes acute appendicitis is hard to diagnose."

Nick had felt the gentleness of her touch on his arm. He looked down at her delicate fingers. It had been a long time since a woman touched him, a very long time, he realized, fighting to keep from reacting to her nearness. For no reason, this woman had managed to slip into his thoughts, even his dreams. He stepped back and managed a nod.

"The doctor will be out shortly to explain more to you about Mrs. Foster's condition." Cari started to walk away, but he stopped her.

"It's pretty serious, isn't it?"

"She has an infection that will take some time.…" Cari waved her hand. "Let me page the doctor."

"Can I at least see her?" he asked, reaching for her arm. He glanced down at her delicate wrist and felt her warmth sear his hand. He released her. "She doesn't have any family close by. I want her to know that she has someone here."

Cari didn't know what had come over her as she all but

stared at Nick Malone. Besides being a very handsome man, whether in a business suit or a pair of jeans and a polo shirt, like now, he also seemed to be a compassionate person.

"I'm sure she'll appreciate you being here, but she's heavily sedated."

"That doesn't matter. I have a picture Danny made her and a card from the family." He reached into his back pocket and pulled out the folded paper along with an envelope. "At least when she wakes up she'll know I've been here."

Cari smiled at this man's sweet gesture. She knew she would have to be careful as she realized how endearing both Malone males were. "Is this the picture from Danny?"

He nodded and handed it to her. Cari unfolded the white paper and glanced at the crayon drawing of a person in a bed. The crooked lettering along the bottom read, "I'm sorry you got sick. Love, Danny." She raised her gaze to Nick's, finding a glint of interest in his gray eyes.

"I have to confess, Danny inherited my lack of artistic talent." Nick gave her a shy grin, reminding Cari of his four-year-old son.

"I think it's wonderful."

"Well, he's close to Claire. She's been the only one who has ever taken care of him."

Cari could understand how protective he was of his son. "Well, I bet she'll love to get this."

"So you're going to let me go into her room?" Nick tossed Cari a grin, which did strange things to her insides.

"All right, I'll take you. But only for a short time."

He raised his hands in surrender and Cari figured he didn't do that often. "I promise I'll only stay long enough to assure myself she's okay and put Danny's picture next to her bed."

Cari nodded, enjoying the sudden smile on his face. She doubted Nick Malone did that very often, either.

Thirty minutes later, Nick came out of the lounge after speaking to the surgeon on Claire's case. It would be nearly three weeks before Mrs. Foster would be able to come back to work, and even then it was iffy. Right now she was on medication to help fight the infection in her system from her ruptured appendix.

It was after eight o'clock when he headed to the elevators. He glanced down the deserted hallway, then toward the nurses' station, but there was no sign of Cari. A little disappointed, he pushed the button and thought about home. Danny would be getting ready for bed, but Nick's mother was probably pretty worried. He'd call from the car and let her know that Mrs. Foster was okay.

The doors finally opened and he stepped into the elevator to find Dr. Landers.

"Hello, Matt. Aren't you on duty a little late?"

The doctor grinned. "I'm taking tomorrow off to play golf."

"And it's not even the weekend. Is that allowed?"

"I take what I can get. Besides, I need to get my game in shape for the upcoming Riverhaven Charity Golf Tournament. I hope you're up for the challenge this year."

"You know I don't play anymore."

"Why?" The doctor gave him a once-over. "You look physically fit. And I've seen those custom clubs of yours. They're the envy of every doctor on staff."

A lifetime ago, Nick had played golf regularly. He loved the game. In college, he'd even thought about turning pro, but his dad's bad heart and Tory's disapproval helped him realize how ridiculous the idea had been. Now he had no time...or desire.

"Get yourself a set. I'll give you the name of the guy who made mine."

"Does it come with a guarantee to help me play better?"

Nick looked away. "Nothing in life comes with a guarantee, Doc. You should know that." If it did, he would be first in line for his son.

"More reason to live every day to the fullest."

How many times had he heard that? The doors opened. Before the good doctor could start his usual lecture on the benefits of the transplant support group, Nick dashed for the front doors.

"Hey, Nick, wait up," Matt called, but Nick didn't slow down.

"I need to get home to Danny. I've been on a business trip the past three days and Mrs. Foster just got out of surgery a few hours ago."

"What happened?"

"The stomach virus she had last week turned out to be acute appendicitis."

"I saw C. Foster on the surgical schedule, but I didn't connect her with the name. Is she all right?"

"She's doing okay now, but it looks like she'll be out of commission for a few weeks. I need someone to look after Danny. And Claire Foster has been the only one he's ever had as his nurse."

"Yeah, poor Danny." Matt Landers crossed his arms over his chest and sighed. "He'll have to interview all those pretty nurses." Matt suddenly grinned. "I think you're going to have a big problem when he's a teenager."

Nick didn't smile. He looked over his shoulder. "Will I, Doctor? Will Danny ever be able to look forward to girls and dating and driving a car at sixteen? Can you guarantee that?"

Chapter Three

Nick watched his sedated son lying on the metal gurney, an IV tube attached to one arm. The small four-year-old wore a colorful print hospital gown, but it didn't brighten the paleness of his face.

Nick took a deep breath, trying to calm his nervousness, his fear. He'd nearly lost his son so many times that he'd stopped counting. But at least in the past two years, since receiving his new heart, Danny'd had only one rejection bout. It made Nick realize how fragile life was, and also made him wonder how long his son would continue to stay healthy.

"Relax, Dad," Matt Landers said, and placed a reassuring hand on Nick's back. "We're doing all the work, and Danny's going to come through this like a champ."

Nick started to speak, when Cari Hallen walked into the room, dressed in surgical green, her sun-streaked hair only partially hidden under a paper cap.

She paused and her eyes met his. A sudden warmth

spread through him, and the hospital's hygienic smell disappeared as her soft scent filled the room. Why now? he wondered. This was the wrong place. The wrong woman. Any woman was the wrong woman. But that didn't stop him from entertaining the thought of how her lips would taste, how her body would... A surge of hot desire shot through him. He quickly glanced away.

Cari went to Danny and ran her hand over his head and spoke soft, soothing words. Nick watched. As much as he tried to be two parents to his child, he knew there was nothing to compare to a woman's touch.

"How are you feeling, Danny?" she asked.

"Sleepy."

"That's good. In a little while, we'll be all done for another year."

Danny raised his hand toward her. "Stay with me?"

Cari's eyes met Nick's. "I'll be right by your side the whole time. And I'll keep talking so you won't get scared."

Who would keep *him* from getting scared? Nick wondered. God, he'd been through this before. It hadn't gotten any easier.

"Well, let's get on with the show," Matt said as an orderly walked up and started moving the bed out.

Nick's heart pounded in his chest as he reached down and kissed his son. "I love you, partner." He walked with them down the hall, holding tight to his son. "I'll be waiting for you when you're all finished," he promised as they approached the surgery ward. The doors automatically opened.

Cari paused, placing her hand on his arm. "You'll have to wait outside."

Panic nearly overwhelmed Nick as he reluctantly let go of Danny's hand and they pushed the bed through to the operating room. But before the doors closed, Cari smiled, a smile that reached out and wrapped around the terror he barely held in check.

"We'll take good care of Danny," she promised.

"I'm going to hold you to that."

Cari nodded, then turned away to catch up with the doctor.

"Danny's the most important person in my life," he whispered to the empty corridor. Slowly he walked down the hall to the waiting room, ignoring the hustle and noise of the busy hospital. All he had on his mind was a prayer that he used to say as a child. He hoped it would help protect his son. He bowed his head and began the litany. Something he'd done a lot of in the past four years.

Cari stripped off her rubber gloves and tossed them in the metal can. She drew a deep breath, pulled her surgical mask down around her neck and released a tired sigh. The procedure had gone without a hitch, but it always took a lot out of her. And with Danny more than usual.

In the short time she'd known him, they seemed to have made an instant connection. Good or bad, Danny Malone had been the first child since Angel's death that Cari had allowed to get close to her. Somehow the charming, dark-haired four-year-old had managed to push his way into her heart. Fate? she wondered again, then slammed the door on the surge of emotions that made her giddy every time she thought of Danny and Angel in the same breath.

Cari hit the button to open the double doors and walked out of the surgery ward. She turned down the hall toward the waiting area, where she found Nick Malone. He was stretched out on the sofa, his forearm resting over his eyes. Was he asleep?

She hesitated inside the small room, taking the opportunity to study this confusing man. There was no doubt Nick Malone loved his son, but with others he seemed aloof. Withdrawn. It was as if he was trying single-handedly to ward off the rest of the world, to protect Danny from any physical or emotional hurt. Of course, that wasn't uncommon for the parent of a heart transplant patient.

About to wake him and tell him the good news, Cari leaned over the sofa, yet something made her pause. Maybe it was that, for the first time, the man looked approachable, almost vulnerable in sleep, and of course devilishly handsome. His coal black hair was slightly mussed, falling across his forehead. She had to clench her hands to keep from brushing it back. He looked fatigued, but his strong jaw was clean shaven, even the cleft in his stubborn chin. His broad chest rose and fell with each breath he took. Her journey continued down to his flat stomach and long, trim legs. There was no doubt that here was a man who was all male and then some.

Cari dragged her gaze back to his face and found he'd raised his arm and a pair of silvery eyes were staring back at her. She drew in a surprised breath as a sudden tingling sensation rushed down her spine.

She straightened, but it took a second or two before she was able to speak. "I came to tell you the procedure is finished and Danny is fine. You can go and see him."

Nick couldn't move. When he'd opened his eyes and found Cari Hallen looking down at him, he thought he was dreaming. But from his body's warm and sudden reaction, he knew she was real. He forced his constricted vocal chords to perform. "Danny's okay?"

Smiling, she nodded, and more heat shot through him. Damn! He had to stop this. Danny should be the only thing on his mind. He swung his legs off the sofa and sat up, checking his watch. "It took longer than usual."

"Not to worry, though, Danny did very well. These procedures are sometimes harder on the parents than the kids."

"Was there any sign of disease?"

"You'll have to talk to the doctor."

Nick stood and glanced behind her. "Where's Matt, anyway?"

"He had an emergency and asked me to come and get you. Danny's in recovery."

Nick grabbed her arm, hating to have to beg for an answer, but he was desperate. "Look, I want to know about my son. I need to know about my son. Did they find anything? Please—you have to tell me."

She smiled at him and he felt emotion clog his throat. "No, they didn't find any disease. Danny's heart is healthy."

Nick let out a long breath. "Thank, God!"

"Dr. Landers will meet you in Danny's room in a few minutes." She started for the hall and Nick followed close behind, smiling and anxious to see his son. But that didn't stop his gaze from involuntarily watching the sway of Cari Hallen's shapely bottom. Hell, even in ugly green surgical pants she managed to get his attention. He rubbed his hand over his face. You need a social life, Malone.

Cari led him into recovery, where he found Danny sleeping. He fought back a flood of emotions as he came up beside the bed and took his son's hand. "How you doin', champ? Cari said you did good."

Danny opened his eyes. "It hurt, Dad, but I didn't cry." His voice was a raspy whisper. "Cari said it was okay to cry if it hurt." Nick knew that his son was fighting the effects of the anesthetic.

"She's right." Nick's eyes rose to the woman standing across the bed. "Even big people sometimes cry."

"I already told you, Larry, I can't make it next week," Nick said into the phone, then listened while the vice president of marketing argued his point. "Yes, I know how important this merger is. It's my company that will sink if we can't work out this deal. But New York? Can't they have the meeting out here?"

Nick still hadn't found anyone to replace Mrs. Foster. It didn't matter that the biopsy had shown Danny's heart to be healthy. Nick wasn't about to fly across the country without a reliable, trained medical person looking after his son.

Nick had been staying at home over the past week, working out of his office. When he really needed to go into the office, it had only been for a few hours, while his mother and Marion handled the baby-sitting. His mother was too fragile and the housekeeper had too many other responsibilities.

"There's another company nipping at our heels on this one," Larry continued. "But I got Micrographics to hold off until they spoke with you. Nick, they agreed to a meeting on Monday, but only if you come to New York."

Nick cursed under his breath. That only gave him four days. "Is this another ploy for a delay?"

"No, Nick. I suggest if you want this merger to come about, you'd better find a way to be at that meeting. They only want to deal with you."

Luckily the outcome of Danny's test had been good news or he would never even consider going on this business trip.

"I'll have Sandy call you after she books my flight," he finally said. "I want you to pick me up at the airport. We need to go over everything before this meeting."

"I don't think you'll regret it," Larry said, then hung up.

Nick slammed down the receiver and cursed again.

"You said a bad word, Daddy," a tiny voice said.

Danny stood in the doorway, dressed in jeans and a Barney T-shirt with a pair of white tennis shoes. "Sorry, son. Do you think Marion is going to wash my mouth out with soap?"

Danny shook his head. "Nope. She puts hot sauce on your tongue."

"Well, we don't want that. Maybe you won't tell."

The child grinned and came into the room. "You mean like it's a secret?"

"Yeah, like that. If I promise not to do it again."

"Okay." Danny climbed up on the chair on the other side of the desk. "What you doin'?"

"I'm working, trying to buy another company so we can make special chips to go into computers."

"Oh." The boy glanced around the room. "Can we go to the park?"

"Sorry, partner. Not today. I have to get ready for a meeting."

"Then can I call Cari? She said she'd take me."

Nick frowned. Cari Hallen had promised to take his son to the park? "She probably has to work."

Danny shook his head. "Not until Friday."

"How do you know?"

"She told me when she called." Danny climbed up on his knees and reached for the paperweight on the desk. "She's called every day since I was in the hospital. Sometimes she talks to Grandma and sometimes to Marion to tell them about Mrs. Foster." Danny's big dark eyes looked up at him. "Cari's my only friend."

Surprised at his son's declaration, Nick was about to deny it, then realized what the boy said was true. "But you have Marion and Grandma. And what about me? We're your friends."

"Can't I have Cari, too?"

Nick opened his mouth but didn't know how to answer.

"I know her phone number by heart. Can I call her and ask her to come over?"

Nick was suddenly intrigued by Cari Hallen's interest in his son. Did her compassion extend to all her patients? He remembered her gentle touch when he'd been so worried over Danny's biopsy. Recalled the little hitch in her breath as their gazes had locked...

"Please, Dad?" Danny said again, the hope in his young eyes too much for Nick to withstand.

"Sure, go ahead." He turned the phone around and watched in amazement as Danny punched out the numbers.

"Hi, Cari. It's me, Danny. No, my dad said it was all right to call you and ask you to come over." The child handed the receiver to his father. "She wants to ask you something."

Nick took the phone. "This is Nick Malone."

"Hello, Mr. Malone," a soft, throaty voice said over the line. "I wanted to make sure that it was okay with you before I accepted Danny's invitation."

He had to hold back a groan after hearing her breathy voice. He wasn't so sure this was a good idea. "Yes, it's okay to visit my son."

"Thank you. I'll need directions."

Nick gave Cari the directions to the house, then alerted the security gate that they were expecting a visitor. It was hard to keep his son under control until his guest finally arrived at the door forty-five minutes later.

Cari parked her car in the circular drive. She turned off the key reluctantly, wondering if she was doing the right thing—getting involved in Danny's life. Maybe it would be better to leave things alone. She thought back to the way his father had stared at her in Danny's hospital room. She wasn't sure if Nick Malone wanted to throw her out or devour her on the spot. Either way, she knew she was in trouble.

Cari drew a long breath and studied the gorgeous Tudor-style home. She knew the Malones were wealthy, but she'd had no idea how rich. The estate was inland, yet when she stepped out of the car she could feel a cool breeze against her face, tasting the salt in the air from the nearby ocean.

She tried not to stare, but she'd never seen anything quite like this. Large, coppery Eugenia bushes, immaculately trimmed, bordered the brick-and-wood structure, and luscious wisteria climbed its way to the second story. Off in the distance, across the beautifully landscaped lawn, she saw a large garage, and farther on was a white building that resembled a stable. There were no horses grazing in the paddock, though. Nor did the pungent smell of animals vie with the sweet scent of flowers.

She made her way along the brick walk and up the steps, but before she could ring the bell, the door swung open and Danny came rushing out. "Cari, you're here." He hugged her around the middle.

"Of course I'm here. I just got a little lost."

"Who found you?" Danny asked.

She laughed. "I sort of found my own way. I just turned around and drove back to where I was supposed to turn. And there was your house."

He took her arm. "Come inside and see my room. I want to show you all my books and games."

Cari allowed herself to be led through the double doors, where she was greeted by a woman in her sixties. Her dove gray uniform dress accented her salt-and-pepper hair, which she tucked neatly into a bun.

"Hello, I'm Marion. I've kept everyone around here fed for nearly thirty years." She reached out her hand and shook Cari's. "It's a pleasure to finally meet you."

"It's nice to meet you, too," Cari acknowledged. "Thank you for having me over."

"Well, I hope you'll stay for lunch."

"Oh, please don't go to any trouble."

"Of course she's staying for lunch," Nick Malone said as he walked toward them. "After her long drive, we owe her the courtesy." He stood beside the housekeeper. "Hello, Mrs. Hallen."

Cari knew she was staring at Nick Malone but couldn't

seem to help herself. He was wearing tan slacks and a navy polo shirt that showed off his wide shoulders and broad chest. The sight stole her breath and riveted her right there to the fancy marble-tile floor.

"Mrs. Hallen," he said. "Will you accept our invitation to lunch?"

"Oh, yes, thank you." Good grief. She was acting as though she had never seen a man before. "And please, call me Cari."

"Then call me Nick."

Nick. Perhaps it was a mistake to suggest they be on a first name basis. Something told her that he didn't welcome that kind of familiarity. But his bold gaze told her differently. She had to fight the urge not to brush a hand through her wind-tossed hair. For a split second, she wondered if her dark slacks and cotton blouse were appropriate. Her self-consciousness took her back to her childhood days, living with foster families and never quite fitting in. But she quickly shook off the feeling, deciding she was dressed just fine. After all, she was here to spend the day with Danny, not to impress Nick Malone.

The boy tugged on her arm. "C'mon, Cari, let's go to my bedroom."

"Just hold on, son. Cari has barely had a chance to catch her breath from her long drive."

The boy looked up at her. "How long will that take?"

Cari and Nick both laughed. "Why don't you go and get your grandmother and tell her that Cari has arrived," Nick suggested.

"Okay." Danny hurried off.

Nick looked at her, amusement in his gray eyes. Cari thought he seemed more relaxed than she'd ever seen him.

"Sorry. My son is pretty excited about your coming by. I hope you can handle his endless energy."

"Mr. Mal—Nick," she amended. "I've worked in pediatrics for the last six years. Believe me, your son is very normal.''

Slowly his smile faded and he looked away. She had the urge to reach out and touch him, stroke that hard, square jaw of his, let him know how lucky he was to have a child. Someone to love.

She couldn't resist, and she placed her hand on his arm. ''Nick? Count your blessings, Danny is healthy.''

His gaze held hers and she watched as he nodded, then his eyes grew more intense. The mood changed and Cari felt herself growing warm. Nick was no longer looking at her as a friend of his son. This was more like a man desiring a woman.

The sound of Danny returning made Cari glance away. After introductions and a short conversation with Eleanor Malone, Danny finally took Cari up the wide circular staircase to the second floor.

She tried not to gawk, but Cari had never seen a house quite so elegant. She smiled. The downstairs was filled with beautiful antiques and expensive paintings. Upstairs, the boy took her into a suite of rooms that were just as lavishly decorated. The sitting area was masculine and comfortable looking, with overstuffed chairs and a sofa in navy and deep green. Across the room, on either side of the fireplace, were built-in wall units that housed a top-of-the-line stereo system. She knew because her husband had priced the same model once, but after discovering the cost, they realized they would never be able to afford it.

''C'mon, Cari. My room is this way.''

Cari followed Danny down a long, carpeted hallway. Before they reached his room, they passed the master suite. Cari couldn't help stopping to glance inside. The large room was painted in beige tones with shutters covering the wide bay window. Against the opposite wall was a king-size bed with a carved wooden headboard and navy comforter. A matching mahogany armoire was placed in one corner, and a thick, nutmeg-colored carpet covered the spacious floor.

"I think you're in the wrong room," a deep, familiar voice announced.

Cari jumped and turned around to find Nick behind her.

"Oh, I'm sorry. Your…home is so beautiful that… I'm sorry. That was rude of me." A blush warmed her cheeks and she turned and continued toward Danny's room.

About an hour later, Nick was sitting in his office when Danny peeked his head in the door. "Dad, can I show Cari where you work?"

Nick pushed his chair back from his computer. "It's not very interesting."

Danny came in, pulling Cari behind him. She smiled shyly. "I'm sorry. I told him we shouldn't disturb you."

"Believe me, I welcome the interruption." He stood up. His gaze followed her as she walked around, apprehensively interested in the surroundings. She seemed to brighten up the room with her presence. "I seem to have wasted most of the morning. The only thing I've accomplished is making a plane reservation to New York."

"Going on a trip?"

"Business." He folded his arms over his chest and leaned against the edge of the desk.

"Dad always goes away to New York," Danny said as he climbed in a chair. "But when he's here, he makes computers."

Cari walked toward the floor-to-ceiling bookcase. "Will you have to be gone long?"

"Longer than I'd like. I'm involved with this merger…" Why was he explaining himself to her?

Danny shook his head. "I don't like it when my dad leaves."

Nick ruffled his son's hair. "You know it can't be helped, especially until this takeover is completed." He didn't like the idea of leaving Danny, especially with Mrs. Foster in the hospital. Not that his son wouldn't be perfectly safe, but if something happened and there wasn't a qualified nurse around—

"What kind of computers does your company make?" Cari asked.

"Actually, Malone Industries designs software. That is, until this merger goes through, then hopefully we'll be packaging the PC and software together."

Danny leaned his elbows on the desk. "My dad makes all my games."

Cari raised her eyebrows. "Really?"

"Well, I have to keep up with the market," Nick explained. "Games are hot. They're also fun to create."

"Yeah." Danny giggled. "And sometimes I get to help him."

"I bet you are a big help." She turned to Nick. "I'm impressed."

For some strange reason, her words thrilled Nick. Too bad his father hadn't felt the same way. When he was alive, Thor Malone had shot down every one of his ideas, thinking integrated circuits were all the company had to do to stay afloat, leaving the computer field to the big companies. By the time Nick took over Malone Industries, it was barely surviving.

"Well, I've worked hard the past few years. I helped design the new chip for the graphics processor." What he didn't tell her was that his design work had been his salvation during several of Danny's hospital stays.

"We already have the patent on a number of chips for the processor, but without Micrographics software, they would be useless. I have to get to New York next week or this merger dream will die, along with millions of dollars of research and technology."

"I hope everything goes well," she said sincerely.

"Thank you."

There was a knock on the door. "Lunch is ready," Marion said as she peered into his office. "Oh, there you two are. I was just going upstairs to look for you. Danny, you can show Cari where to wash up."

The boy took Cari's hand and escorted her out of the room. And Nick was left with Marion and her knowing look.

"What?" He pushed away from the desk.

"She's awful nice, isn't she?"

"Yes, Marion, she's nice."

"Oh, they get along splendidly, Mr. Malone. When I went up a little while ago, Cari was reading to Danny and he was sitting on her lap just as content as could be. I haven't seen him like this in...well, I don't know how long."

Nick didn't say anything. He knew Marion was thinking about his son's mother. Tory's absence from Danny's life had been her own choice. He clenched his hands, remembering his ex-wife tearfully telling him that she couldn't handle her child's illness. The worst blow was her blaming him for their son's imperfect heart.

All at once the housekeeper's voice brought him back to reality. "What did you say, Marion?"

"I said maybe you should ask her to stay here next week while you're away on business."

He froze. He'd only made that decision a little while ago. "How did you know I was going away?"

"You were on-line with your computer, so your secretary called the house line to confirm your reservation. If you're only going to be gone a short time, I bet Cari could stay here and watch Danny. Oh, sir, that child adores her."

Yes, that was obvious. They both seemed to be taken with each other. What Nick didn't understand was why Cari affected him so strongly. She was pretty enough, but not what you'd call a classic beauty. Her eyes were almost too large for her heart-shaped face, but the crystal blue color was certainly mesmerizing. She was too fair for his taste, but her hair was the color of sunshine. And her legs… Immediately Nick thought of his ex-wife, and how her beauty had disguised her inner ugliness for so long.

The sound of Marion's voice brought him out of his reverie. "I talked with Mrs. Foster this morning. They're releasing her from the hospital," the housekeeper said. "But she's going to spend the next few weeks with her sister in Gilroy. She won't be able to come back to work for at least three weeks. Don't you think you should find someone to replace her? Temporarily, of course."

There was no question that Marion had never been fond of Claire Foster. She thought the nanny was too stringent about Danny's upbringing. But the woman had just been following his orders to prevent his son from overdoing.

"I'll think about it," he said.

The housekeeper raised an eyebrow, then silently left the room. What was that supposed to mean? he wondered. More than likely Marion wanted to add to her suggestion in favor of the woman upstairs. Well, what choice did he have? He picked up the phone, dialed the hospital and asked for Bess Linley.

"Bess, Nick Malone."

"Hello, Mr. Malone. How is Danny doing?"

"He's doing just fine. I called you for another reason."

"What can I do for you?"

He released a long breath. "I need Cari Hallen."

After lunch, Cari and Danny went back up to his bedroom. "Will you read me this one?" Danny held the book up to Cari.

"Danny, I've already read you three stories," she reminded him, watching the stubborn pout on his face. She had seen that look many times on her own daughter's face.

If Danny had Angel's heart, could he have picked up her characteristics? The boy climbed on her lap.

"P...please," he whispered. "I promise I'll take my nap after this one. It's my very favorite."

Cari made room for the stocky child on her lap. "You said that about the others." She bit back a grin as the boy rested his warm body against hers. Cari closed her eyes and inhaled the wonderful fragrance that was only a child's, a mixture of soap and peanut butter, with a little perspiration tossed in.

She closed her arms around Danny, enjoying the sweet moment. And for a few stolen seconds, she dreamed that she was holding her own child. Suddenly her heart ached with the loneliness of the past two years, the emptiness she felt every time she saw a child that wasn't hers—that would never be hers. Her family was gone, and she would never hold her little Angel again. She closed her eyes. Maybe Danny could be the closest thing.

Suddenly she felt a small hand on her cheek. "Cari, are you asleep?"

She opened her eyes and smiled. "No, sweetie, I'm just dreaming."

His face creased into a frown. "About your little girl?"

Cari nodded. "Yeah, about my little girl."

"Did you used to call her sweetie, too?"

Cari had to bite down on her lip, then managed to answer, "Sometimes. But mostly we called her...Angel."

Danny's expression was thoughtful. "Grandma says that people go to heaven when they die. That's where Grandpa lives and so does your little girl and her daddy."

Cari nodded. "They're all together." *And I'm here all alone,* she cried silently.

Danny patted her arm. "I'm sorry she died, but I'm glad you're my friend."

She hugged him. "I'm glad I'm your friend, too."

She reached for the storybook, but froze when she read the title on the cover. *The Velveteen Rabbit.* Oh, God. Angel's favorite. Her bunny book, she used to call it. Her daughter would climb up on her lap, dragging her stuffed Honey Bunny along with her, anxiously wanting to start the bedtime story.

Cari glanced down at the four-year-old child now in her lap. Danny was doing the same.

"Cari, read the words," Danny insisted as he opened the book.

"Sure." She cleared her throat. "There was once a velveteen rabbit..."

Nick hadn't heard a sound out of either one of them in more than an hour. It was Danny's naptime, and he walked down the hall toward his son's room. He didn't want his son overtired. Guest or no guest, he wasn't going to let Cari Hallen upset Danny's routine.

He reached the doorway and stopped. Cari was sitting in the rocking chair, holding Danny in her arms, and they were both sound asleep.

Cari's head was tilted to the side, her blond hair partially covering her slightly flushed cheek. His son was curled in her arms, his head resting against her full breast, his small hand tucked around her slim waist. Nick was captivated by the scene, shocked to find he was envious of his son's closeness with this woman. It had been ages since he'd wanted a woman or had the time for a personal relationship. Why now? Why had Cari Hallen suddenly caused a yearning in him? He studied the sleeping woman, his eyes drawn to the gentle rise and fall of her breasts.

He walked across the room and, careful not to disturb him, picked up his son and carried him to the bed. After covering him with a blanket, he returned to Cari. He leaned forward and touched her arm. She rolled her head against the back of the chair, making a purring sound. Nick's body immediately reacted as he glanced down at her shapely legs encased in slim-fitting pants. He bit back a groan and decided he had better wake his sexy guest quickly.

"Cari…" he whispered as he shook her shoulder gently.

She blinked, and blinked again, revealing blue eyes glazed with sleep, compelling and magnetic. Her slightly mussed hair made her look as if she had been in bed for more than sleep.

"Nick…?" She spoke his name in a sleep-husky voice.

Nick stood. "You fell asleep," he said, careful not to make eye contact.

Embarrassed, Cari sat up and combed her hand through her hair. She saw Danny asleep on the bed. "Did you put him to bed?"

"Yeah. He's fast asleep." He looked back at her. "You two must have played hard. It was nice of you to come by today."

"I enjoyed it, but I guess I forgot how tiring it can be."

They both studied the slumbering child. Nick saw the longing in her eyes. "Danny told me about your husband and little girl," he began. "I'm sorry."

"Thank you. Sometimes it seems like a long time ago." Cari drew a long breath and then released it. "Other times it seems like only yesterday."

"How long ago was it?"

Cari stood. "Two years. My husband and daughter were in a automobile accident. Tim died instantly…my daughter three days later." She swallowed. "They say it gets easier with time, but the pain of losing a child never goes away. I'll miss Angel forever."

"It's hard to lose a loved one." There was silence for a long time, then Nick finally spoke. "C'mon, let's get you a cup of coffee before you head back."

"Thank you. I could use one."

Nick tugged the blanket over his son's small form as Cari reached down and brushed a lock of hair off his forehead. The child stirred but didn't wake. She glanced up to find Nick watching her. His eyes had a haunting, faraway look in them. When he turned and headed for the door, she quickly followed. Once in the sitting area of the suite, he offered her a seat.

Cari tried to hide a yawn as she sat down on the over-stuffed sofa. "I'm sorry I fell asleep. I guess I was more tired than I thought."

He pulled open the louvered doors to a tiny kitchenette, took two mugs from the cupboard and reached for a cof-feepot. "Are you putting in a lot of hours at the hospital?"

Cari shook her head. "In fact, I'm barely getting three shifts a week. I just happened to work late last night."

"It's hard to make a living that way."

"I'll be okay for a while," she lied. The fact was she could use a little extra money. "Hopefully before too long the new wing will need me full-time."

"I'm sure they will." Nick was watching her so intently that Cari felt uncomfortable.

She started to speak, when he interrupted her. "How would you feel about staying with Danny next week while I'm out of town?"

Cari opened her mouth, then quickly closed it. Her heart raced with excitement. She couldn't believe it. He wanted her to stay with his son. With the child who might have received Angel's heart.

"If there's a conflict with the hospital—"

"No!" She stood up. She'd do anything to be able to spend time with Danny. "I have to work over the week-end. But there's nothing on the schedule for me next week. I'll talk with Bess and make sure I'm cleared."

"I've already spoken with her," Nick admitted. "She recommended you very highly. I'll match your salary at the hospital, plus a bonus since you'll be here twenty-four hours a day, looking after Danny. You'll have to stay here at the house, of course." He cocked an eyebrow. "Will you have a problem with that?"

Cari watched Nick pace back and forth in front of her.

Would there be a problem? There was something happening between them and she wasn't quite sure how to handle it. Then there was Danny. And that overruled any thought of turning down the job. ''No, there's no problem. When do you want me?''

Chapter Four

The following Sunday afternoon, Cari arrived at Malone Manor. As soon as she stepped into the entry, Danny came running down the stairs.

"Cari! Cari! You're here."

"I'm here," she answered, watching the boy skip the last step and fall onto his knees. But before she could react, Danny was back on his feet and racing toward her, his usually groomed hair flying in different directions, his cheeks rosy. He looked as if he'd just woken up from his nap.

He skidded to a stop in front of her. "Will you take me to the park?"

"Yes, but not right this minute."

Her response did nothing to dampen the boy's enthusiasm. "Will you read me stories and tuck me in bed at night?"

Marion closed the door behind Cari. "Yes, and she'll give you your medicine and make sure you take a nap," the housekeeper added, then glanced at Cari. "The boy is a handful, just like his father was." There was a twinkle in the woman's eyes.

"Danny and I will get along fine," she said evenly.

"Of course you will. Welcome to Malone Manor, Cari. Just leave your bags here and my husband, John, will take them up to your room."

Danny reached for her hand. "Did you know that your room is next to mine?"

"No, I didn't."

"When my daddy goes to New York, he says I can wake you up every morning. Is that okay?"

"Yes, that'll be great. You can make sure I don't over-sleep and lose my job."

"That's silly, I'm your job."

"Well then, I'd better make sure I don't lose you."

They both laughed. "C'mon, we're gonna have tea with Grandma."

"Sounds lovely."

Cari allowed Danny to lead her through the large entry and past an enormous dining room with a long mahogany table and Queen Anne chairs that would easily seat a dozen people. The boy opened a pair of french doors that led into a den, beautifully decorated in soft shades of blue and antique white.

The glossy, honey-colored hardwood floors were adorned with a large area rug. A floral-patterned sofa and easy chair were grouped in front of a gray marble fireplace, whose brass fixtures were polished to a bright gold hue.

Seated in her electric wheelchair, Eleanor Malone appeared in the doorway of the adjacent bedroom. She wore a light pink dress and her white hair was styled into a french twist. Cari thought the woman looked beautiful.

"Grandma, Cari's here," Danny announced as he raced across the room.

"I see, child." The older woman gently stroked her grandson's hair. "Good afternoon, Cari."

"Good afternoon, Mrs. Malone."

Marion entered, carrying a tray with a teapot and two cups and saucers and a bottle of fruit juice for Danny.

Mrs. Malone pushed the button on her chair and approached a large coffee table in the center of the room. "Please join us for tea, Cari."

"I'd love to." Cari went to the sofa and Danny followed.

"I'm not old enough for tea yet," the boy announced. "But Grandma said you're never too young to learn eddiecut."

"That's etiquette," his grandmother corrected.

"How about good manners?" a familiar male voice inquired.

They all looked toward the doorway to see Nick Malone.

"Dad, Cari's here." Danny jumped off the sofa and ran to his father.

Cari drew a sharp breath as her eyes took in the man in the custom-tailored charcoal gray suit. A crisp white shirt and maroon-striped tie accented his dark complexion.

"I see that, son," he said, but his silver gray gaze locked with Cari's. "Good afternoon, Cari."

"Good afternoon, Mr. Malone." She felt a tingling down her spine and quickly glanced away as his bold gaze traveled over her.

Eleanor Malone spoke up. "Well, Nicholas, to what do we owe the pleasure of this visit? I thought that you'd be in conferences all day, preparing for the merger."

Nick pulled his attention away from Cari, finding it easier to ignore his mother's cunning smile. "I thought it would be easier to work from my office here, and then leave directly for the airport later tonight." At least that's what he'd told himself when he'd left the plant in near turmoil. But the real reason, he now knew, was his concern for his son. He'd never left Danny with anyone besides Mrs. Foster.

He glanced over at the blond woman in the long, blue print skirt, which unfortunately revealed nothing of the shapely legs beneath. His gaze moved up to her slim waist and the short-sleeved sweater that covered her full breasts. His palms began to itch. Quickly he raised his eyes and took in her long, slender neck and noted the soft blush on her cheeks. Damn! Cari Hallen was a lovely woman. But was she the right person to care for his son?

"Have you had a chance to get settled in?" he asked.

"Oh, yes. Thank you. My room is lovely." She beamed a smile at him. "And I'm so close to Danny."

And just across the hall from me, he thought, wondering what all that golden hair would look like spread across a pillow, what it would feel like against his skin...

"Dad," Danny said, interrupting his wandering thoughts. "Cari's gonna take care of me real good when you're gone."

"I know, son. I wouldn't leave you here otherwise. But I need to discuss your schedule with her." Nick wasn't surprised to find Cari having tea with his mother. Eleanor had been almost isolated since arthritis had put her in a wheelchair and she seemed pleased to have company.

She placed her teacup on the table. "Nick, you can at least allow the girl to finish her tea before drilling her on the routine around here."

Well and truly admonished, Nick had to struggle to hold back a grin at his mother's tenacity. Something he hadn't seen in a long while. "I apologize for the interruption. Please, enjoy your tea. When you finish, Cari, I'll be in my office."

Cari watched Nick Malone leave the room, almost relieved when the door closed. She hoped he hadn't seen her nervousness. She was a professional and had always presented herself that way. The last thing she wanted to do was lose this job.

"Please, Cari, don't let my son intimidate you," Eleanor said. "The Malone men have always felt the need to be in control of everything and everybody." She sighed. "I believe the stress of running the business killed my husband, Thor. He couldn't seem to turn it off after hours. I hoped my son was going to be different, but it doesn't appear so."

The older woman looked thoughtful as she stroked Danny's hair. "The past few years have been rough on Nick. He's had to handle so many things on his own. I'm afraid I haven't been as helpful as I'd have liked."

Bess had already told Cari that Danny's mother, Victoria, hadn't been in the picture since before the boy's surgery. Cari wondered if the woman ever visited her son. And she was more than a little curious as to whether she and Nick still had a relationship. "Well, maybe I can at least ease his worries about Danny," she offered.

"I hope so. Nick needs to loosen up and have some fun." Eleanor glanced at her grandson lovingly. "He seems to feel he can't have a life outside this house and office. I tell him all the time that we have more than sufficient staff to help care for us. Don't get me wrong, Cari. I love having both my men here with me. I just don't want to become a burden."

"Oh, Mrs. Malone, I doubt your son thinks of you that way."

A bright smile wreathed the older woman's face as she reached across the table and patted Cari's hand. "I can't begin to tell you how very glad I am that you're here. We need a little life in this house."

"I'm alive, Grandma."

Both Cari and Eleanor laughed at the child sitting patiently on the sofa. "Very much so, Daniel. And you have behaved like a perfect gentleman."

The boy's big brown eyes lit up. "So can Cari take me to the park now?"

Cari set her bone china cup on the saucer. "How about tomorrow after breakfast?" she suggested.

"Okay," the boy said, obviously disappointed.

"And because you've behaved so well, as a reward, how about I read you two stories at bedtime?"

"Wow!"

"Daniel, why don't you go check and see if John carried Cari's suitcases up to her room?"

"Okay, be right back," he called as he raced across the room and out the door.

Both women smiled as the energetic child disappeared. Eleanor sighed. "I wish Nick would spend more time with him. One day he'll realize how precious this time is."

Cari sighed, lost in her own thoughts. Yes, she mused, sometimes we don't appreciate our blessings until we've lost them. She felt her throat tighten. What she wouldn't give to have Angel back with her.

As if she had read her mind, Eleanor gasped. "I'm sorry, Cari. I forgot about your daughter."

Cari raised her hand. "It's all right. I don't mind talking about Angel. She was my life."

The next thirty minutes they spent getting to know each other, and then Danny returned, eager to tell Cari about his new computer and games. She wondered whether or not he had any friends his own age.

When Marion appeared to clear the dishes, she told Cari that Mr. Malone would like to see her in his office.

Cari glanced at her watch. She jumped up. "Oh gosh, I didn't realize how much time had passed."

"Slow down," Eleanor said, waving her hand. "My son can stand to wait awhile. He's too used to having his way."

Cari was planning to give Nick Malone his way. Within reason, of course. After all, he was her employer. She thanked Mrs. Malone for the tea, told Danny she'd see him later and excused herself. Getting directions from Marion, she headed down the hall to the double doors next to the staircase. She drew a deep breath, brushed her hair off her shoulders and knocked.

"Come in," Nick's voice rang out, deep and clear.

She turned the knob and stepped into the large paneled room. She had visited this room once before but was still in awe of the masculine beauty of the oak bookcases and all the leather-bound books. Behind the huge oak desk she found Nick. He was minus his jacket and tie, and his shirt-sleeves were rolled up, revealing his forearms as he worked the keyboard at the computer. He had a scowl on his face, but it didn't take away from his good looks or the unsettling effect he had on her.

He glanced at her, his gray eyes unreadable as stone. Darn. Why did he make her feel as if she were tardy for class?

"Sorry to pull you away from your afternoon tea, but we have a lot to go over before I leave for New York tomorrow." He motioned to the chair in front of his desk.

As she sat, he picked up a piece of paper and handed it to her. "This is a schedule of Danny's day. You'll find the times for his medicine and nap noted."

Cari had trouble hiding her shock as she glanced over the hour-by-hour routine of a four-year-old child. Where was the playtime…visits to the park…time with friends?

"He doesn't have any fun time," Cari commented, staring unbelievingly at this man.

"There's free time listed," he argued. "Two hours in the morning and in the afternoon after his nap."

Cari leaned back in her chair and shook her head. "Did you have a schedule when you were four years old?"

Nick looked taken aback. "Look, Cari. That's not the point." He stood and came around the desk, then rested his hip on the edge. "I feel this routine is important for

Danny's health and well-being. I really don't like his routine varied.''

"Fun is good for a child's well-being, too, and that can't always be scheduled. Sometimes it's spontaneous." She glanced up and realized how close he was to her. She tried diverting her gaze downward and discovered his slacks didn't hide the taut muscular tone in his thighs. Oh, Lord. She swallowed the sudden dryness in her throat and concentrated on matters at hand. Danny. "And I feel it's important that kids get fresh air and sunshine. The park would be the perfect place." She tossed him a challenging glare. "Do you have a problem with that?"

"Weather permitting. Of course, Mrs. Foster only allowed a park visit about once a week."

Cari nodded and glanced back at the paper. "It says here that Danny is on the computer for two hours. I'm sorry, but I'm not what you would call computer literate."

A smile began to spread across his face and Cari was mesmerized by the complete change it made in his chiseled features. "No need to worry, Cari. My son is more than capable of teaching you whatever you need to know."

She found herself returning the smile. "Good, I always wanted to learn."

Nick stood. "Well, unless you have any more questions, we both need to get back to work."

"I'll just go and find Danny," Cari said anxiously as she jumped up and nearly collided with him. Their eyes met. The blatant interest in the silvery depths of his gaze unnerved her. She backed away, flustered, and tripped over the chair.

Nick caught her by the arm and jerked her forward. Their bodies touched and Cari immediately felt a tingling when her hand made contact with his solid chest. She drew a breath and inhaled the masculine scent of his cologne, nearly making herself dizzy.

"I'm sorry, Mr. Malone." She tried to push away, embarrassed by her clumsiness, her uncanny reaction to his touch…to his look.

His gaze bore down on her. "My name is Nick, Cari."

She stilled in his arms, riveted by the powerful jolt of awareness that arced between them. "All right…Nick."

He seemed satisfied and released her. "Now, go and unpack, and if there's anything you need, just let Marion know. I'll see you at dinner."

This time Cari made sure to watch where she was going as she headed for the door and made her escape.

Nick rested on the edge of the desk, staring at the door Cari had closed behind her. His body was a searing reminder of how Cari's touch had affected him. Her hands on his chest had left an imprint and he could still feel the heat. He recalled how her hair had danced around her face, and the rosy blush had colored her cheeks. Had she been as aroused as he? Damn! What was he thinking? She was going to be his son's nanny. Temporarily. He rubbed his hands over his face. He had reacted so strongly to Cari only because he hadn't been with a woman in a long time. No wonder he was feeling like a randy teenager.

Nick returned to his chair. Well, he could easily remedy that situation while he was in New York. Over the past few years during numerous trips to the east coast, he had made the acquaintance of willing females. Surely within the week he would be able to find time to relax…and release some tension. He smiled as he picked up the phone.

The next day, Cari sat down on the park bench and tried to catch her breath. Where did the child get his energy?

She'd thought she was in pretty good shape, but after a morning at the playground with Danny, pushing him on the swings and chasing him up the slide and across the monkey bars, she needed to rest. And this was only her first day. She still had to survive five more.

Cari smiled as she recalled waking up that morning. As

with every morning, her thoughts had been of Angel. But for the first time in more than two years, a child ran into her bedroom to greet her with a hug. Angel had never been shy with her affection, and it seemed Danny wasn't, either. He let her know that he was happy she was staying with him.

Cari admitted to herself that she was worried about the strict schedule Nick had left her. She couldn't in good conscience keep a four-year-old accountable every waking hour. Cari would bet a week's pay that Nick Malone had never had a schedule when he was a kid.

"Hey, Cari! Look at me!"

She shot off the bench like a coiled spring when she found her young charge standing at the top of the biggest slide in the park.

"Daniel Malone. You aren't supposed to be up there." She hurried toward him. The boy didn't wait for the rest of her lecture. He carefully sat and headed down the slide. Fast. All Cari could do was race to the bottom and try to catch him. Well, she made it there, but when she reached for the giggling child, his weight threw her backward. They landed in the cushioning sand with a thud. Cari gasped for much needed air as she sat up.

"Are you all right?" She held Danny out in front of her for inspection.

"That was cool," he said.

"Cool? That was dangerous, young man. You're too little to go…" Her words died out when she saw the boy's wide grin. She hugged him close to her drumming heart. "I know it was fun, Danny, but maybe you should practice your landings on the smaller slide."

He gave her a pouty look. "That's for babies."

"Oh. I beg your pardon, Mr. Man. I keep forgetting you're a big guy of four whole years."

He hopped up and down and giggled again. That's when

she discovered his skinned elbow. "Look, you did hurt yourself."

Danny just shrugged it off. "I want to go again." He started to pull away, but Cari held on to the squirming child.

"Okay, but only once more. And you need to go slower." She sat him down and showed him how to spread his legs and let his rubber-soled tennis shoes regulate his pace. His head bobbed up and down in agreement as she reluctantly let him go. He ran to the ladder without a glance. Boy, this child was independent. Wonder where he got it? Her thoughts immediately went to Nick. She had a feeling that Nick Malone had given his mother a few fits when he was a little boy.

Standing back, she watched Danny climb the ladder, his chubby legs barely reaching each step, but he made it to the top. Then she went to stand near the bottom, but not close enough to let the other kids know that he might need help.

Danny called her name. "Watch me!" he ordered.

Cari's pulse raced as she waved back and prayed that she was doing the right thing. With a grin that was the most beautiful sight she'd seen in a long time, the boy took off down the long silver slide. She didn't breathe until she saw Danny spread his short legs and slow himself. Then, after reaching the bottom, he jumped off the end, started in a dead run to Cari and threw his arms around her waist.

"I did it, Cari! I did it! Just like you said." He threw his head back and asked, "Can I go again?"

"I think twice a day is enough for beginners. Maybe we can stop for ice cream before we head home for your nap."

Just like any four-year-old, his attention span was short, and his new interest was a treat before going home. Cari knew it was a bribe, but Danny needed a little break in his strict routine.

She wondered what his father would say....

It was after eight o'clock that night when Cari brushed the hair off Danny's forehead. He was finally asleep. She sighed as she enjoyed the simple pleasure of seeing the small child safe and secure in his bed for the night. She placed a soft kiss on his head, smelling the wonderful fragrance of his soap and shampoo. He stirred in his sleep, then turned to his side.

She could sit here and watch him all night and never get tired. It had been these simple pleasures she missed the most: cuddling her child, reading her favorite story...tucking her into bed, knowing she was going to be safe.

She walked to the doorway and dimmed the light so she could check on Danny later, then she continued into the sitting area. She thought about a cup of coffee but decided a caffeine-free soda might be better. After taking a glass from the cupboard, she went to the refrigerator and filled it.

The suite was quiet. The past couple years she had gotten used to solitude. She walked to her room, turned on the lamp next to her bed and placed her drink on the coaster. The last thing she wanted to do was leave a mark on the antique nightstand. She glanced around the beautiful bedroom that she'd been given during her stay. The rich, cobalt blue carpet was thick and soft, tempting her to go barefoot. The eggshell walls added a softness and accented the honey oak furniture. She drew back the ivory satin bedspread and placed it at the end of her double bed. Stacking two feather pillows against the headboard, she sat down on the firm mattress.

Cari had never had many nice things. Although she and Tim had planned on owning their own home, they hadn't managed to save enough money. But material possessions had never meant much to her. Family had been all Cari yearned for. And Tim had felt the same. He wanted a big family, too. They'd had so many plans....

There was no doubt that the Malones had it all. Or did they? All their money couldn't protect them from the pain they had to live through with Danny.

Suddenly the phone rang, and Cari jumped. She knew it was the private line and picked up the receiver next to her bed. "Hello?"

"Cari..."

The familiar male voice caused her heart to race. "Nick. What are you doing calling so late?"

"Checking on my son."

"Oh, of course. I just meant that it must be nearly midnight in New York."

He sighed. "It is. And it's been a long day." She could hear the fatigue in his voice. "How's Danny?"

"Sound asleep. Like you should be."

He gave a long sigh. "Another mother is the last thing I need."

Cari felt the warmth rush to her cheeks. "I just...just meant that you need sleep, too."

"Thanks for your concern, Cari, but for quite a while I've managed to take care of myself."

"I'm sure you have," Cari said, although she still had her doubts. She already knew that his wife hadn't been in his life for a long time. But had there been other women who tried to fill the void?

"How did your first day go?"

"It went great. Danny and I went to the park."

"You didn't let him get overtired, did you?"

"No, your son has a stubborn streak. He doesn't quit easily when he wants something."

"What did he charm you into?" Cari could hear the amusement in his voice.

"One more of everything," she answered. "But I ended

up only having to read him one story before he fell asleep about thirty minutes ago."

"So he took his medicine without any trouble?"

"Of course." Cari was getting irritated with his questioning. "Has Danny ever given you any trouble about taking it?"

"No."

"Your son is a very bright child, Nick. He understands more than you think he does."

There was a long silence, and Cari wondered if she'd said too much. But it needed saying.

"Oh?" There was another pause. "What are you trying to tell me?"

She bit her lip. "It's just that Danny wants to be a normal kid."

"Ah, Cari. Don't you know that I would give anything for that to be possible, but it isn't going to happen."

The last thing Cari wanted was to pursue this over the phone. She changed the subject. "How are the meetings going?"

"All right. We made some headway today, I think. But tomorrow we're negotiating some of the finer points of the deal. That's probably when the trouble will start."

"Well, I wish you luck."

"Thanks. How are you spending your evening?"

Cari leaned against the pillows and cradled the receiver next to her ear. "I'm just lying here in bed about to read a book."

"You're welcome to use the suite. There's a television and stereo. I know you're having your meals with my mother, but if you prefer to eat by yourself—"

"Oh, no. I enjoy having dinner with Mrs. Malone."

"I appreciate that," he said. "My mother hasn't had much company lately."

Cari wondered if the same thing was true for Nick. She

doubted he entertained much, unless it was for business. "I enjoy both her and Danny's company very much."

"It's been rough these past few years for you."

It touched her to hear the concern in his voice. "I've had my work at the hospital." Cari's voice softened. "But, yes, it's been lonely."

"I'm sorry, Cari. I didn't mean to bring back bad memories."

Memories were all she had left. "It's okay. The nights are the worst. It seems when you're alone in the dark, your mind just won't turn off...." Her throat seemed to close up.

There was a long pause, then finally Nick said, "You want to talk about it?" Then he rushed on to say,

"I mean, since you're new to Santa Cruz, you can't have too many people to talk to."

Once again this man surprised her with his compassion. "Thank you, Nick. I'll keep that in mind. But I think right now what I could use is some sleep. Your son is an early riser."

"Okay, but if you need...anything, let me know," he said in a low, husky voice.

She smiled. "I will."

"Good night, Cari."

Snuggled down, suddenly warmed by his husky voice, she murmured, "Good night, Nick."

Nick hung up the phone, Cari's soft, sultry voice still lingering in his ear. He knew the last thing he was going to have tonight was a good night's sleep.

He stretched out on the bed and laced his hands behind his head. Spending time on the phone with a woman was something he hadn't done in a long time. So why had he waited until after his son's bedtime to call Cari? He'd found out everything he needed to know about Danny when he called his mother earlier.

He'd never been much for idle conversation. Not unless it was for business. That had been one of his ex-wife's complaints—that he'd been too distant. No communication. Even their lovemaking had been lacking…among other things. Nick closed his eyes, not wanting to rehash that chapter of his life. It had been over for nearly three years. Ever since the day in the hospital when Danny's doctor told them that their son needed a donor heart to survive.

Tory had lost it. She'd cried, then gotten angry, throwing accusations at Nick, telling him that it was all his fault that their child had problems. He was the one who carried the flawed gene.

Nick felt the stab of pain in his chest as if it were happening all over again. Tears clouded his eyes. Damn! Would the guilt ever go away, knowing that he was the cause of his child's imperfect heart? He could finalize merger after merger and make all the money in the world, but what good would it do? It could never guarantee his son a long life.

He drew a deep breath and Cari Hallen's face reappeared in his thoughts. He pictured her in bed, curled up on her side in slumber, her sunny-colored hair spread across the pillow in waves. He immediately grew hard and closed his eyes. A man could forget a lot, lost in her rich blue eyes, her luscious curves. He closed his eyes against the wanting…the hunger…

"Damn!" He jumped off the bed and headed for the shower to cool off—determined not to allow Cari Hallen to complicate his and Danny's lives.

Chapter Five

By the end of the week, Nick had completed the deal with Micrographics. He hadn't gotten everything he wanted in the merger, but it wasn't worth another day of debating issues. On Friday, he caught the first flight out of New York. He was exhausted by the time he arrived home. With briefcase in hand, he stepped out of the limo and walked to the front door. The only thing on his mind was crawling into bed. That was if Danny would allow him a few hours of sleep.

His thoughts turned to Cari, and he realized he was a little anxious to see her, too. He had spoken with her nearly every night during the past week, but he'd never let on that he might make it back a day early. He managed a smile as he opened the front door and went inside. The house was silent.

"Hey, is there anyone around here to greet a weary traveler?" he called out. No response. He tried again. "A weary traveler bearing gifts?"

His smile faded when he didn't hear the familiar foot-steps of his son running to greet him. He checked his watch. It was only twelve-thirty. Danny wouldn't be nap-ping yet, he thought as he headed for the kitchen, where he found Marion.

"Mr. Malone, you're home," she said with a warm smile.

He glanced at the bare table, where his son usually ate his lunch. "Where's Danny?"

She ignored his question. "Your mother is about to have a cup of tea. I'm sure she'll be eager for you to join her." The housekeeper quickly pulled a cup from the cupboard.

"Is Danny with her?"

"No. Cari took him out."

Nick didn't mind that. It was a warm summer day. "To the park?"

The gray-haired housekeeper turned around, but her eyes didn't quite meet his. "I'm not exactly sure of their destination, sir. Maybe you should talk to your mother."

Marion didn't know where Cari had taken Danny? Nick yanked his tie loose as he strode down the hall to his mother's suite. He found her sitting in her chair, watching one of the many talk shows on television.

Eleanor glanced up and smiled. "Well, hello, son. I didn't expect you home until tomorrow."

He kissed her on the cheek. "We finished sooner than expected. Where's Danny?"

"I take it the merger went through?"

"Yes, Mother, it did. Can you tell me where Danny is?"

"Of course. He's with Cari."

He clenched his teeth and prayed for patience. "And just exactly where would that be?"

"Let me see, today is Friday," she said, looking thoughtful. "I believe they went to the beach."

"The beach?" Nick could barely restrain his anger. "Why would you allow her to take him to the beach?"

"Because Cari thought it would be a wonderful treat."

"Treat?" he demanded. "A treat is a piece of candy. Not...not... What beach did they go to?"

Eleanor shrugged. "I believe they went to Twin Lakes State Beach." She studied her son. "If you're disappointed Danny isn't here, Nick, you should have let us know that you were coming home."

"Disappointed? Mother, I'm angry." He took a calming breath. "The woman I trusted with my son has taken him to the beach without my permission. He can't even swim."

"Oh, but he can," she said with wonder in her voice. "Cari's been giving Danny swimming lessons in the pool."

Nick's temper had reached its limit, but he refrained from saying any more, knowing his mother had never approved of his strict parenting. He turned and left the room. Eleanor was more engrossed in her television program than in the whereabouts of her grandchild.

Nick climbed the stairs two at a time and he began stripping off his tie and shirt. By the time he was in his bedroom he was bare-chested. He tossed the wadded garments onto the bed and grabbed a pair of jeans and cotton T-shirt from the dresser. After putting them on, he went to the closet and slipped into a pair of tan Top-Siders. Grabbing the keys to his BMW, he took off down the stairs.

Within thirty minutes he had made it to Twin Lakes State Beach. He pulled into the parking lot and drove up and down the aisles, looking for Cari's car. He was determined to find them, even if he had to comb every beach along the coast. Cari had no right to take his son out without asking him. His hands gripped onto the wheel as he searched the lot. Finally he spotted the faded red Volkswagen bug. It was Cari's all right. He recognized the bright yellow sunflower sticker on the back window. Good God! He hadn't even thought about that damned rattletrap she drove. She shouldn't be carting Danny around in a car that looked as if it would break down at a second glance.

He pulled into the vacant spot next to the car and climbed out. Making his way to the sand, he stopped to scan the area. There had to be hundreds of people here.

He removed his shoes and headed toward the beach. There were kids everywhere. Some were building sand castles, others were in the water, and more than half of them seemed to have dark hair and be about four years old. After approximately fifteen minutes, he decided to check out the lifeguard tower, thinking Cari would be sensible enough to stay close to help in case... Damn! Why did she have to take Danny out of the house?

Suddenly, Nick heard familiar laughter. He stopped. It was Danny's laugh.

He jerked around and saw them. Hand in hand, the two were running along the beach, skipping through the waves as the water surged toward the shore. Danny was wearing a bright green T-shirt and a pair of matching shorts. On his head he had on a too large baseball cap.

Nick's gaze drifted to Cari's long, golden hair dancing in the sunlight as she skipped along the waves. His breath caught as he lowered his gaze to her blue, one-piece swimsuit. It was modest compared to a lot of beach attire, but the clinging nylon revealed every curve of her shapely body. Her legs were slender and long, long enough to cradle a man....

Nick's body quickly reminded him of where his thoughts were going, and he shook his head. He wasn't here to stimulate his libido. He was here to get his son. He marched off in their direction, calling out Danny's name.

Immediately the child looked up.

"Daddy," the boy cried. Danny ran toward him and threw his arms around Nick. "You came home."

"Of course," Nick said, and crouched down to be eye level with his son. "But you weren't there to meet me."

"Cari brought me to the beach."

"I can see that," he answered, and glanced up at Cari to find her nose a bit red. "Looks like you two have been out in the sun a little too long."

"Only an hour. And we've been in the shade most of the time," she said, pointing to a bright green-and-yellow umbrella.

"Cari gave me her Seattle Mariners cap so my nose wouldn't burn," Danny said. "And she put some stinky stuff all over me."

"I made sure that he had plenty of sunscreen," Cari added, acting as if she'd done nothing wrong.

"Well, we shouldn't chance it," Nick began. "I think we should go back home." He tried to stand, but his son refused to let him go.

"No, I don't want to go back," Danny cried. "We haven't built a sand castle yet."

"We'll do it another day."

"No, you'll never bring me back," the boy said stubbornly. "Cari promised me for today. She said every kid has to build a castle...just 'cause they're a kid. And I can pretend to be anything I want to be." Tears formed in the child's eyes. "When Mrs. Foster is better, she'll never take me to the beach. She *never* takes me anywhere."

Nick hadn't realized how many of the simple things in life his son had missed. Was he being unfair to him by trying to protect him? He glanced around the same beach that his own mom had taken him to. Where he had built castle after castle, sometimes not going home until dark.

He took Danny's hand. "Maybe we can stay for a little while."

"Oh, boy!" Danny hugged him. "I love you, Daddy." But before Nick had a chance to cherish this precious moment, Danny took off running.

"C'mon, Dad. We got shovels and everything."

Nick looked at Cari. She was smiling at him. "You've made your son very happy."

With Danny out of earshot, Nick needed to make a few things clear to Cari. "When I talked to you the other night, why didn't you tell me about your plans?"

She shrugged. "I didn't know then."

"You knew I wouldn't approve. And you were right. I don't like being tricked."

"I didn't trick you, Nick. I felt Danny needed this." She moved closer as the wind whipped her hair across her face. He resisted the urge to brush it away. But he'd be lying if he didn't admit that he was dying to touch her.

"He needs to feel normal," she continued. "You can't keep him locked up in the house forever."

"So, you're the expert?"

"No, your son is." Just then Danny's laughter rang out. They both looked in the direction of the child to see him chasing sea gulls. "Let him have his day, Nick."

Nick had never seen his son look this excited…this happy. What would it hurt? If something happened, he had his phone in the car and Cari was a nurse. Maybe this once. "I guess we better get over there to protect the birds."

Cari stood by and watched as Nick jogged toward his son. He tossed his shoes on the beach towels beneath the umbrella and charged at Danny, grabbing him up in his arms and swinging him around. They were both laughing when Nick tumbled them to the sand, careful that the child landed on top of him. They both erupted in a fit of giggles.

Cari sighed, feeling a little envious. She'd had Danny to herself for nearly a week. But it was his father he desperately needed to be with, especially since his mother hadn't been to see Danny since before his surgery. That was something Cari could never understand. A mother deserting her child. Her sick child.

The past five days with Danny had been like a gift from heaven, easing some of the loneliness that had consumed her life in the last two years. Danny was a special child, just as her Angel had been.

No, she couldn't let herself dwell on such thoughts. Besides, she had no proof. But she knew there was a connection, a reason she had been so drawn to the child. Was it because there was a possibility her daughter's heart was beating in Danny's little chest? Cari closed her eyes as her own heart began to race with hope.

Off in the distance, she heard her name being called and she opened her eyes. Danny was motioning for her to come and help. She waved back and, after pulling on her cover-up, joined the two of them for the big dig.

It hadn't taken Danny long to establish himself as supervisor of the project, bossing Nick and Cari into doing the work. Cari was surprised to find Nick taking orders so readily. Of course, the man's muscular shoulders and arms could shovel a lot more sand than a four-year-old's. And once his shirt had been discarded, he could move more freely.

Cari nearly gasped when her gaze skimmed over his well-developed chest. His olive skin was void of hair except for a faint dark swirl around his navel that disappeared into the waistband of his jeans. Oh, Lord! The man was gorgeous, she thought, finding his nearness disturbing and exciting at the same time.

Nick looked at her. "Is something wrong?" he asked.

"No." She shook her head, knowing she'd been caught practically drooling. "We're going to need some water."

Grabbing a couple of the plastic buckets, she hurried toward the ocean. Maybe she should pour the seawater over her head to cool off, she thought, disgusted with herself for acting like a silly teenager. She'd never reacted to a man this way, not even Tim.

The rest of the afternoon passed quickly, and finally the

castle was finished. The two Malone men stood side by side, looking rather proud of themselves.

"Oh, Danny," Cari said. "This is the best castle I've ever seen." She studied the cockeyed structure of wet sand, which in a child's imagination resembled a castle.

"Really?" he asked, then turned to his dad. "Do you think so?"

"It's the biggest and best I've ever seen," Nick said encouragingly. "I wish I had a camera."

Cari handed him a flag made out of a toothpick and a scrap of paper. "Now, as the king, you have to christen your castle."

The child looked thoughtful. "How do I do that?"

"Now, you are the lord of all the land you see," Nick began, sweeping his hands wide. "It is your job to put the flag in the tower so all the kingdom will see it and know that you are their king and protector." Nick bowed at the waist. "If I may assist you…" He picked up Danny and held him over the sand castle.

Danny managed to plant the flag and Cari cheered as the paper waved in the soft sea breeze.

"I did it," Danny cried, jumping up and down. "I made a castle." He looked up at Cari. "Is it time to roast our hot dogs? Did you bring enough for Daddy?"

Cari's stomach suddenly lurched, but she refused to look at Nick, certain he would disapprove.

"Yes, Cari," Nick began. "Did you bring enough for me?"

Cari's eyes were drawn to his. Instead of anger and disapproval, she saw something else. And within a single heartbeat, every cell in her body responded to the man. They weren't even touching, but his eyes were relaying erotic messages. She quickly turned away. "I have plenty of food. But I'll need some wood for the fire."

The late afternoon temperature had dropped a few degrees and the air was cooling off. Still Nick hadn't put on his shirt.

"It's getting a little cold," he said. "Danny needs a jacket."

Cari quickly reached into the bag and pulled out a sweatshirt. "Here, Danny. This should keep you warm until we get a fire going." She tugged the shirt over his head as she and Nick exchanged glances.

"Maybe we should just go home?" he suggested.

"No, Daddy," Danny cried. "I never cooked hot dogs in a real fire."

Cari put a protective arm around the boy's shoulders. "We'll be fine, Nick. If you get a fire going." She dared him to play the bad guy.

"Okay, son. Let's get some wood."

Danny took off down the beach.

Nick grabbed his shirt and pulled it over his head. Feeling the soreness in his shoulders, he knew he was going to pay for his afternoon exertion. He glanced at the woman on the blanket, who was giving him that innocent look. As soon as they got home, he was going to let her know that she was never going to take his son out of the house again without his permission.

His gaze wandered to the small child racing ahead of him, and his heart ached because he had to take things like this away from Danny. But it was for his own protection.

They pulled up in front of the house when it was just starting to get dark. Nick couldn't believe they'd stayed at the beach so long, but once they had the fire going, it kept them plenty warm. He also realized that his son was pretty good at getting his own way. After they roasted hot dogs and marshmallows, the stories started, and the next thing Nick knew it was nearly seven o'clock. They packed up everything in his car, including one sleepy four-year-old, and, with Cari following in her own car, headed back home.

Nick unfastened his son's seat belt and carried him into the house. Cari was behind him as they made it into Danny's bedroom. She went to the dresser and got out pajamas while Nick carefully stripped the sandy shoes and clothes off the sleeping child. Then Cari took over and slipped him into the lightweight pj's. They had to wake Danny enough to give him his medicine, but he was exhausted from the day's activities and in no time was under the covers and sound asleep again.

Nick brushed his son's dark curly hair off his forehead, seeing traces of marshmallow on his cheek. Danny could bathe in the morning, he thought. He walked to the door and turned around in time to see Cari place a soft kiss on his son's cheek. He felt a strange stirring in his own body. The simple pleasure of spending a day at the beach with this woman had been the most wonderful thing that had happened to both him and Danny in a long time. But they weren't the typical American family. They never would be. He turned and walked into the suite, where he waited for Cari.

Nick watched her as she came into the room. Dressed in her beach clothes, jeans and a sweatshirt, her hair in a ponytail and her feet bare, she looked about sixteen.

"I'll go get the things out of the car."

"That can wait, I need to talk to you," Nick said, preventing her departure. It was time to set her straight. "How many other outings have you and Danny had while I was in New York?"

"Just the park a few times, and today's trip to the beach."

Nick raised an eyebrow. "You're sure?"

Cari looked confused, then squared her shoulders. "Look, Nick, you hired me to watch your son. I didn't take a job as warden."

Nick clenched his hands. "I left you a schedule. I expected you to follow it."

"I did. We fit everything in, and with the time left over we went to the park. Today was the only exception, and it wasn't planned until this morning. Danny said he'd never been to the beach, and since it was such a warm day, it sounded like a good idea."

"If you had called me, I would have told you no."

"Good thing I didn't call, then," she muttered, and saw Nick's glare. "Look, I care very much for Danny, and I would never do anything to hurt him. Your son needs to get out of the house. You should have seen him at the park with the other kids—"

"What do you mean?" Nick interrupted. "Kids his own age? You let Danny play with strangers?"

"Sure, why not? Children play with other children at the park."

He began to pace. "As a nurse you should understand that kids that age always have some kind of cold or infection. There's no telling what Danny was exposed to."

"Nick, calm down. You can't keep your son away from other children. It's not healthy. Besides, I didn't put him at risk."

He stopped and whirled around. "You put him at risk every time you took him out of this house."

"But Danny can't survive without people, friends his own age."

"He has so far." Nick's hands were shaking. Why did everyone think they knew what was best for his son?

"Surely Dr. Landers has told you that Danny needs to be treated as normally as possible."

"But Danny isn't normal," Nick stressed.

Cari shook her head. "Have you ever considered going to one of the hospital's support groups? Other parents are going through what you are."

That was it. Nick walked to the desk and pulled his

checkbook from the drawer. He scribbled down an amount, a quick signature, and tore the check out. He went to Cari and handed it to her.

"Here. This is payment for staying with Danny this week. Since I'm home and Mrs. Foster will be coming back soon, we won't be needing your services any longer."

Cari was still angry thirty minutes later. Nick Malone was being pigheaded. But she was being foolish to think she could change him so fast. Now she couldn't see Danny anymore. She should have stopped herself from getting so attached to the boy. Hadn't she always known that Mrs. Foster would be returning as primary care giver for Danny? That this job was only a temporary one? Yes, of course she'd known, but there was this fleeting hope...

Cari zipped up her bag, then looked around the bedroom to see if she'd forgotten anything. Nothing. But then, she hadn't brought that much with her. She released a tired sigh and walked through the connecting bathroom into Danny's room. In the dim light, she could see that the child was sleeping soundly, but she still went to the bed. Biting down on her lower lip, she tried to fight back her emotions. She'd come to love this child and had hoped that somehow she could be a small part of his life. But it wasn't meant to be.

Cari brushed back a lock of his curls. "Bye, Danny," she whispered. "I'll miss reading you *The Velveteen Rabbit.*" Retreating through her room, she picked up her bag and headed down the hall. She had one more thing to do before she left the Malone home. At the bottom of the stairs, she turned away from the front door and went straight to Nick's office.

Cari set down her bag, then, before she lost her nerve, she knocked hard. Without waiting for an answer, she pushed open the door. Not surprised, she found Nick sitting behind his desk. He was so engrossed with something on the computer screen, she doubted he even heard her knock.

He shot her a sharp glance. "Is there something else?"

So she was wrong. She squared her shoulders and marched across the large room. "Yes, there is."

Nick got up and rounded the desk. He still had on his jeans and shirt from the beach. His recently acquired tan definitely added to his good looks. "I thought we said all that needed to be said upstairs."

"*You* said everything," she clarified. "I barely got a word in. I just don't want Danny to suffer because of what happened…between us."

"What do you think I'm going to do, lock my son in his room for the next week?"

Cari didn't answer.

He gave her an incredulous look. "You're kidding, right?"

"You lock him up in this house," she accused. "Danny needs fresh air and to interact with other kids his own age. He needs to experience life, Nick. I know you're afraid that something will happen to him, but you're not allowing Danny to live his life. You're not giving him *any* life."

"Hold it." He raised a hand. "I love my son. I'm only doing what's best for him."

"No! You're doing what's best for you."

The room was silent as Nick stared at Cari in disbelief. How could she think that he didn't love Danny? She hadn't any idea what his life had been like.

"How dare you," he began in a controlled voice. "I'm the one who's been there with Danny. From the time the trouble started at his birth when they discovered his heart condition." *The birth defect I caused,* he reminded himself silently. "I stayed with Danny day and night. Two years later as his condition worsened, I was the one praying they'd find a donor in time. He came so close to not making it..." Nick's voice faltered. He closed his eyes and drew a deep breath. "God, Cari! Do you have any idea what it's like? Then when you get a sliver of hope, you promise God that you'll do everything in your power to cherish that life."

He saw her trembling hand cover her mouth, saw the tears glistening in her eyes, eyes filled with a torment so powerful it nearly shouted. Then it struck him. Her husband, her daughter had both died.

"Hell, Cari, I'm sorry." He came across the room and without any hesitation drew her into his arms. "I'm so sorry. That was a cruel thing to say. Of course you know."

He cradled her small frame, trying to absorb some of the pain he'd caused. She remained rigid, then finally sagged against him as her arms circled his waist.

"It's okay to cry, Cari," he coaxed.

"No ." She shook her head. "If I give in, I might never stop."

"Yeah, I know." He closed his eyes, feeling her sweet softness against him. He inhaled her honeyed fragrance while his hands gently stroked her silky hair. Pressing his lips against her temple, he soothed her back with his hands. After a while things began to change between them. It was as if he had just discovered that he was holding a woman in his arms. His body ached, and suddenly the only comfort he wanted to share with Cari was in bed. He placed another kiss at her temple. When her breathing grew ragged, he worked his way to her eyes, feeling her respond to his touch. His lips caressed her warm cheek and he felt his control slipping.

He told himself to push her away, knowing he was acting crazy. Any carnal thoughts would only lead to trouble. Trouble he didn't need. Cari raised her head and her sapphire blue eyes locked with his, exposing her need and loneliness. With a shaky hand, she reached out and touched his chest, and Nick felt every muscle in his body respond.

Ignoring all the warning signs, he cupped Cari's cheek and lowered his mouth to hers. When she released a whimpering sound, it only made him hunger more, and he pulled her against him, crushing her to his chest. God! It had been so long since he'd held a woman.

Cari's hands moved around his neck, making his whole body tighten with desire. Blood rushed to his head and to his groin. The feel of her seared him to his soul. Somewhere in the mist of their passion he knew he had to stop before it was too late. Finally, he managed to tear his mouth from hers. Breathing hard, he looked down at the surprised expression on Cari's face.

"I'm sorry, that shouldn't have happened," he lied, then quickly turned away, avoiding her eyes.

After a few seconds, Cari managed to say, "You're right. I didn't come in here for…that. I'm sorry, too. Goodbye, Nick."

He heard the door click shut and fought to keep from stopping her. At that moment he wanted nothing more than to go after her and finish what he'd started. But he couldn't. There was no room in his life for Cari Hallen. It was just him and his son. He went back to the computer, knowing he had plenty to fill his life. He had his work.

And, for a while, he had Danny.

The following week, Cari walked into the nurse's break room and tossed her purse into her assigned locker. She glanced in the mirror and checked her french braid. She should be smiling since she had gotten moved to full-time status in the cardiac unit. This was what she wanted. A new job. A new life. But that was before she had gotten emotionally involved with little Danny Malone. How could she walk away from her daughter's heart recipient?

At times her misery was so acute it was a physical pain.

She had to figure a way to move on with her own life. Working full-time would help, but it could never fill the ever aching loneliness.

Her thoughts turned to Nick and the memory of his heated kiss. It had kept her awake since the night she'd walked out of the Malone home. She had been foolish to let it happen, but she'd never regret the feel of Nick's touch, his mouth.... Never in her life had she reacted to a man like that. She felt a stab of guilt, remembering her marriage.

"Hey, Cari, wait up," Matt Landers called out.

She smiled at the good-looking doctor, wondering why she couldn't be attracted to this man instead of pining after Nick Malone. "'Morning, Dr. Landers."

"Good morning, Cari." He too smiled, and every nurse at the desk turned her attention toward the two of them. "You got a minute?" he asked.

Cari glanced over her shoulder to see the whispering conversations going on among the staff. "Of course," she answered, and they walked toward the end of the hall for some privacy.

"I've got a favor to ask," Matt said. "Would you be willing to attend the Parents of Heart Recipients meeting tonight?"

Cari gaped in surprise. No one in the hospital knew that her daughter had been a donor. "I don't know..."

"Look," he continued. "I know it's short notice, but we haven't been able to find a replacement since Cathy went on maternity leave. Some of the nurses have been volunteering, but I feel the program needs a regular liaison from the hospital. Someone the parents can trust. So they can feel free to talk over their fears and problems."

Cari still couldn't speak. Would this be too close to her own pain? "Why do you think I'd be able to handle this job?" she said at last.

Matt folded his arms over his chest, his brown eyes

gentle and understanding. "Because you've lost a child and you're a compassionate person. I've seen you with the kids around here and I feel you'll be a tremendous help to these parents. They need everything from medical advice to emotional support." His hand rested on her shoulder. "I think it will help you, too, Cari."

Cari knew he was talking about Angel, but her thoughts quickly went to Nick and Danny. She hadn't been so helpful to them. "Okay. What time and where do I go?"

A happy grin spread across the doctor's face. "It's at seven o'clock in room 108. What time do you get off?"

"Five."

"How about you come to my office after your shift and I'll take you out for a hamburger?"

Cari tensed. Was he asking her for a date?

Matt must have noticed her apprehension. "Cari, I thought that since I'm going tonight, also, I could fill you in on what to expect. I know we doctors have reputations—"

"No," Cari interrupted. "The only reputation you have is as one of the best cardiologists on the West Coast. It's just that with the grapevine around here..."

The doctor glanced over his shoulder to see the group at the desk watching them. "If only I was able to live up to everything they've been speculating about me over the past three years. In reality I don't have time to date, let alone form relationships."

"I'm sure there are plenty of nurses more than willing to go out with you."

"No, thank you. I think I'll stick to golf on my time off."

"You need to make the trip, Nick," Larry Keaton said. Nick just glared at the second-in-command at Malone Industries.

"I was there two weeks ago. If Micrographics wants any more meetings, they're coming out here."

"But—"

"Save your breath, Larry," Nick interrupted. "You've known me since college, and I'm not about to change my mind."

Nick studied his best friend. The tall blonde was still lean, but before Larry had reached his thirtieth birthday, he had already lost most of his hair. Cindy, his wife, hadn't seemed to notice, though. Larry's college sweetheart looked at him with the same loving eyes she had ten years ago. It was something Nick had envied. A lasting relationship, a husband and wife who were there for each other— who loved each other.

"Well, how does the production time look for the chip?" Nick asked.

"We're on schedule, but Haskins is holding us up."

"Figures." He had a hunch the CEO of Micrographics might pull a power struggle. "What does George want from us? This merger will prevent a hundred layoffs at their San Jose plant."

Larry shrugged. "We knew going into this that getting your IAU chip into production wasn't going to be easy." He picked up his briefcase. "I'll set up a conference call for next week."

"I owe you one, Lar," Nick said, knowing how hard his vice president had worked on this project. How hard they'd both worked on this dream of building their Internet Access Unit. Nick might have designed the chip, but Larry had sold it.

"You owe me more than one," he teased, "but who's counting."

"After we start production on the software, I want you and Cindy to get away for a few weeks."

Larry looked puzzled. "Cindy? Who's Cindy?" Then a

big grin broke on his face. "Will you be in the office tomorrow?"

"Do you need me there?"

"Hell, yes!" Larry grew serious. "But if you haven't found a replacement for Mrs. Foster, don't worry about it." He waved his hand, then walked out.

Claire Foster, Nick thought. He needed to call her and find out when she was coming back. He was more than eager to get things back to normal. He picked up the receiver and punched in the numbers. It was time his son had some structure back in his life. Between his grandmother, Marion and...Cari, the child had been spoiled.

Besides, he needed to get back to the office full-time. The phone rang and Nick leaned back in his chair.

"Hello," the familiar voice answered.

"Claire, this is Nick Malone."

"Hello, Mr. Malone. I've been meaning to call you."

"I hope it's good news," he said as he watched his son walk into the office, wearing the now familiar Seattle Mariners cap. Nick put his hand over the mouthpiece and whispered, "It's Mrs. Foster."

Danny climbed up on his father's lap and propped his elbows on the desk. "Is she better?"

"Danny wants to know if you're better?" Nick asked.

"Tell him my recovery is coming along as expected."

Had she always spoken so formally? Nick wondered. He glanced at Danny. "She's just fine, son. We're all anxious to have you back, Claire," he continued. "Do you think you can give us a date?"

"Well, Mr. Malone. I know I should have called you sooner, but I had a lot of difficulty making this decision. I know I've been in your employment for nearly five years. But since my illness, I've realized how much I miss my family. My sister is also widowed and I've decided to stay with her in Los Angeles. Permanently."

"I'm sorry to hear that. We're going to miss you," he

said politely, all the while fuming inside and wishing he didn't have his child in the room so he could swear out loud. He finished the conversation and said his goodbyes, promising to send her things within the next week.

"Well, Dad, when is Mrs. Foster coming back?"

"She's not, son. She's going to be staying with her daughter and grandchildren."

"Really? Oh, boy!" His son's eyes lit up. "Now you can get Cari to stay with me. I have to tell Grandma and Marion." He climbed down and raced for the door. Before Nick could tell him otherwise, Danny stopped and looked at him. "So, are you gonna call her, or can I?"

Chapter Six

It was nearly dark the next evening when Nick stood outside the old stucco apartment building in Watsonville. He was here under protest and against his better judgment. The last thing he wanted was to let Cari Hallen back into his life. Yet here he was, ready to do just that. Between Danny and his mother, they had talked him into asking Cari to take over his son's care. So before he had time to come to his senses, he had rushed here straight from work.

He glanced around at the faded structure with the peeling paint, wondering what amount they could possibly charge for rent. The grounds were neatly kept, but there wasn't any security. His attention went to the fragile-looking front doors. No dead bolts. Hell, couldn't Riverhaven Hospital afford to pay their nurses enough to live decently? He walked into the building and found Cari's apartment.

A few seconds after he knocked, he heard the lock click.

The door opened a crack and Cari's face appeared behind the security chain.

"Nick? What are you doing here?"

"I've come to take you out of this place," he said.

Cari paused, then she closed the door to release the chain and swung it open.

He didn't wait for an invitation before stepping inside the dark apartment.

"Will you please tell me what this is all about?" she asked.

Cari wore a pair of faded jeans and a light pink sweatshirt. Her hair was pulled back into a ponytail, reminding Nick of their day at the beach, and triggering a reaction in his body that surprised him. He buttoned his suit coat, turned around and checked out his surroundings. The small living room was sparely furnished with two chairs and a sofa. A small television sat on the bookcase. This was no place for Cari.

Cari's voice broke through his thoughts. "Nick, how did you know where I live?" she asked.

"You worked for me, so Bess gave me your address and phone number."

She glanced away. "You could have called."

"Why? So you could make up an excuse to keep me away? So I wouldn't know you're living in a dump like this?"

Pride squared her shoulders. "Look, Nick, you have no business coming into my apartment and talking to me this way." She glared at him. "I only got a full-time position this past week, and my moving costs were a little more than I expected. In a couple of weeks, I plan on finding another place closer to the hospital."

Nick had no idea why he was being so protective, but he knew he wasn't going to let Cari spend another night in this place. The glint of a silver picture frame caught his eye. He strolled over to the table and picked it up. The smiling little girl in the photo had her mother's blue eyes and yellow hair.

A familiar feeling tugged at his heart, and he wondered how Cari had handled the loss of such a precious child. He turned around. "Is this your daughter?"

A ghost of a smile touched her lips. A smile that was achingly sad. "Yes, that was right before she... Angel was two-and-a-half."

He carefully set her daughter's picture back and glanced at the man in the next photo. He didn't ask who it was. For some crazy reason he didn't want to hear about Cari's past, especially one she had shared with another man—a man she had loved.

He walked toward her. "I want you to take care of Danny."

She blinked but didn't say anything.

"Mrs. Foster decided to stay with her daughter in Los Angeles."

"She's not coming back?"

"That's right, and I need someone to take care of Danny. I can't keep working at the house with this merger going on."

"You want me to watch Danny while you look for someone else?"

"No, I want you to take the job...permanently."

Cari gaped. She couldn't help it. Not only was Nick Malone standing in her apartment looking devastatingly handsome in a charcoal gray suit, but he wanted her to come back and stay with Danny. Her heart pounded and she had trouble finding her voice. She wanted to jump up and down and shout that she'd love to, but she knew the best thing would be not to get involved in the Malones' lives. If the secret ever got out... She looked up at Nick, thinking about another concern. Her cheeks warmed as she remembered their kiss.

"Do you really think it's a good idea?"

He rubbed his hand across the back of his neck. "Danny thinks it is." His gray eyes met hers, and there was a spark of genuine emotion. "Regardless of what you think of me, Cari, I listen to my son."

"I never said you didn't love your son," she said, excited at the prospect of caring for the child again.

"Well, whatever you think of me, we have to come to an understanding. My son seems to have adopted you." Nick shrugged. "I've come to realize that Claire Foster wasn't the motherly presence that Danny needed. Maybe that's the reason he's transferred his affections to you."

Cari's heart soared. She felt the same way. "I feel close to Danny, too." She truly believed that Danny was Angel's heart recipient. Maybe that was the best reason for her to walk away, knowing at least that her daughter's short life had made a difference. But Cari couldn't. Danny needed her. And right now, Cari needed both the Malone men. She'd been so alone. She was a woman who needed a family. "What about you?"

He frowned. "What about me?"

"How do you feel about me coming back to work for you?"

"Honestly, if I didn't feel it was a good idea, I wouldn't have asked you to take the job. As for what happened in my office…"

"You mean the kiss."

"Yes, the kiss." His gaze met hers. "We'd both be lying if we denied that we weren't affected by it. But you can rest assured that I have no intentions of starting a personal relationship with you. This is strictly a business arrangement."

Cari was a little hurt that he was able to dismiss what had happened between them so easily. She hadn't. But if she planned to share a future with Danny, she could never let Nick know how much he affected her.

"Of course. I wouldn't come back under any other circumstances." She locked her hands together, hoping he wouldn't see her trembling.

"Good. Now pack what you need for a few days. You're coming home with me now."

Cari felt a thrill of excitement at Nick's demands but quickly came to her senses. "Wait a minute. I have a few questions of my own."

She watched his jaw tense, then he relented. "Okay."

"I will work five days, but I want two days off so I can continue working at the hospital."

"You don't want any time off for yourself?" he asked.

"I don't need any," she answered. It was true. She didn't have any family and she was new in the area. "I prefer to stay busy. Also, I have a support group I work with once a week. I'd like to continue."

"I don't see any problem. Just let me know when those times are and I'll make sure that I'm home. Now it's my turn." He drew a long breath. "You are not to take Danny to the beach, the park or any other playground without checking with me first."

Cari folded her arms across her chest and tried to remain calm. "Okay, if you promise to take time off so *you* can take Danny to the beach and on picnics."

"Picnics?"

"Yes, picnics. You remember, fried chicken, apple pie, ants...."

A smile tugged at his stubborn mouth. "Agreed. Anything else?"

"Not that I can think of, but I'd like to leave things open so we can discuss changes and new activities."

He raised an eyebrow as if to argue again, but changed his mind. "Okay, get your things. We're expected home for dinner."

"Dinner." She looked down at her jeans. "Look, why don't I come tomorrow?"

"Not on your life." He motioned in the direction of the

bedroom. "I was instructed not to return unless you were with me. So grab a nightgown and a toothbrush, whatever you need to get through the night. I'll send someone by tomorrow to tell the manager that you're moving out and pack up the rest of your things."

Cari stopped. "No, Nick. I'm not giving up my apartment." She needed to keep it just in case things didn't work out.

He walked toward her, his jaw clenched. "You think if this doesn't work out I'm going to throw you out on the street?"

Cari refused to look away. She wasn't going to let this man railroad her. "I'm not worried about that." *I've been on the street before,* she thought. "I'm more concerned about what it will do to Danny if I have to leave again. He needs me."

He didn't say anything for a long time, then spoke her name in a husky voice that sent her pulse racing. "Cari, I'll do everything I can to make this work, but if for any reason it doesn't, you'll have a month's severance pay."

Cari had never had much financial security in her life, and since there was only herself to worry about, the offer of money didn't matter to her much. But she didn't know if she could stand to be torn out of Danny's life again. That *did* matter. A lot.

"So," Nick said, "you ready to go home?"

"Home." Cari nodded, only wishing it were true.

The next few days passed without any problems. Cari had gotten settled in the same bedroom as before, and Danny had been there in the mornings to wake her. She looked forward to his hugs. There were other benefits to her job, too. Nick had given her a substantial increase in pay, insisting that she would earn it since she'd be on call twenty-four hours a day when he was out of town.

What made Cari the happiest was Bess agreeing to allow

her to stay on part-time at the hospital, making her eligible for medical benefits. Since the meager savings she'd had had been eaten up by the move to Santa Cruz, Cari needed all the help she could get. Maybe holding on to a vacant apartment wasn't a good idea, but it seemed the only independence she had. Even if she didn't want to think about it, her job wasn't guaranteed. She couldn't forget that Nick had dismissed her once before because of a difference of opinion.

That didn't seem to be a problem this time. Cari hadn't seen much of Nick since her return to the house. Most mornings, he'd been gone before she'd gotten downstairs for breakfast, and some nights he hadn't made it home for supper. She couldn't help but feel disappointed over the man's absence. Was he avoiding her? she wondered, recalling how hesitant Nick had seemed about being in the same room with her. But what about Danny? She could administer the child's daily medication and monitor his health, but Danny needed his dad. Cari also discovered that she wanted Nick to be around more, too.

"Cari. Cari, you're not listening," the child's voice broke into her thoughts.

She glanced down at Danny, sitting next to her at the desk. "What, sweetheart?"

His big brown eyes rounded. "You didn't hear what I said?"

"I'm sorry."

He smiled. "It's okay. I'll tell you again." He picked up a color-coded disk. "This is the target disk. You put it in here." His chubby little hands slipped the red card into the computer slot. "Now, you go to the picture of the cat." Again his hand went to the mouse and somehow managed to move the arrow to the big picture of the cat on the screen. "Then you push the button." He took her hand and brought it to the mouse. "Now, you do it."

The entire week since she'd arrived, they'd worked on

Danny's computer. Cari figured that she needed to learn more so she could keep up with the child. One thing she had to give Nick credit for was all the time he'd spent with his son at the computer, creating programs that were not only educational but entertaining.

"Oh, okay. Here goes." She followed his instructions and pushed the button, listening to the sound of the computer copying on the disk.

Danny's eyes lit up. "You did it," he cheered. "Wasn't it fun?"

Cari tickled him. "For you it is, 'cause you know what you're doing. How did you learn all this stuff?"

"My daddy, he's made me lots of games. You want to see more?" He reached into the shelf next to the screen and searched for another colored disk with a picture on it.

"Does your dad ever take you outside, like to the park?"

Danny shook his head. "No. He's afraid I'd get sick. So was Mrs. Foster." He studied her. "Are you afraid I'll get sick?"

Cari smiled and brushed his wavy hair from his forehead, noticing a few freckles scattered across his nose, probably from their trip to the beach. "Sometimes, but I'll make sure you take care of yourself. That's the reason you should eat all your vegetables and take your vitamins."

"Even carrots?"

"Especially carrots. They make your eyes strong so you can see the computer screen."

"And so I can read when I go to school."

Couldn't put anything past this child. She wondered how Nick was going to deal with school. "That's right, you're going to be five soon."

His head bobbed up and down.

"After Christmas. Then I go to kindergarten."

A pain shot through Cari. Angel would have started school the same year. "You're growing up so fast. You're not a baby anymore. Pretty soon you'll be going to school every day.''

Danny's smile slowly faded. ''Cari, will the other kids make fun of me 'cause I had to get a new heart?''

It was after midnight when Nick climbed the stairs to the suite. He was exhausted. He'd spent the day at the San Jose plant working on a design problem. Would this project ever run smoothly? he wondered as he tugged off his tie. He stuffed it into his suit jacket and opened the door to the suite.

Setting his briefcase on the table, he walked into the kitchen area and opened the refrigerator. He found a casserole and smiled. Marion had sent up dinner. Even though he hadn't eaten since lunch, he didn't feel like food. He grabbed a can of juice, popped open the lid and took a long drink. The cold liquid felt good going down.

He gathered up his things and started toward his bedroom, hoping for a good six hours of uninterrupted sleep. He had a production meeting at eight in the morning. He reached for the light when he caught sight of something on the sofa. Cari. Curled up in the corner, her head resting on one of the throw pillows, her pale hair fanned out around her face, she was sound asleep.

He walked silently into the sitting area, then sat down on the edge of the oak-and-glass coffee table. He started to wake her, but something stopped him. Maybe it was the long lashes resting against her rosy cheeks, or the flawless skin that made his fingers ache to stroke her softness. He drew a long breath, and her subtle fragrance swirled around him like a heady cloud, filling his senses with her delicate scent. Shifting his gaze to her full mouth, he swallowed back a groan, knowing too well how intoxicating she tasted. He continued his unguarded journey to the rise and fall of her full breasts. Her yellow cotton gown and robe were modest enough, but didn't hide the faint outline of her nipples through the fabric.

Cari wasn't tall and willowy like the women he was usually attracted to. In fact, she was barely average height; she didn't even reach his chin. His gaze moved to her slim waist, then to the shapely flare of her hips. Smooth, curvy legs peeked out from beneath her robe, and crossed at her delicate ankles. Each of her ten toes was painted bright pink.

Damn! He didn't want to be attracted to this woman, but she always seemed to be on his mind. She was so compassionate with Danny. He had noticed the changes in his son almost immediately since her return. He found he looked forward to seeing her, hearing her soft laughter ringing through the house, making him hope and dream again.

He couldn't be in the same room with Cari Hallen without wanting to strip off her clothes and bury himself so deep inside her that it satisfied the lonely ache that kept him awake night after night. Nick swore under his breath and Cari stirred, making a throaty purring sound. His pulse raced through his veins as she blinked and her eyes locked with his.

"I was about to wake you."

She quickly sat up. "I'm sorry. I must have fallen asleep. I was waiting up for you."

That idea excited him, but reality quickly took over. "Is something wrong with Danny?"

"No. I just wanted to ask you something."

"What?"

"Would it be all right if I take Danny to the park tomorrow?"

"If the weather is warm, I don't see any problem."

Cari studied Nick hungrily. She hadn't seen him in days, not since production started on his new computer chip. The long hours were taking their toll. There were dark circles under his eyes. "You look tired. Why don't you take the day off, too? We're going to stop by the store and get a kite. I can pack some sandwiches and make a day of it."

"Like the beach?"

Cari felt herself blush as she watched Nick begin to smile. How handsome he looked once the scowl was gone.

She tucked her bare feet under her robe. "Okay, so I get carried away when I plan things. I guess it's because I'm used to working full-time. I had so little time to spend with Angel that I had to cram everything into my days off."

Nick's expression turned to concern. "You must miss your family a lot."

"Yes, I do." Memories crowded in, making her smile. She couldn't pinpoint when it had happened, but talking about Angel had become easier. "Angel was crazy about the park. Of course, in Seattle we got so much rain that whenever the sun came out, the child was ready to go. And once we got there, she never wanted to come home. Then she'd turn on the tears and it would nearly break my heart...." Cari stopped as her eyes met Nick's. "Sorry, I didn't mean to get carried away."

"Please, don't apologize, Cari." He reached out and placed his hand on hers. "I've heard that daughters have a way of wrapping mothers around their fingers." His extraordinary eyes were filled with warmth and compassion.

This was the first time she'd ever felt comfortable around him. "Actually, Tim was worse than I was," she admitted. "Just wait. If you ever have a daughter, I bet you'll spoil her rotten, too."

Abruptly, his smile was gone and he stood. "That's something I'll never know." He walked to the other side of the room and picked up his briefcase. "I'm going to bed. You should, too. Have a nice time at the park tomorrow. 'Night, Cari."

Stunned, Cari watched as he disappeared down the hall.

She heard him go into Danny's room, then a few minutes later his own bedroom door closed.

What in the world had she said to set him off like that? "Oh, Nick," she whispered. "Why are you shutting everyone out?"

Cari and Danny came downstairs for breakfast the next morning together. Already the child had a million questions about their outing to the park.

"But I never flyed a kite before," Danny insisted.

"It's flew," Cari corrected. "And you're going to learn. Just like you taught me to copy a disk, I'm going to teach you to fly a kite."

"But what if I can't?"

Cari stopped when they reached the bottom step. "Can you run?"

Danny nodded. "Real fast."

"Okay, hold up your hands." The child did as he was told and she quickly examined each chubby little finger. "Well, these hands look like they can hold on to a string. Yep, you can definitely fly a kite."

"Oh, boy. Oh, boy." He jumped up and down. "I'm gonna go tell Grandma." He took off running, and Cari hurried to catch up. But once she reached the kitchen door, she froze in her tracks. Nick was sitting at the table, having breakfast with his mother, and an excited Danny raced in and began talking nonstop about his day.

Nick glanced up at her and smiled, then turned back to his son. Cari leaned against the doorjamb, focusing her attention on the older Malone. She was no longer getting resistance from Nick. Had he finally accepted her and decided she wasn't going to harm his child?

As usual, Nick was dressed in a dark business suit, a crisp white shirt and a brown and blue paisley tie. Most women dreamed about men in a pair of tight jeans and cowboy boots, or bad boys in black leather jackets. Not her. This *GQ* man was more than enough to stir her libido.

"Good morning, Cari," he said in a low voice that sent a shiver through her. "Are you sure you're ready for today?" He nodded to the enthusiastic child now chatting with his grandmother.

"My, you are going to have a big day, Daniel," Eleanor Malone said. "You better eat a good breakfast." The older woman looked up at her. "You, too, Cari. If Daniel is anything like his father, I have no doubt he will keep you hopping."

Cari took her place at the table as Nick shot his mother an irritated glance. "I'm sure Cari isn't interested in my childhood," he said.

Marion appeared and placed a plateful of scrambled eggs and two pieces of fresh fruit in front of Cari.

"Better eat up," Nick said teasingly. "We wouldn't want you to keel over from exhaustion."

"Yeah, Cari," Danny said. "I want to fly my kite all day."

Nick tried to suppress a grin as his gaze caught hers. "Sounds like you've got a busy day planned." He nodded toward her plate. "Maybe Marion should bring you more."

"I have plenty, thank you," she said, curious as to what had put him in such a playful mood. Well, she could play, too. She picked up her fork. "It is going to be a busy day. We're going to the park, and after we catch a strong breeze and get our kites high, we're going to have lunch."

"Fried chicken," Danny cheered.

Nick's gaze narrowed. "Are fried foods such a good idea?"

Uh-oh. So much for acceptance. Here, true to form, came the resistance. "Every once in a while doesn't hurt," Cari stated. "Believe me, Danny eats more than his share of nutritious food. I thought today we could make an exception."

What in the hell was she trying to do? Nick wondered, knowing he would be the bad guy if he said no. Or maybe she'd planned it this way.

Ever since Cari came storming into their lives, she had managed to change everything, including his calm and orderly life-style. And what was worse, she was making him think about taking the day off and going with them. Hell, he had a plant full of employees waiting for him to complete the beta test on the new software. After yesterday's glitch, he wasn't even sure how to fix things. He'd lain awake trying to think of a possible solution, but the only thing he could conjure up in his head with any success was Cari in her yellow nightgown.

"Is it okay, Dad?" Danny asked, jarring Nick back to the present.

"I guess this one time, son."

"Oh, boy!" The child started to get down from the table.

"But first you have to finish your breakfast."

"Will you come with us, Daddy?" the boy asked. "It'll be fun, like the beach."

"I'm sorry, son." Nick hated the disappointed look on Danny's face. He was too young to realize how much his father wanted to go with them this morning, but he couldn't. He pushed his chair away from the table and stood. "I need to get to work." He went around the table and kissed his mother, then mussed his son's hair. "See you later, buddy."

"Will you be home for dinner?" Cari asked.

He looked at her, suddenly realizing that her presence made it seem as if they were a real family. His gaze drifted to her soft, full mouth. *If you were waiting for me, I would drive like hell to get here,* he thought, then quickly came back to reality. No woman would be waiting for him.

"I'll try." He turned and went out the door but didn't get too far before Cari called his name. She caught up with him in the entry.

"Nick, I know you said you would try, but please, it's been nearly a week since you've been here. Danny hides it well, but he misses you."

He closed his eyes and sighed. "Look, I said I'll try."

"You worked through the weekend. Don't your employees have families they want to be with, too?"

"Yes, but they also need their jobs to support those families," he said determinedly.

Cari lowered her eyes. "I'm sorry. Of course, a lot of people are depending on you. Perhaps you'll be home tomorrow?" She looked up at him hopefully.

Hell, he couldn't promise her that. If things didn't go well today, he had to keep working straight through until they did. "How about if I promise to be home for dinner and spend a couple hours with Danny before bed?"

She smiled and a small dimple appeared in her cheek. "He'd like that. But be ready to listen to him nonstop about his day. Angel was so excited after a day at the park. I had a terrible time trying to settle her down for the night. I usually had to read her an extra story."

Nick watched Cari's eyes light up at the mention of her daughter.

"Then if that didn't work, I had to rock her..." She stopped and a rosy blush appeared on her face.

"Look, don't apologize," Nick assured her. "I want you to feel free to talk about Angel."

She nodded shyly, and he wanted to pull her into his arms for assurance. Damn! What was he thinking? He had to get out of there. "I've got to go."

"Wait, I almost forgot. I have to leave for my support group meeting by six-thirty."

Frowning, he nodded. "I said I'd be here."

Cari watched as Nick walked out the door. She smiled.

They'd been together almost a week and not one argument about Danny—other than the minor disagreement over fried chicken. Now, if the man would just stay home. Of course tonight he had to be here, but she wouldn't. Walking back to the kitchen, Cari was a little disappointed she'd miss Nick tonight, but Danny would benefit from spending some quality time alone with his father.

Cari found Danny finishing his food. "You ready to go?"

Nodding, he scooted off his chair. "What color kite do I get?"

"Any color you want. You get to pick it out."

"Oh, boy."

"We just need to go upstairs and brush our teeth and comb your hair."

The child was already running out the door before she could tell him to slow down. She shook her head and looked at Eleanor Malone. "I believe he's a little excited."

"Well, it's about time," Eleanor said. "That boy has been cooped up in this house too long."

Marion appeared and began clearing the table. "That old Claire Foster was the worst. She'd barely allow Danny downstairs, let alone trips to the park."

Cari had had suspicions about the older woman, but knew that in her own way she had cared for Danny and was only trying to protect him from exposure to germs. "Well, if I don't get upstairs, Danny will probably have toothpaste all over the bathroom."

"And I'd better head to my room," Eleanor said as she turned her chair from the table. "I'm missing 'Regis and Kathie Lee.'"

Marion stacked the breakfast dishes. "You go on up. I'll have your picnic basket packed before you get back."

"Marion, you don't have to do that. I was planning to stop by a fast-food chicken place."

The housekeeper looked insulted. "You think I'm going

to let my Danny have a picnic without a fresh-packed lunch?''

Cari laughed. "I guess not." She headed out of the kitchen just as the phone began to ring.

Her hands full of dishes, Marion called over her shoulder for Cari to answer it.

Cari went to the phone hanging on the wall and picked up the receiver. "Malone residence."

"I'd like to speak with Nick Malone, please," a soft, sultry voice asked.

"Mr. Malone has already left for the office."

"May I have that number?"

Cari knew anyone who needed to contact Nick had his office number. "I'm sorry, I can't give out that information."

She heard the frustrated sigh on the other end of the line. "Then how am I supposed to get ahold of him?"

"If you'd like to leave your name and number, I'll give it to Mr. Malone."

"I've tried that, but he never seems to get my messages."

Cari knew that was possibly true, since Nick hadn't been home much. "I'll put it on his desk and tell him when he returns home tonight." Cari reached for a pen and paper next to the phone. "Your name and number, please." She waited.

"My name is Victoria Malone...."

Cari's hand stilled. Nick's ex-wife. Danny's mother. What did she want?

"Did you get that?"

"Would you repeat your number?" Cari said, too shocked to have heard her the first time.

Victoria stated the number again. "Tell him it's imperative that I talk with him as soon as possible. It's concerning our son."

A million things were going through Cari's head. "I'll

tell him." She hung up the phone. What would Victoria Malone possibly want with her son after all this time? She'd been out of their lives for three years. Suddenly a pain shot through Cari.

What if Victoria Malone had decided she wanted her family back?

Chapter Seven

"It gives me great pleasure to introduce our new hospital liaison, Cari Hallen," Matt announced.

At the sound of the applause, Cari stood, then quickly sat back down as she nervously glanced over the large number of people who'd showed up for the support group meeting. Both mothers and fathers had come, and some even brought their children with them. The preschool kids played in the corner, the smaller ones were held protectively by their parents.

"Many of you might know Cari from Riverhaven. She works part-time on the cardiac floor and has assisted me a few times on some of the biopsies." Matt smiled as he looked at Cari. "Her favorite patients are the kids. That's how I got her to volunteer so readily." Laughter broke out in the room. "Seriously, Cari is here to share her expertise and help answer some of the questions you have about caring for your children."

For the next thirty minutes Matt continued to run the

meeting, explaining about some new findings and procedures, then turned the meeting over to her. Still a little
nervous, Cari began taking questions from the anxious parents, while Matt excused himself to answer his pager.

Finally the meeting concluded about nine. Cari went to
the refreshment table and poured herself a much-needed
cup of coffee. She was approached by a woman in her
early thirties carrying a little girl about a year old. Cari
felt a tightening around her heart, that familiar ache whenever she saw a little girl.

"Hello," the woman said. "I'm Sharon Bennett and this
is my daughter, Heather."

"Hi, Sharon." Cari looked down at the fair-haired child.
"Well, hello, Heather. You're a cutie."

The little girl grinned, showing off her two front teeth
as she reached her arms out to Cari.

Cari had no trouble taking the innocent bundle. Cradling
the little girl in her arms, she inhaled that wonderful baby-
powder smell. Cari felt her emotions welling, but holding
this child was like a fix. She needed to feel this sweet life
in her arms. Although she'd missed her Angel desperately,
Cari took some consolation in knowing that she had made
the right decision to give up her daughter's organs. It had
been a soul-wrenching decision, but seeing how healthy
Danny and this little girl were, she knew it was the right
one. She hugged Heather tight against her breast. She was
a precious gift, and she wouldn't be here if not for the
unselfish parents who'd braved their grief and signed the
release forms for organ harvesting...giving the gift of life.

"Heather doesn't usually go to anyone," her mother
said. "I guess she got used to your voice during the meeting." Sharon smiled. "I wanted to thank you for coming.
Since Dr. Landers started these meetings, I haven't missed
one. They've been my salvation." She glanced down at
her entwined hands. "Heather was born with Left heart
syndrome. She received her new heart before she was a

month old, but she's had two bouts with rejection.'' She looked up at Cari once more. "I've been blessed to have Dr. Landers and this group for support. Heather's been healthy for the past four months, but I've been afraid to leave her and I have to work."

Cari moved the baby to her hip, not willing to give her up yet. "Have you thought about you and your husband working different shifts until Heather is a little older?"

"I'm not married," Sharon said matter-of-factly. "Heather's father isn't involved in our lives. I've been fortunate, though. My boss has been very understanding when I've had to take time off work." She looked over her shoulder at the couple talking with Matt Landers. "I connected with Bill and Cathy Morgan and she's been watching Heather during the day. Hopefully, next year, Heather will be able to attend the day care where I work."

Cari touched the child's nose. "Well, she's a real sweetheart." Little Heather smiled on cue and waved her arms.

"That's what Cathy says. She has two boys. Do you have any children?"

Cari's breath caught. "I had a daughter. But...she died."

"Oh, gosh, I'm sorry, Mrs. Hallen," Sharon said as tears formed in her hazel eyes.

"It's okay, Sharon. Really. And please call me Cari." Cari handed the child back to her mother.

"If I had known—"

"Sharon, really, it's okay. My daughter and husband died over two years ago in a car accident." Cari felt as if the room were suddenly closing in on her. She needed to get some air and fast.

Sharon just nodded, looking terribly uncomfortable as she hugged her baby.

"Look, I'd better be getting home. I have to work tomorrow." Cari excused herself, and without waiting for Sharon to speak, she headed for the door.

Once outside the hospital, Cari drew a deep breath of cool ocean air. What was wrong with her? She'd worked with children at the hospital without falling apart. Maybe she was just tired, after her long day with Danny. They had barely made it home before supper. Danny had had a little trouble getting his kite to take flight, and he'd been determined to do it on his own. His stubbornness nearly exhausted her patience. When she'd left the house about six-thirty, both father and son were discussing the day's outing. She also wondered if Nick had gotten the phone message from his ex-wife that she had left on his desk. The big question, would he call her back?

Some of the parents began filing out of the building and waved goodbye to her. It was time for her to leave, too, she decided, since Danny would probably be waking her up before the sun.

Walking toward her car in the employee lot, she reached in her pocket for her keys. She unlocked and opened the car door, then climbed in behind the wheel. But when she put the key in the ignition and turned it, nothing happened.

"C'mon, start," she coaxed as she tried again, but still nothing. No doubt it was the starter, Cari thought. The mechanic had warned about needing to replace it soon. And that was before she'd left Seattle. She sighed tiredly. Now she was stuck.

"Having problems?"

Cari jumped at the sound of the male voice. She turned around, relieved to find Matt Landers. "Oh, Matt. You scared me."

"I'm sorry." He nodded to the car. "Is there anything I can do?"

"It's my starter."

He glanced around the employee lot. "Well, you can leave it here overnight and call a mechanic to look at it tomorrow. I'll give you a ride home."

"I can't ask you to go out of your way...."

"Why not? I asked you to take time out of your busy schedule to come tonight. C'mon," he began as he pulled open the car door. "I'll buy you a cup of coffee and you can tell me why you took off so quickly."

"Did anyone else notice?"

"Just Sharon. I think she was afraid that she upset you."

Cari shook her head. "No, she didn't. I guess holding her little girl brought back some memories." She looked up at the handsome doctor as they walked across the lot to his cream-colored luxury sedan.

"Cari, if this is going to bother you—"

"No," she protested. "It's not a problem. I need to do this. It's just that little Heather reminded me of Angel."

Matt put his arm around her shoulders as they continued to walk. It wasn't anything sexual. He was just comforting her as he would any one of his patient's parents. "I'm sorry, Cari. I wish I could say it'll get easier, but I can't. I've never had a child." He sighed, and Cari could see his anguish. "I've lost patients and had to tell the parents. It's not a part of the job you can be trained for, especially when people expect you to be a miracle worker."

He released the car alarm and opened the passenger door. Cari got in, inhaling the scent of rich leather. Matt walked around and climbed in the driver's side but didn't start the car. "I meant what I said, Cari. If these meetings are going to cause a problem—"

"No!" Maybe it was time to tell him about Angel. "Matt, there's something I should tell you." She gave him a sideways glance but still didn't speak.

"Cari," he said as he touched her hand, "I promise, anything you say to me will never be repeated."

Cari bit her lip and tears welled up in her eyes. She had hoped when she came to Santa Cruz, she could leave the sad memories behind.

"Two years ago when my husband and daughter were in the car accident, I was on duty at the hospital. Tim was already pronounced dead by the time I got down to emergency. But Angel...she was put on life support. The doctors ran every test imaginable to see if there was any hope that she might survive. But her head trauma was too severe. Two days later, they declared her brain-dead.'' Cari stared out the windshield as a tear ran down her cheek. She quickly swiped it away. ''But before they took her off the respirator I consented to have her organs harvested.''

Matt squeezed her hand. ''Oh, jeez, Cari. If I had had any idea, I would never have asked you to be liaison.''

''No, Matt.'' She turned to face him. ''Just like my work at the hospital, I need these meetings.'' She didn't tell him that being with Danny Malone was her biggest need. ''Seeing these children being given another chance helps me realize how right I was in donating Angel's organs. And the fact won't change that every time I see a little girl, I'll long for my child.''

In the dimly lit car, she could see the compassion in his eyes. ''I knew you were one heck of a nurse, but you're also one heck of a brave lady, Cari Hallen. You've gone through a lot. If there's anything I can do to help...''

Cari smiled. ''You have...by listening. I was in a support group in Seattle and they helped me through some pretty rough times. But I felt I needed to move on...to get away from the memories. I love it here in Santa Cruz and I love working at the hospital.''

''Well, the kids are crazy about you. I only wish you'd remained on staff full-time. I'm glad you're with Danny, though. He needs you right now. I just hope Nick realizes how lucky he is to have you.''

Nick. The last thing she wanted was for him to find out about her donating Angel's organs. Not now—not yet. ''Matt, please don't say anything to Nick about this. I wouldn't want him to jump to the wrong conclusion.''

''Cari, Nick would be the first to understand. Remember, his son received a heart from a generous parent like yourself.''

She glanced away. But would he feel the same way if he found out the truth.

"C'mon, I promised to buy you a cup of coffee.'' He started up the car. "I'll even throw in a piece of pie, and you can fill me in on things at the Malone mansion.''

Nick had been pacing the past hour. It was ten o'clock. Where was Cari? Surely the meeting didn't last this long. Maybe she'd had an accident. He began walking again.

Suddenly the intercom buzzed. Nick answered and the guard at the front gate told him Cari had arrived.

Nick hung up, marched down the stairs and yanked open the front door.

"Where have you been?''

She glanced up and gasped. "Nick. What are you doing up?''

"Isn't it obvious?'' He folded his arms across his chest. "I'm waiting for you.''

She ignored him. "Well, I'm home now. So you can stop waiting.'' She started for the stairs and he went after her.

"Aren't you going to tell me where you've been?''

Cari stopped on the landing. "The meeting ended about nine o'clock. When I went to my car it wouldn't start, so Matt offered to give me a ride home.'' She shrugged. "And I'm back.'' She continued up the stairs.

"That was over an hour ago.''

Cari pushed open the door to the suite. "Matt was hungry. We stopped for pie and coffee.''

He'd just bet Matt Landers was hungry. "Do you think it's a good idea, you going out with a doctor from the hospital?''

"It wasn't a date. Matt and I are just friends.''

Yeah, right. Men and women weren't friends.

"Besides," Cari continued, "I didn't realize I had to tell you my whereabouts every minute."

"You don't." He noticed her sad expression. He couldn't help feeling protective. "I was just worried. Didn't your father ever worry about you?"

Cari's chin rose. "I never had one."

"What do you mean you never had one? Everyone has a father." He paused, waiting for her to explain.

"I never knew who mine was. There was just me and my mother. And she died when I was eight. I don't think a series of foster fathers count."

Nick froze. Fathers—plural? He knew she didn't have any family, but... "Hell, I'm sorry."

"Don't be, it was a long time ago."

The last thing Cari wanted was to stand here and rehash her past with Nick. It had been a long, tiring day. But this might be the best time to clear the air. "This is a switch. It's usually me who's waiting for you to come home."

"I have good reasons why I have to be gone," he said defensively.

"The reasons don't matter. The only thing that matters is that you should be here with your son. He needs you, Nick."

"He has you to take care of him," he challenged.

"It's not the same. Danny wants his father." Cari suddenly remembered the phone call from Victoria Malone. "Or his mother."

Nick glared at her, hatred blazing in his eyes. "She'll never be a part of my son's life."

"But what if Danny—"

"Never," he interrupted. "Tory isn't going to get anywhere near Danny."

"But she is his mother."

"What kind of mother leaves her child when he's dying? She told me she couldn't handle his illness." Nick raked a hand through his hair. "Well, she sure as hell could take my money. And believe me, the divorce cost me. But the million was worth it. I got sole custody of Danny.''

Cari wondered if it was worth it. Nick had paid more than monetarily.

''Look, Cari.'' He came across the room to stand in front of her. ''Tory is selfish. If she wants to come back into Danny's life, you can bet it's for a reason, and believe me, love has nothing to do with it. You have no idea what that woman is capable of.'' There was pain in Nick's eyes. ''I will not allow my son to be hurt. Besides, she has no rights. She gave those up when she walked out on the both of us. The only communication I'll have with my ex-wife is through my lawyer. I've already contacted Craig Reed about Tory calling the house.'' His gaze leveled on Cari. ''Just make sure that you tell me every time she calls. And never is she to be allowed to speak with Danny.''

Cari nodded. ''I promise. I'll do everything possible to protect Danny.'' She watched his anger turn into relief.

''Thank you. I'll see that you're compensated for your trouble.''

''Nick, stop. I don't want your money. I happen to care about Danny.''

He looked remorseful. ''I know that.''

Nick had never met anyone like Cari. The people he knew all seemed to be out for the almighty dollar, except for a small circle of his close friends. He reached out and stroked her cheek with the back of his hand, all the time knowing he was treading on dangerous ground. But even staying away from the house hadn't dispelled his feelings for this woman. If anything they'd only intensified.

''You know you've been keeping me awake nights.''

She looked up at him. ''Nick, this is a bad idea.''

''Of course it is.'' He lowered his head, bringing his lips within a whisper of hers. She smelled so damn good. Even in the short time she'd been at the house, he'd grown accustomed to her scent. "But it doesn't stop the fact that I want to kiss you." He smiled to himself, hearing her intake of breath. "And if you're truthful, I think you want to kiss me, too."

Cari's gaze darted away, then finally met his. "Yes."

His mouth closed over hers, swallowing her sexy moan. He wrapped his arms around her back, praying for caution, but when he pulled her heavenly body against his, he knew he was doomed. Nothing else seemed important except the woman in his arms. Oh, he needed her...badly.

Cari's arms circled his neck as he deepened the kiss, parting her lips with his searching tongue, delving within to taste all of her. His hands roamed over her, and he could feel her tremble at his touch. Her movement along his body fueled the desire he'd been suppressing for weeks. With a groan, he pulled her tight against him, trembling as her warm hands slid over his chest, setting him aflame.

He tore his mouth from hers but didn't pull away. "Cari," he breathed painfully against her thoroughly kissed lips. "I don't know how much longer I can keep my hands off you." He took teasing nibbles from her lower lip. "Tell me to stop."

She drew a ragged breath. "Stop...."

Nick closed his eyes at the sound of her husky voice. "That wasn't very convincing."

Cari sunk her fingers into his hair, tugging him closer. She settled her lips squarely on his, coaxing them apart and tasting him deeply. He groaned again as he pressed his arousal against her, letting her know what she was doing to him.

Nick tore his mouth from hers, staring down at her fervent blue eyes. She was so lovely. He began planting kisses down her neck...her long, lovely neck. His hands made fast work of the tiny buttons on her blouse, then parted the fabric. He felt her body quiver beneath his touch as he cupped her full breasts through the sheer bra. When his fingers skimmed her delicate nipple, a throaty gasp came from her throat.

"God! You're so beautiful," he whispered before his mouth covered hers again.

Suddenly a voice cried out. Nick broke off the kiss, realizing the sound was coming from his son's room. "Danny. Something is wrong." He tore off down the hall.

Cari stood dazed. She drew several breaths, trying to clear her head. My God! What had happened? Once again Danny's cries echoed in the room.

"Danny," she whispered. Quickly buttoning her blouse, she followed the sound of the distressed child. Her heart racing, she rounded the corner to his room just as Nick was helping his son out of bed, leaving the evidence of an upset stomach all over his blankets.

"Oh, Danny." She looked at the pale four-year-old. "Let's get you cleaned up."

"I got sick," he said, fighting back tears.

"I know." She began stripping off his soiled pajamas. "But we'll make you feel better." She was still breathless as she glanced up at Nick. This was no time to think about what had nearly happened in the other room. "Just as soon as I get you cleaned up. Does your stomach still hurt?"

The child nodded. "Real bad."

Nick stepped in and placed his hand on Danny's forehead. "He's warm, too." Concern was etched on his face. "He probably caught something from the kids he's been playing with."

There was no mistaking the accusation in his tone. How had he known about Danny's new friends? "Danny couldn't possibly catch something that fast. He probably just ate too much."

"Yeah, too much junk."

"He didn't have junk," Cari insisted.

Suddenly Danny's hand went to his mouth. Nick swung his son up in his arms and rushed him into the bathroom.

Cari followed closely and they made it to the toilet just in time. She got a washcloth as Nick tried to comfort his son.

The tears came. "I don't feel good," Danny cried, and went into Cari's arms. She cradled the boy, praying that the child only had a minor stomach virus. But the angry look on Nick's face told her that whatever Danny had contracted, his father was holding her responsible.

"How about you sit in a cool tub while I change your bed?"

"Don't leave me, Cari." Danny hugged her tighter.

"I won't." She looked at Nick, but he had already left the room. She reached in the tub to turn on the water, then stripped off Danny's pajama bottoms. After checking the water, she coaxed the child into the tub.

Ten minutes later, careful not to let Danny catch a chill, she wrapped him in a big towel and carried him into the bedroom, where she discovered Nick had already changed the bedding.

"Look, Danny. Your dad put on fresh sheets."

The child was still pale and lethargic. She set him down on the edge of the bed as Nick walked back into the room.

"How are you doing, son?"

"My stomach hurts," Danny mumbled as Cari helped him into a pair of lightweight pajama bottoms.

She went through the bathroom into her adjoining bedroom and grabbed her medical bag. She returned to Danny's bedside, and after finding a Thermoscan thermometer, she touched it to his ear and got an instant reading of one hundred and one. She pulled out her stethoscope and placed it against Danny's back to listen to his breathing. To her relief, his lungs seemed fine. His heart rate was a little high, but nothing out of the normal range.

Cari started to tell Nick but discovered he had disappeared again. If there was only some way she could calm his fears—and her own. With a trembling hand, she brushed Danny's hair off his forehead. She was pretty sure this wasn't anything more serious than the flu, but when it was your own child... Her heart swelled as she smiled at the sick boy. Danny was like her own. She would never allow anything to happen to him.

Nick reappeared. "I called Matt," he announced, his hard gaze shooting sparks of resentment.

His lack of confidence in her hurt. Didn't he trust her to care for his son? "What did he say?"

"He wants to talk with you."

Cari followed Nick across the hall into the master bedroom. He directed her to the phone next to the king-size bed.

"Hello, Dr. Landers."

"Hi, Cari. I guess Danny isn't going to let any of us get any sleep tonight. What are his vitals?"

"His respiration is twenty-four, pulse one hundred and ten. Temperature after a cool bath is one hundred and one."

Cari tried to listen to Matt's instructions, but all the while her eyes locked with Nick's, the tension between them increasing with frightening intensity.

"Monitor him for the next few hours," Matt said. "If he gets worse, bring him to the hospital. Let me speak to Nick."

"Dr. Landers wants to talk to you." She didn't miss his hostile glare as she handed him the phone.

She waited until the conversation was finished. Nick hung up the phone, then he turned around to face her.

"I want to know where you've been taking my son to make him sick!"

"I didn't do anything," she insisted. "Kids catch things. It's part of being a kid."

"Don't hand me that, Cari. Danny doesn't get sick," he said through clenched teeth, "because I keep him away from anyone with anything contagious."

Cari had had enough. "You keep him away from everyone, including yourself." Her breathing was ragged. "You want your child to live in a sterile vacuum. It's not fair to him."

"Who are you to come in here and tell me how to raise my son?"

"I'm the person you hired to take care of him."

"Daddy! Daddy!"

They both rushed into the bedroom to find Danny sitting up in bed and crying. "Don't be mad at Cari," he pleaded. "She didn't do it on purpose. Please! I love her." He began to sob in earnest.

Nick's chest tightened. He'd made his son cry—his sick son. He went across the room and sat down on the bed.

"Sh, Danny." He hugged him. "It's okay. I'm not angry at anyone. I'm just worried because you're sick." He looked at Cari and saw the concern in her eyes. Maybe he had overreacted and blamed her to salvage his own guilt. He had to admit that he was impressed with her capable calm in handling the situation.

He also couldn't forget how he'd held her in his arms not thirty minutes ago and thought of how much he'd wanted her. The painful aching of his body told him how much he still wanted her. But it wasn't possible. He had to think about his son. "Why don't you go to bed? I'll stay with Danny."

Cari shook her head. "I need to be monitoring him," she said, moving to the bed. She touched Danny's forehead again. "Danny, do you think you can handle a little something to drink?"

He nodded. "I'm thirsty."

"Okay, sweetie. I'll be right back." Cari headed for the kitchen and filled a small pitcher with water and crushed ice. She knew Danny would probably prefer apple juice but doubted his stomach could handle it. She opened the cupboard and reached for Danny's favorite glass.

Cari closed her eyes and gripped the edge of the counter, fighting back her own tears.

Why had Nick's accusations hurt so much? She knew that he was just worried about Danny. Other parents had gotten angry and she'd never let it bother her. She was a nurse—a good one. Danny had the flu, that was all. And with his symptoms, there wasn't any reason to think otherwise. Yet.

Three hours later, Danny's fever still hadn't broken. In fact, it stayed stubbornly at one hundred and one. Nick was back on the phone with the doctor, and within ten minutes, Danny was bundled in a blanket and they were on their way to the hospital. In a way Cari was relieved. Let Matt handle Nick.

Danny wasn't crazy about the idea. He clung to Cari during the ride to Riverhaven and began to cry again when the emergency room nurse tried to examine him. Nick stayed right beside Cari, helping to soothe Danny. The next six hours weren't much better, but as Danny dozed off and on, Nick was close by her, touching her hand to calm her fears, or maybe to share them. Finally, Matt announced that Danny's temperature had returned to normal and the crisis was over. It turned out to be a stomach virus.

By nine o'clock Danny was back home in bed, watching cartoons. Nick was downstairs explaining to his mother what had happened and apologizing to Marion about the soiled sheets in her laundry room.

After checking on Danny, Cari went into the connecting bathroom for a much-needed shower. Ten minutes later, under steaming hot water, she managed to feel almost human again. She wondered if Danny would allow her the luxury of a nap today. Pulling on her robe, she wrapped a towel around her wet hair and began applying moisturizer to her face, when the door swung open. Thinking it was Danny, she asked, "What do you need, honey?" Her words died when she caught sight of Nick's reflection in the mirror.

"Oh," she gasped, and whirled around. "I thought you were Danny." Her heart was thumping as she looked up to find Nick leaning against the doorjamb. He was wearing last night's jeans and a polo shirt. His black hair had a sexy mussed look and she could see the morning stubble on his strong jaw. Would it feel rough and raspy to the touch?

"Sorry, I didn't know you were in here." His piercing gray eyes did a lazy once-over of her short satin robe and she felt her nipples tingle in response.

"I'll be finished in a few minutes," she said, feeling a sudden dryness in her throat.

Nick shook his head as if coming out of a trance. He held up Danny's favorite cup. "His highness asked for a glass of water. Would you mind?"

She stepped back and allowed him access to the sink. The room seemed to shrink in size. Like a lovesick teenager, she simply stood there, gazing at Nick's broad back as he leaned over the sink. All she could think about was last night...his kiss. She imagined she could still taste the scent of his cologne on her lips. Good grief. She was a mess and going downhill fast.

She was about to leave when he set the cup on the counter and turned toward her. He was close—too close. "I wanted to thank you for the way you handled things last night." He looked a little sheepish. "As you already know, I really blew it."

Cari was surprised at his confession. "You were just concerned."

"I was paranoid." His silver eyes met hers. "And I made you think I didn't trust your judgment, which isn't true."

Cari glanced away. "People say things when they're upset."

Nick reached out and cupped her chin. Her sad, vulnerable look tore at him, especially when he knew he had caused it. "I had no right. You've made Danny happier than I've seen him in a long time." Reluctantly he released her. "But it doesn't change the fact that I'm afraid every time my son leaves this house. And after yesterday's outing, I thought—"

"You thought I put Danny in harm's way."

"Not intentionally."

"Not unintentionally, either."

He was speechless. Did she know him that well? He glanced down at her skimpy robe, at the soft curves barely hidden by the silky material. Could she also read his mind and know how much he wanted her right this minute?

"I care about Danny," Cari went on. "I'd do anything to keep him healthy. But, Nick," she said, pointing toward Danny's bedroom, "that child needs to feel normal. He needs to do things that other kids do, be with other kids."

Nick tensed. This was something they weren't ever going to agree on. "I know I've been cautious with Danny, but with good reason. Not only do I worry about rejection, I worry about my child being exploited by the press." He raked a hand through his hair. "There's been a lot of publicity about this merger along with a lot of money that has exchanged hands. Danny could even be a target for kidnapping."

"Oh, my God, is that really a possibility?"

Nick shrugged. "There's never been a problem, but I've always kept Danny close to home. So from now on, I would like more details on your whereabouts. Since your car is so unreliable, maybe you should let John drive you around, or use one of the cars here. And take a cellular phone."

She nodded. "Of course. It just never occurred to me."

"Outside of the press bugging me, I've never had anything to worry about," he said, wanting to ease her mind but not wanting her to take Danny and his security lightly. "I don't want anything to happen to you, either."

He hadn't meant to admit that, but now that he had, he realized it was the truth. This beautiful woman with her sad eyes and gentle touch had slipped past his defenses and become important to him. His heart jolted as his eyes did a slow journey downward. His breath caught as he saw her hardened nipples through her robe. And suddenly the vivid memories of last night began playing in his head. The feel of her in his arms—his hands on her soft skin. Would they have made love if Danny hadn't gotten sick? Yes, he realized, they would have.

He reached out and slowly pulled the towel from her head, captivated as her long hair tumbled free. He combed his fingers through the damp, silky strands. Cari made a throaty sound and closed her eyes.

Damn! This woman was too hard to resist. He cupped the back of her head and drew her close. He'd shut off all the warning signs as he lowered his head to her...

"Dad, are you gonna kiss Cari?"

Chapter Eight

Nick jerked around to find Danny standing in the doorway. In pajamas and dragging his stuffed bear, affectionately known as Joey, the four-year-old was looking curiously at his father.

Nick felt his cheeks burn. Damn! This was all he needed—to have to explain the situation to his son when he didn't even understand it himself. "Good morning, Danny," he began as he went across the bathroom and knelt down in front of him. "What are you doing out of bed?"

Danny grinned. "I feel good." He looked up at Cari. "Can I have something to eat?"

Cari gripped the lapels of her robe together. "Sure. If you'll wait a few minutes until I get dressed, I'll bring you a tray."

"Can I eat in my bed?"

"You bet." Nick swung his son up in his arms. "I'll even eat with you. How about I stay home today and take care of you? We'll give Cari the morning off so she can catch up on some sleep.''

"You don't need to do that—" Cari began, but Nick stopped her.

"I know I don't need to, but I want to." Nick could see her exhaustion. "None of us had much sleep last night, so you're officially off duty," he announced. "I'll be taking care of Danny today."

Too tired to argue, Cari agreed. She grabbed the discarded towel off the floor and went into her bedroom. Once inside, she closed the door and leaned against it for support. What had happened to her? First last night, and again today in the bathroom. She had been more than ready to fall into Nick Malone's arms. She shut her eyes, savoring the memory of his touch, the feel of his hands on her skin. Never in her life, not even with Tim, had she felt so alive.

No! Cari's eyes darted open. This couldn't happen. She had only taken this job to be close to Danny. She couldn't get involved with Nick Malone, not with her secret....

She walked to the bed as her thoughts turned to the little boy she had come to adore in the six weeks she'd been in Santa Cruz. But what if last night had turned out differently? What if Danny *had* been rejecting his heart?

He hadn't, though. Cari recalled that during the night, every time she had listened to Danny's heart, it had been beating loud and strong.

Pulling back the comforter, she sat down, finished drying her hair and folded the towel. Finally exhaustion took over and she had to lie down, promising herself just to rest a few minutes. She tried to stay awake but knew that it was useless as her eyelids drifted shut. A calm, serene feeling began to take over, pushing her into a deep sleep. Then the dream began.

A tiny two-year-old girl dressed in a pink rosebud-print dress, her blond curls dancing around her face as she ran through the grassy field.

It was Angel.

The soft breeze caught her heavenly laughter as the child chased after the butterfly. "Mommy! Mommy! Look, it's a butterfly." The tiny voice of her daughter was a beautiful sound to Cari's ears. She never thought she'd hear the word "Mommy" again. Never thought she'd see her precious little girl again.

Cari ached to hold her daughter. When she tried to lift her arms, she couldn't. She fought, but it was as if a heavy weight were holding her down.

Angel stopped and looked around. Her small hands brushed the wayward strands of hair from her face and a frightened look appeared. "Daddy! Where is Mommy?"

"Angel, I'm here!" Cari tried to call out, but the words she worked so hard to form fell silent.

Her daughter's face puckered up and she began to cry. "Mommy! Where are you, Mommy?" Panic was etched on the child's face as she took off running. "Mommy!"

"I'm here! Angel! Mommy's here!" Cari fought harder to overcome her resistance, but to no avail.

Then a familiar voice drew her attention from her struggle. It was Tim. She was relieved as he appeared next to their daughter and picked her up in his arms. Cuddling the sobbing child against his chest, he rubbed her back, and soon the girl's cries slowed. Angel raised her head. "Daddy, I can't find Mommy."

"Sweetheart, remember, I told you Mommy can't be with us now."

"But I want her to be," the girl insisted.

"Oh, Angel, don't you remember what I told you?" her father began. "She is with us. Just like part of us is with her."

"In here?" The child's tiny hands touched her chest.

"Yes. In a special place in our hearts," he said, smiling. "And when it's time, she'll be with us."

Angel began to smile. "Soon? I miss her, a lot."

"And she misses us. But you can close your eyes and see your mommy."

Angel did exactly that. "I see her, Daddy," she gasped with excitement. The child waved. "Hi, Mommy. I miss you. I love you."

Cari's throat clogged up. "I love you, too, Angel. I love you, too," she whispered as the picture began to fade, then when it came back into view it was Danny's face in the scene. Cari smiled. Yes, her daughter was with her, and as long as she had Danny, she always would be.

During the next few weeks, Cari could see things had changed a lot. Nick had been spending more time at home. He hadn't worked a weekend since the scare with Danny. Most mealtimes, he had made it home. Although he had been friendlier with Cari, he never stepped over the line. The kiss they had shared the night Danny had gotten sick had never been discussed or repeated. There had never been a chance: Nick and she were never alone.

Cari realized it was for the best, but she had this strange longing that never seemed to go away. She wasn't fooling herself. She cared more for Nick than she'd ever thought possible. Tim had been a good husband, but their quiet, sedate existence was always centered around their child. If Tim had survived the accident, she doubted their marriage would have made it, not without Angel.

It was the future that concerned her now. Danny was healthy, and she was blessed to be a part of his life, but in a few months he'd be five, and starting kindergarten in a little less than a year. She didn't think Nick would want her around while his child was in school.

"Cari! Cari!" Danny burst into her room, scrambling onto her bed, where she was folding clean clothes and putting them away.

"What's got you all excited?"

"Daddy said if it's okay with you, if he takes tomorrow

off from work, we can all go to the beach. Is it? Is it okay?''

Cari couldn't help but smile. It was fun to see Danny act like a normal kid. "He did, did he?"

"Yes. Can we, please?"

The past few weeks, Danny and Nick had been able to spend more time together, though this was the first outing they'd planned.

"Why don't you and your father go alone?"

"No, you hafta go. We need help with the sand castle like before. And Dad said that this time we can build a really big fire 'cause it's colder. Dad said Uncle Larry's got a special place—"

"Slow down, son, before you pass out."

Cari looked up to find Nick standing in the doorway. He was wearing a gorgeous navy pin-striped suit. His tie was pulled from his neck and his collar button undone. Why was it that every time she was around this man, she seemed to have trouble breathing?

"Sorry, I guess I should have warned you. " His smile was irresistible, just like the man.

"No problem." Cari felt her body warm and realized she was staring at his mouth...remembering. She quickly glanced away. "I...I just didn't realize you were home." It was only four-thirty.

"I've been working on a prototype for a new computer game and promised Danny I'd let him test it out."

"It's really neat, Cari," Danny volunteered, his brown eyes round with excitement. "It's all about dinosaurs. Where they live. What they eat."

Nick leaned against the doorjamb, still grinning. "It's educational, geared more for schools. Not arcade material." His silver gaze met hers. "How do you feel about tomorrow? Would you like to go with us?"

Cari walked to the dresser. Even though Nick wasn't officially in her room, he was close enough to make her feel the intimacy. "Wouldn't you prefer to spend time alone with Danny?"

"We've been together every night for the past week. But he likes to spend time with you, too." He rested his hands on his son's shoulders. "You're an important part of his life."

Cari drew a breath, feeling her emotions begin to surface. She wanted to be important in Nick's life, too. She worked hard not to hoard Danny's time and to help build a relationship between father and son.

"We love you, Cari," Danny announced. "So come with us."

Cari was jolted, even though the words came from a four-year-old. So badly, she wanted to believe them. She smiled. "Sure, I'll go."

Nick's four-wheel-drive vehicle pulled off the coast highway onto a dirt road lined with large trees. Between the traffic jam outside of Santa Cruz and Danny's are-we-almost-theres, it took them well over an hour to get to their destination. But with the Pacific Ocean in her sights, Cari knew the trip was worth the trouble.

Suddenly a weathered, two-story brown house with white shutters came into view. They passed through an archway covered with rose-colored bougainvillea and followed the brick driveway that led them to the beach house. The brush was thick around the structure, but Nick explained that was how Larry liked to keep it. More privacy.

"It's beautiful," she said, and got out of the car.

Nick watched Cari as a cool breeze caught her hair and blew it against her face. She brushed it back and smiled into the bright sunlight. The past few days, he'd noticed some changes in Cari. She seemed less reserved, more open. Most important, the sadness in her eyes had nearly disappeared. Someday, he promised himself, it would be gone completely.

"Can we go in the water now, Daddy?"

Nick looked down at his son. "We talked about this at home. It's October. It might be too cold to swim today. If the weather warms up later, we'll see."

"Okay, then I want to make another sand castle."

"I think what we have to do first is unpack the car, then we'll go down to the beach. Are you big enough to help?"

Danny nodded. To prove it, he pulled the canvas tote of sand toys out of the back seat and lugged the big bag to the patio. Nick withdrew the key that Larry had given him and went to the front door. The Keatons had owned the beach house for about five years, but Nick had never made it down here before today. Not that he hadn't been invited. But he'd used any excuse to keep from attending the Keatons' social gatherings. He hadn't been much on socializing since the divorce. But mostly it had been to protect Danny. He refused to put his son in any situation that could harm him.

Today they didn't have to worry about that.

Nick opened the front door and was surprised at the warm, homey atmosphere. A braided rug covered the polished hardwood floor. There was an overstuffed sofa placed in front of the huge slate fireplace and pictures of the Keatons' three kids lined the mantel.

All of a sudden Nick felt a twinge of envy. He picked up a photo of Larry's youngest daughter. Although he'd sent a lavish gift when Jill was born, he hadn't seen her more than a few times over the last four years. She was close to Danny's age. Larry's two boys were...what? Six and seven, at least. Nick frowned, knowing that since Danny was born, he'd lost touch with his friend. His best friend. A friend who'd stuck by him and helped rebuild the business after his father died. Who was still there when he needed him.

Danny came into the room and dropped a bag on the floor. "Hey, this is neat. Does Uncle Larry live here?"

"He and his kids come here sometimes."

The child went to the fireplace. "Will you make a fire, Daddy?"

"Later when it gets cold."

Cari came in with a grocery bag. "Where do you want this?"

"In the kitchen." Nick walked around the oak table and four chairs. He took her bundle, then led her into the small alcove. "Larry said everything is turned on. He and Cindy were just here a few days ago." He pulled open the refrigerator to find it stocked with milk, bread and a dozen eggs and bacon. What caught his eye was a bottle of wine and a note attached. Nick tore the paper from the bottle and opened it.

Hey, Nick,
It's about time you took Cindy and me up on our invitation. There is plenty of food and drink and enough wood to keep you warm and cozy for days. So relax, and you, Cari and Danny enjoy yourselves. Feel free to spend the night. There's enough room for everyone. Pop some corn in the fireplace, put a Michael Bolton CD in the stereo and see what develops. If there's anything else you need, just look around, you'll probably find it.

Larry

P.S. Don't worry, I'll handle things at the office.

Nick wasn't surprised by Larry's note. What surprised him was the fact that he was actually thinking about taking his friend's suggestion.

Cari walked in, carrying another bag. She was wearing typical beach attire. But she filled out the white shorts and navy shirt like no other woman he'd known. He'd always been attracted to tall, willowy women, no hips, no breasts.

His gaze lowered to Cari's backside as she bent over and put their food supplies in the refrigerator. Cari definitely had a shapely backside, and long, smooth legs that could bring a man to his knees. Nick's body stirred to life.

He'd been avoiding her like crazy. He had to do something to stay sane, remembering the kiss they'd shared just a few weeks ago. If Danny's cries hadn't interrupted them, they would have shared much more. He couldn't let that happen. Cari needed to find someone who could give her what she needed—marriage and more children. He wasn't able to do either. But that didn't stop the sudden heat that surged through him, along with an overwhelming ache for Cari's touch, her hands on his body.

As if she heard his silent cry, she turned around and her blue-eyed gaze met his. Did she have any idea how hard he had to fight to keep from going across the room and dragging her into his arms?

It was Cari who finally broke the spell. "Is that a note from your friend?"

Nick blinked and reality returned. "Yes. Larry suggested we take full advantage of our opportunity here... and spend the night."

She gave him an astonished look. "Do you want to? Spend the night?"

He found himself shrugging like a lovesick adolescent. "I took the day off. We could start back early in the morning."

Her excitement seemed to build, too. "I brought my medical bag with Danny's medicine and extra clothes. I guess that only leaves something to sleep in."

Nick's breath ceased at the thought of her naked body lying in bed. "Well, uh, Cindy probably has something you can wear."

She smiled. "You're lucky to have such nice friends."

"Yes, I am." And he was crazy for even thinking what he was thinking, and with his son... Where was Danny, anyway? Panic seized him, yet before he could even make it out of the kitchen, the child called to him.

"Hey, Daddy. Cari. Come out here and see."

Nick went to the sliding glass door off the kitchen, yanked it open and stepped onto a large patio. The beach house sat on a grassy rise about a hundred yards from the water. They walked to the railing where Danny stood.

On each side of the property, their view was kept private by high walls and shrubs. It was as if there were no one else in the world but this place.

"It's beautiful," Cari breathed.

"This is my favorite place in the whole world," Danny announced. "I want to stay here forever."

Nick patted his son on the shoulder. "We can't stay forever, but how about we stay for the night?"

Danny's eyes lit up. "You mean sleep here?"

"Yes, I mean sleep here tonight," Nick repeated.

"Oh, boy." Danny jumped up and down, then ran back to the house. "I never sleeped anywhere but the hospital."

"That's slept," Nick corrected.

"Can I go look for my new bed?"

"Yes, but be careful about touching stuff. Remember we're only borrowing this house."

Danny bobbed his head, then took off to investigate his new surroundings.

Later in the afternoon, Cari sat on the beach as Nick and Danny ran through the surf. It was a little cool for swimming, but somehow the four-year-old convinced his father that he would only get his feet wet. At the sound of laughter, Cari shaded her eyes against the sun's glare and watched Nick and Danny jog along the beach.

This had to be the most perfect day, she thought. It was like being a family again. Since she'd taken the job, it had been just her and Danny most of the time. Now with Nick involving himself more in his son's life, and in hers... She felt the familiar stirring in her lower body when she looked at Nick as he lifted his son onto his broad shoulders. Holding on to the child's hands, he began to dance through the water. His athletic grace didn't surprise Cari as he spun around in circles then pretended to trip and almost fall. She'd never seen Nick Malone so relaxed, so happy...so lovable.

The twosome turned and headed toward her. She pulled up her legs and felt her pulse racing. Good Lord, the minute the man got in her vicinity, she started feeling all giddy.

"Hey, Cari, have you seen Danny anywhere?" Nick asked.

"Danny?" she said as she glanced up and down the beach, but never up at the child on Nick's shoulders. "No, I haven't."

"Hey, I'm up here," Danny cried out, then burst into a fit of giggles.

"Well," Nick began, "if you see him, tell him it's time for his nap."

"I'm here," Danny screamed out. "And you said no nap today."

Nick glanced upward. "There you are. Have you been hiding from me?"

The child shook his head as his dad lifted him from his shoulders and placed him next to her. Cari wrapped a towel over the boy's damp legs, making sure he wouldn't get cold. The sight of Nick brushing the sand from his bare chest snagged her attention. To her disappointment, he reached for his shirt and pulled it over his head.

"Did you miss us?" he asked as he took a seat on the blanket and rubbed a towel over his legs.

"I had my reading." She held a romance novel in her hand.

His eyes were bright with amusement. "Do women really expect men to be like that?" He nodded at her book.

She couldn't look away.

"We can always hope."

"Oh, so you do like all that romantic stuff?"

She glanced away. Did he know she had been lusting after him? "Yeah, I guess I do."

"Yuck," Danny volunteered, and wrinkled his nose. "All that kissy stuff."

Nick rustled his son's hair. "Just wait, son, when you get older…" His words died quickly along with his smile.

Cari's heart went out to him. She knew what Nick must be thinking. But right now, she was more concerned about him pulling away from his son, again.

"Danny, do me a favor. Go up to the house and bring us some cans of juice." She handed him a small net bag. "You can put them in here."

The child got up and started up the slight incline to the house.

"Be careful," she cautioned.

"I'm a big boy," he insisted as he trudged through the sand toward the house.

Cari turned to Nick, who was braced on his elbows, staring out at the ocean. "Nick, listen to me. I know it's impossible not to think about Danny's future. It's with you every day."

He remained silent, but she saw his jaw tense.

"I can't tell you that there isn't a possibility of complications. But so far, Danny's been healthy. And there's no reason why he won't continue that way."

"But for how long?" An ocean breeze ruffled his dark hair. His gray eyes, staring into hers, begged for answers. Answers she didn't have. She only had hope… encouragement. She almost told him then, told him that the guarantees he so desperately sought were as important to her as they were to him. But fear kept her silent, kept the secret locked in her throat. The secret that a part of her daughter lived on in Danny.

"There are limited statistics on heart transplant patients, and you probably already know all the numbers. But the younger the child is going through the surgery, the better chance he has of survival."

Nick closed his eyes. God, how he hated that word. He also hated the fact that every time he saw the fading scar on his son's chest he was reminded that he was the cause of it. He had been the one who transferred his flawed gene to his son.

Cari's voice broke into his thoughts. "Just live each day as if it's a precious gift," she whispered. "Have no regrets."

Hearing the obvious pain in her words, he turned to see the tears in her eyes. She was no longer talking about Danny. She was talking about her daughter, Angel.

He sat up and without hesitation drew Cari into his arms.

"God, Cari." He pulled her against him, feeling her tremble. "I wish there was something I could do." He was so lousy when women got emotional.

She raised her head. "Don't think about what the future may hold, because it's impossible to know." She wiped a tear off her cheek. "Think of your time with Danny as a gift and cherish it for as long as you have it. Enjoy what you and Danny have together." Her liquid blue eyes searched his. "Promise me, Nick."

At that moment he couldn't deny her anything. "I promise."

Later that evening, Nick put another log on the dying fire, then turned around to discover that Danny had fallen asleep next to Cari on the sofa.

He smiled, seeing his son's angelic face so peaceful. "I guess it was the last marshmallow that did him in."

Cari licked the white creamy substance off her fingers as she glanced down beside her. "I expected him to give up sooner. Must be the Malone stubbornness that kept him going the last hour.''

"Well, whatever it was, he needs to be in bed.'' He leaned over and scooped his son up in his arms. The child made a whimpering protest, but it quickly died. Cari went up the stairs ahead of them and hurried to get the blankets pulled down before Nick came into the small bedroom. Nick placed Danny on the bottom bunk, and the boy rolled to his side. Cari covered him, then dropped a kiss on his cheek.

"Good night, Danny. Sweet dreams.''

There was a tug at Nick's heart as he watched the tender scene. He knew what her touch was like, and how his body craved it. He knew he shouldn't feel this way toward her, but it didn't stop him from wanting some of her loving. Maybe just tonight, he could forget the pain of reality, the pain of causing his son's problems. Maybe Cari could help him forget.

"'Night, sport.'' He, too, kissed his son.

He took Cari's hand and led her out of the room. Once in the narrow hall, he closed the door and drew her to him, forgetting any silly notion of keeping his distance. With the feel of her body against his, he wondered why he even tried.

Nick braced his hands on either side of her face and lowered his head to hers. He held off the kiss, using his tongue to trace the curve of her sweet mouth instead, and the contact sent heat through him. Then he lost his reserve as Cari's arms went around his neck, urging him closer. Her lips parted invitingly and she welcomed his delving tongue as he took her mouth in a hungry kiss.

A shudder of pleasure rippled through Nick and nearly knocked him off his feet. He leaned against the wall for support, drawing Cari to his aching body. All the time their mouths remained locked, their tongues tasting, stroking, unable to get close enough.

Finally, Nick tore his mouth away and rained tiny kisses over her cheeks, eyes, chin, then returned to her lips. Each kiss was longer, deeper, wetter, until finally they were both gasping for air.

"You're making me crazy," he whispered as he began nibbling down her slender throat to the pulse beating rapidly in her neck. He sucked gently on the delicate skin. Cari moaned and drew his mouth back to hers in another hot, arousing kiss.

They were both burning up. Cari's hands went to his shirt, tugging it free from his jeans, and then her palms were moving over his chest. He was going out of his mind. His hands found their way under her shirt and stroked her soft, warm flesh, then he reached up to cup her breasts.

"Cari...I can't keep my hands off you," he breathed against her mouth as he rubbed his thumbs over the taut nipples.

Cari was trying to think clearly. She shouldn't be doing this. She worked for Nick Malone, she cared for his son. More important was the secret. But none of that seemed to matter. She needed this man's hands on her skin, making her feel alive again. "Touch me," she cried.

Nick swept her up in his arms, and Cari gasped. They exchanged a look of need, then she laid her head against his shoulder and he carried her into the master bedroom. A large four-poster was near the bay window, and the room was bathed in moonlight. He walked across the hardwood floor and set her down.

Cari's gaze met his, then she glanced away shyly. But Nick refused to let her hide from him.

"Cari..." He brushed a hand through her silky hair. "I want to make love to you." He breathed deeply, inhaling her sweet fragrance. "I need to know if you want the same."

She looked up at him, her eyes wide and honest. "Yes.... I want you to make love to me."

Nick began to tremble as he pulled her into his arms, and his mouth closed over hers while his aroused body relayed his need. God! He never knew he could want a woman so much.

He pulled back and yanked his T-shirt off and tossed it aside. Then he helped Cari with her top. Next came her shorts, then his jeans and underwear. He threw back the quilt on the bed and guided her down to the cool sheets. The only hesitation came when he reached behind her and unfastened her bra. The air seemed trapped in his lungs as he removed the delicate lace to expose her beautiful breasts. The sheer garment found its way to the floor, and he lay down beside her on the bed.

He reached out a shaky hand and gently stroked her skin. She made another whimpering sound that caused his blood to boil. Then he lowered his head and drew her breast into his mouth. At first he laved the nipple slowly, then his hunger took over. Using his teeth, he nipped at the bud until it grew hard, then moved to the other breast, giving it the same attention.

Cari was slowly going out of her mind. She clenched her hands in the thickness of Nick's hair as his hands and tongue gave her sweet, exquisite pleasure. Heat spiraled from her womb and a heavy ache settled deep inside her. She shifted restlessly on the bed and Nick's body moved over hers. Their legs were entwined and she strained against his hardness.

"Nick, please," she cried huskily, unable to get enough of him.

"Tell me what you want," he demanded, keeping his hand on her breast, his eyes staring into hers.

Cari knew she loved Nick more than she ever thought it possible to love a man. And right now nothing else mattered but those feelings. "I want you!" Her voice was shaky with emotion.

A groan rumbled in his throat as his mouth locked on

hers in another heated kiss. It drove her need to desperation. He raised his head to look down at her.

"I'll be right back," he promised, and got up from the bed. He went into the bathroom but returned within seconds and was back beside her. He ripped open a foil packet and she watched boldly as he slipped on the protection.

Turning toward her, he explained, "I found a rather large supply in the medicine cabinet." After stripping off her panties, he raised his body over hers and placed a sweet kiss on her lips. "Remind me to thank Larry," he whispered.

Before Cari had a chance to speak, Nick was doing unbelievable things to her body once again. His hand slid between them to the soft mound of curls above her thighs. His fingers gently stroked her as his legs nudged hers farther apart.

Cari opened herself to him readily. He created a searing heat at the very core of her, while his mouth continued to caress her breasts.

"Nick, please!"

He positioned himself more fully against her undulating hips.

Cari's breath caught on a sob as he joined their bodies with a slow, sure stroke. He released a groan and Cari watched as he fought for control. "Am I hurting you?"

Cari wrapped her legs around his hips and pulled him deeper. "No. You feel wonderful."

Trembling, Nick closed his eyes, feeling Cari's tight heat wrapped around him. "You feel...damn! You feel so good." A hoarse sound escaped his throat as he tried to stay in control. He began to move in a slow, even rhythm, then too quickly his thrusts increased and their passion soared. He felt Cari's tension heighten and she gasped his name. That triggered his own release. He squeezed his eyes shut as a shudder raced through his entire body, and he lost himself in her. In heaven.

Nick collapsed on top of her, and for a long moment they both fought to catch their breath. Nick rolled to his side and pulled Cari along with him, making room for her in the cradle of his arms. She rested her hand on his chest, feeling his still-labored breathing.

"You okay?" His expression showed his concern.

Cari trailed her fingers over his chest, already missing their intimate connection. "Uh-huh," she murmured. Regrets would overwhelm her later, she knew. But for now she just wanted to bask in the sweet security of Nick's arms.

"Yeah, I'll agree with that," he said, and placed a kiss on her mouth, then another. Before long they realized their hunger was building once again.

Nick made a second trip to the bathroom and returned carrying a handful of foil packets. He dropped them on the nightstand. "I think my buddy, Larry, deserves a raise." He climbed back into bed and pulled Cari into his arms. Soon their hands were busy caressing, soothing and exciting each other again.

This was Cari's fantasy night. There were no problems or secrets. She was going to keep the world on hold for a few hours. For now there was only hope in her heart. And a budding dream that she might possibly start a new life. A life with Nick and Danny.

Chapter Nine

The next morning, Nick rolled over in bed and opened his eyes. He blinked at the blinding sunlight coming through the window. Immediately he turned away from the brightness and checked the clock on the bedside table. Eight o'clock. Releasing a groan, he recalled how little sleep he'd gotten last night.

His thoughts went to Cari and he turned to the empty side of the bed. She was gone. But he could never erase the feeling of her naked body tucked up against his all night, or the taste of her sweet mouth, or the little throaty sounds she made.... His own body soon came to life.

Damn! He couldn't think about their lovemaking. He sat up and ran his hand through his hair in frustration. He had to figure out what to say to her. "Thanks for last night. It was great, but..." Nick shut his eyes. That was the last thing he wanted to say to her. What they had shared was incredible. He'd never known a woman like Cari. But it shouldn't have happened.

Nick threw the blanket back and climbed out of bed. Naked, he went to the dresser and opened a draw to discover some sweats and a few pairs of underwear. Larry had told him to borrow what he needed, and Nick did. He started for the bathroom, when he found the portable stereo on a table next to the window. On top were several Michael Bolton CDs.

He frowned, went into the bathroom and turned on the shower. He needed to clear his head and think of some explanation for Cari.

Fifteen minutes later, Nick made his way to the kitchen. But he nearly turned back when he found Cari standing at the stove dressed in a short teal blue robe. His gaze traveled up her bare legs to where the silky material covered her shapely thighs. He swallowed the dryness in his throat, knowing exactly what was hidden underneath.

Danny's voice drew his attention away from his wayward thoughts, but when Cari turned around to the table, the air froze in his lungs. She looked beautiful. Her long blond hair was mussed from sleep, and her face, free of makeup, had only a slight blush on her cheeks. She handed Danny a plate of pancakes, then raised bright blue eyes to his. A smile appeared.

"Good morning." Her voice was husky soft. Once again he was reminded of last night.

Danny looked up and smiled at him, too. "You're an old sleepyhead, Dad. But Cari said you needed rest 'cause you work too hard." The boy picked up his fork and stabbed at his pancakes. "Are you going to go to work today? Can we stay here and play?"

Nick never took his eyes from Cari. "Yes, I have to go to work, son. So after breakfast we need to start back." He saw the smile on Cari's face fade, saw the questions in her blue eyes. Nick didn't want to leave, either. He didn't want reality to intrude just yet. His palms itched to grab her and drag her back upstairs and make love to her the whole day. But it didn't matter what he wanted. He couldn't. There was no future for the two of them. As badly as he wanted to, he couldn't make any promises.

Cari's heart dropped to her stomach. She knew that the man she had made love to last night was gone. Nick was having second thoughts.

"Can we come back?" Danny asked.

"Maybe next summer."

Danny's smile faded. "But it's my favorite place. Can I take my shells home?"

Cari didn't like what was happening. "Danny, why don't you go and round up your things, then we'll take one last walk on the beach."

The child got up and went out the back door. Cari turned to Nick. "Is something wrong?" She felt awkward, too. How did you handle the morning after? The only other man she'd ever made love with had been Tim.

"No," he said, and walked across the kitchen to pour some coffee.

Cari didn't know what she expected this morning, but this was definitely not it. "I'm sorry if you regret..."

He turned around and faced her. "Look, Cari, it's not that...it's just... Aw, hell!" He marched to the sliding glass door and stared out at the beach. "I just don't have time in my life for a relationship."

Cari felt as if he had struck her. "I don't remember asking for a commitment," she said in a whisper. What else could she say? Never mind that she'd dreamed about just that, ached for that commitment, a sense of belonging, a family...children.

He swung around and glared at her. "You deserve one. You're a very special woman, Cari. Any man would be lucky—"

"Please, stop." She closed her eyes. "You don't need to explain." She fought like crazy to keep from crying.

She didn't need to make a bigger fool out of herself. "Why don't we forget last night ever happened?"

"I can't do that, Cari." He came to her, and when he touched her, she trembled. "You're special to me." The sincerity in his voice drew her gaze to his. Did he really mean it? Or was he only trying to spare her feelings? But before she could find out, Danny came in carrying his bag of toys.

Nick immediately released her. "We can't talk now. Maybe tonight?"

Cari shook her head. "I can't. I have my support group meeting."

He looked disappointed.

"You could come along," she suggested, then rushed on. "You can meet some parents of heart recipients."

She held her breath, seeing the turmoil in his eyes.

"I need to go into the office for a few hours this afternoon. What time do you need to be there?"

"A little before seven."

He nodded. "I'll be home." He glanced around. "We need to clean up before we leave."

"I'll do the kitchen." She started to pick up the plates from the table, but he stopped her.

"Cari, you can help by going upstairs and getting dressed."

Awareness shot through her. "I'm sorry," she said as the faint odor of his soap drifted to her. "When Danny woke up this morning, this was all I could grab before he came bursting into the bedroom."

He arched an eyebrow. "Well, I suggest that you go get dressed now."

She was unable to speak, but her heart soared, knowing he wasn't immune to her. She nodded and hurried out of the room and upstairs.

Later that night Cari stood in front of her group, feeling Nick's eyes on her every move. Most of the parents were used to her presence and had no problem opening up to her and Matt with their worries. The questions seemed to be endless, but never once did any come from Nick. Cari guessed he wasn't used to doing things in a group. She had come to the conclusion that he was a loner, or maybe he was just lonely.

The meeting ended about nine and Cari went to the refreshment table and poured herself a cup of coffee. She turned around and found Nick across the room talking with Matt. That was good. Maybe the doctor could get him to open up, maybe even get him to bring Danny along the next time.

As if he knew she was watching him, Nick looked over at her and her heart did a somersault. She smiled nervously, remembering last night and how tenderly he'd made love to her. How he'd taken the time to bring her pleasure. Suddenly Cari's body grew hot, her breasts ached at the thought of his hands....

"Who's the good-looking man?"

Cari jerked around to find Sharon standing beside her. She forced a smile. "Hi, Sharon. I didn't see you."

The young woman grinned. "I guess you were distracted." She eyed Nick appraisingly. "Is he your friend?"

"My employer," she corrected. "Nick Malone."

"Didn't his son have a heart transplant a few years ago?"

Cari nodded. She didn't want to say too much, knowing how Nick valued his and Danny's privacy. "Yes, and he's doing fine."

"I'm glad to hear that," Sharon said.

Cari noticed that her new friend was without her daughter. "Where's Heather?"

"She's staying with my mom tonight. She's been cranky all day, probably cutting a tooth."

"I hope everything is okay. I remember when Angel was getting her teeth, she kept me up all night."

To Cari's surprise, there wasn't the usual pain that hit her whenever she tried to talk about her daughter. She smiled. Was it the dream she had had a few weeks ago? Seeing her little girl so happy? It had given her peace. And now she had a part of Angel with Danny.

She noticed Nick walking toward her and her pulse began to race. He was so handsome dressed in charcoal slacks and a maroon-and-white plaid shirt.

"You ready to go?" He spoke with cool authority.

"Sure, but first, Nick," she began, "I'd like you to meet Sharon Bennett. Sharon, this is Nick Malone."

Nick was cordial and shook Sharon's hand. "Nice to meet you, but if you'll excuse us, we need to be going." He took Cari by the hand and tugged her toward him.

Cari watched Sharon's smile drop as Nick pulled her away. She wanted nothing more than to dig her heels in and refuse to leave. But she didn't want to cause a scene. "Call me, Sharon, if Heather isn't better by morning."

The young woman nodded as Nick continued to push Cari through the crowd. All she could do was wave her goodbyes. Just as soon as they got home, she was definitely going to give Nick Malone a piece of her mind.

Danny had been asleep for an hour by the time she got upstairs to check on him. Cari was a little disappointed, even though Marion had taken good care of him. She liked to spend bedtime with the little guy. She placed a kiss on his cheek and got up and walked out. After closing the door, she went into the living area of the suite, where she found Nick. He had a drink in his hand and he was pacing in front of the fireplace.

Cari folded her arms. "Now, are you going to tell me why you were so rude to Sharon?"

"I wasn't rude, I just needed to get the hell out of there."

"Why?" Still confused, she came further into the room.

"I just didn't belong."

"You belong. Your son has had a heart transplant."

He swung around, his eyes blazing with fear. "Don't you see I can't sit there and rehash everything? For two years I went through hell. I never thought Danny would survive. But he did. Now I have to protect him." His gaze softened. "I sat beside my son after the surgery and promised him that I wouldn't let anything happen to him again. These people tonight were discussing their children's bouts with rejection. One mother told about her daughter who had to have a second transplant."

Cari could see his pain, his agony. "But, Nick, they survived. And they're trying hard to give their children a normal life."

"No!" He raised his hand to wave off her words. "They're so fragile. Oh God, I can't let anything happen to Danny."

A sob tore from his throat and tears flooded his eyes. Cari hurried to him, wrapping him in a tight embrace. They sank to the sofa. She held him, felt the shudder of his tears, wanted to assure him that Danny would always be safe, but she couldn't. She knew too well there was no way of predicting the future.

Finally, Nick raised his head, but he didn't release his hold on her as he searched her face. He held her, and Cari's heart pounded hard in her chest from wanting this man. Suddenly the mood changed, and Nick pulled away. Cari immediately felt the loss and ached to reach out and pull him back.

"I'm sorry," he said, and she could sense his embarrassment.

"You needed to share your pain with someone." She

wished he would allow her to help. "Besides, how many times have I cried on your shoulder about Angel?"

He finally turned to her, no trace of emotion left. "That was different."

"I don't think so. Just because I'm a woman and you're a man?"

"That's one hell of a big difference."

"Nick, I know what it's like to lose someone you love. But you can't refuse to let them live, either."

Nick looked away. He didn't want to hear Cari's lecture. No matter if she was right. "Danny's a little boy."

"Danny is a very active, nearly five-year-old boy. Who can't wait to start school."

"I thought I'd hire a tutor to come to the house."

"Oh, Nick, think about it. He would be a prisoner right here in his own home. You wouldn't want that."

Nick had known this was going to happen someday. During the two years since the surgery, Danny had been content to have his world revolve around the house and his family. But lately, since Cari had come into their lives, the child had wanted more. Friends. That scared Nick the most, his son contracting some disease from another child. He'd been so lucky that Danny had been healthy, and he was going to do everything possible to keep him that way. But maybe Cari had a point. He couldn't sacrifice Danny's happiness because of his own fears. Maybe it was time to let go some.

He sighed tiredly. "How about if I let go a little? I've been thinking about investigating one or two of the private schools in the area."

She smiled. "And Danny should be able to have a few friends over to the house."

He couldn't answer for the longest time, his thoughts were in such turmoil. "Maybe Larry and Cindy can bring their kids over. Their little girl, Jill, is about Danny's age."

Her face brightened. "Oh, Nick. What a great idea."

Nick found Cari's smile irresistible, like the woman herself. He reached out and drew her into his arms. He told himself it was to thank her for caring for his son, but after what they'd shared last night, he realized his feelings were a lot stronger than he wanted to admit. It wasn't fair, though. Cari had already lost a family, and she deserved to have a second chance at a loving husband and more children. And he wasn't the right man to provide her with either of those things. But somehow that didn't stop him from leaning forward and placing his lips on hers.

Cari gasped as he pushed her back on the sofa and his mouth settled on hers, hard and possessive. She trembled all over, wanting the closeness but knowing Nick didn't want anything permanent. But there was a connection between them; with Danny and Angel, there always would be.

With his hard body pressed against hers, all Cari could think about was satisfying that ache deep inside her. She raised her hips to get closer, but the constriction of clothes prevented it.

Without a word, Nick picked her up and carried her down the hall into his bedroom. Panic seized her as his large bed came into view. The beach house had been different. Now, whenever she passed Nick's room, she would always remember... It would put them both in an awkward position. And she would not be able to handle seeing the regret in his eyes tomorrow.

He set her down next to the bed, his hands cupping her face as his mouth came down on hers. She felt herself weakening as his tongue delved deep, simulating what he was planning to do to her. When he pressed his aroused body against hers, she felt her knees give way, but his strong arms caught her and gently laid her down on the bed. All the time her body screamed yes. Yes, she wanted to make love to Nick. But a tiny voice in the back of her mind was crying no. She finally heard it.

No! Cari shoved at Nick's chest until he finally released her. Somehow she managed to get up and walk to the other side of the room.

"Cari, what's wrong?"

Trying to catch her breath, she glanced away from the tempting man sprawled across the bed. "I can't."

"Can't what?" He sat up.

"I can't have sex with you, Nick."

He looked frustrated. "If you're worried about protection…"

She raised her hand to stop him. Yes, she was, but not the kind he was talking about. What could protect her heart? "We can't make the same mistake as last night. Besides, you were the one who wanted to cool things."

He stood and came to her. "Maybe I've changed my mind."

Cari's heart soared at the thought. But she also knew that Nick was too guarded with his feelings to let himself care about her, to ever let himself love her. And if he found out her secret…

"No, Nick," she said, trying to keep the tremor out of her voice. "You were right this morning. This isn't a good idea. I work for you. I take care of your son. Think of what it would do to Danny if this—" she spread her arms "—affair didn't work out. He would be devastated."

Nick combed his hand through his hair and turned away. "I guess you're right."

Cari bit her lip to hold back the tears. She had to struggle to sound in control. "I am right," she said. But still she stood there, her body shaking, willing herself to leave, to get out of there before she weakened. Finally she turned and started for the door, praying that he wouldn't call her back, and hoping that he would. But the only sound she heard was her pulse pounding in her ears as she made it across the hall and into her bedroom.

To the familiar loneliness.

* * *

Cari had spent a restless night. She kept waking up thinking about Nick, fighting to keep from making the short trip back to his bed. She knew that, if only for a short time, she could find comfort in Nick's strong arms and satisfy her hunger and her loneliness. But she wanted more. Maybe she wasn't meant to have a home and family again, but she wasn't going to settle for a fling, either. That alone kept her in her own bed until about six o'clock the next morning.

Cari got up and checked on Danny before she went to take a quick shower. After turning off the water, she stepped out of the stall and grabbed a towel. Wrapping it around her body, she caught a look at herself in the mirror and discovered the dark circles under her eyes.

Great! All she needed was the entire household to know she had spent a sleepless night. She reached for her makeup case and took out her foundation. Applying her makeup also gave her time to think about what she was going to say when she saw Nick today. If the man had any compassion, he would have already left for the office.

An hour later, she and Danny were coming downstairs to join his grandmother for breakfast. At the bottom step, Cari glanced at Nick's office, wondering if he was inside working. The door was open and there wasn't a light on. With a sigh of relief, she started for the kitchen.

She forced a bright smile and walked through the doorway. "Good morning," she said to Eleanor, who was seated at the end of the table, then froze when she discovered Nick seated at the opposite end.

"Good morning to you, too, Cari." The older woman gave her a curious look. "My goodness, you're in a good mood today. The trip to the beach must have agreed with you."

Cari felt herself blush, but Danny drew everyone's attention away from her. "It agreed with me, too, Grandma," he said as he took his usual seat at the table.

"It sure did," she said, then her eyebrow cocked toward the other end of the table. "Too bad it didn't do as much for your father. He's been as grumpy as an old bear since he came down for breakfast."

Nick looked up at his mother. "I apologize, Mother. I have a lot on my mind." He went back to eating his food.

Cari made her way to the table and sat down across from Danny. She tried not to look at Nick, but it was impossible. The man drew her with his magnetism. He was, as usual, impeccably dressed in a dark business suit. When she walked by him she caught a whiff of his familiar aftershave and her breathing became difficult.

"'Morning, Nick," she greeted him, not wanting to let on that something was wrong.

He gave her a quick nod.

"Well," Eleanor began, "I want to hear all about the trip to the beach." She held on to her delicate teacup protectively with both her arthritic hands.

"I already told you all about it yesterday, Grandma," Danny said. "But I still need to clean my bucket of shells. Cari said she'd help me, didn't you?"

In her daze, Cari heard her name and looked at Danny. "Oh, sure, I will."

Eleanor frowned. "Are you okay, Cari?"

"Just a little tired," she lied, feeling self-conscious when Nick glanced up and her gaze met his. "I'm fine, really."

"Well, it wouldn't hurt for you to take it easy today." Mrs. Malone turned her attention back to her son. "Oh, Nick. You never said how the meeting went last night."

Cari watched his jaw firm. "It went fine."

Eleanor smiled. "Good. Did you meet a lot of parents?"

"Yes, Mother, I did."

"Were there children Daniel's age?"

"I didn't ask," he murmured, and set his fork down.

"Well, when is the next meeting? Maybe Daniel can go with you."

"Go where?" Danny asked, looking confused.

"It doesn't matter, son," Nick said, and stood. "I don't plan on attending any more meetings. Now, if you'll excuse me, I need to get to the office." His steely gaze met Cari's. "Would you mind following me out? I need to go over something with you."

Before Cari had a chance to agree, Nick was already out the door. She had to hurry to keep up with his long strides. He didn't slow down until they reached the office and he was behind his desk. He started putting papers into his briefcase.

He was no warmer toward her in here, either, Cari thought. It was hard to believe this was the same man who had made love to her two nights ago, and just last night... How could he turn off his feelings so easily?

"What is it you want to discuss?" she asked.

"I'd prefer it if you would keep Danny at the house today."

"Why?"

Nick finally stopped and looked at her, as if no one had ever questioned him before. "Because he's had a busy few days and I'd like him to rest today. Is there a problem with that?"

"No—no, of course not," she stammered, trying to control her rising anger. "Look, Nick, I know you're upset with me, but that's no reason to punish Danny."

He stopped what he was doing and came from behind the desk. "Whatever gave you that idea?"

Did Cari really think that he would stoop so low? Nick wondered. He couldn't deny she had bruised his ego when she walked out of his bedroom, and even though he knew she had been the only one thinking clearly, it hadn't stopped him from wanting her—or still wanting her.

His gaze roamed over her. She was dressed in a pair of

khaki pants and navy blouse, and even though they were oversize, they didn't hide her shapely figure. And he knew every lush curve.

Damn! Did she have to look so beautiful? She probably hadn't lost a minute's sleep last night while he'd spent hellish hours wide awake as her sweet scent lingered, causing every part of his body to ache. Several times he'd gotten up to go after her and drag her back to his bed. But he'd always stopped himself. He knew the best thing was to keep as far away from each other as possible.

"If you think this has anything to do with us, you're wrong," he began. "You and I are a separate issue. We both agreed wholeheartedly that a personal relationship between us is a bad idea."

He watched her back straighten and her eyes flash with hurt. "Yes, but I also thought you agreed not to close Danny up in the house anymore."

"I assure you, Cari, that's not my intention. After I finish with my meeting this morning, I'm coming home to pick up Danny and take him back to the plant with me." He couldn't help a wry smile. "Do you think he'll enjoy that?"

She blinked in surprise and he saw the joy that sprang into her eyes. "Oh, Nick, he'd love it. But aren't you worried about all the germs he could catch?"

He looked a little sheepish. "Maybe I overreacted a little about that. And I'll keep him pretty close to my side."

"What time do you want me to have him ready?"

"I want to surprise him, otherwise he'll drive you crazy all morning." He couldn't help himself and moved closer. "I think you can use a break, too. You've had a busy few days…with very little sleep."

A soft blush covered her cheeks. Was she remembering the beach house? Nick wondered. God! He hoped so. He'd never forget the memory of their night together. What it felt like to caress her soft skin, stroke her willing body to the point of near completion, then hold back until, finally, he drove deep inside her, time after time.

Nick bit back a groan. No! He couldn't let himself think about it. He grabbed his briefcase off the desk. "I'll call you before I come home. About noon."

She nodded. "Bye, Nick."

He walked out quickly, trying to figure out how he was going to keep his hands off her.

"Well, aren't you going to say thank-you?"

Nick looked up from his desk at the plant to find Larry Keaton standing in the doorway. "Thank you."

Grinning, his friend walked into the glass-enclosed office and shut the door, muffling the assembly-line noise. "That's all the details I get for helping you to…?"

Nick arched an eyebrow. He recognized the eager look on his friend's face. "If you think I'm going to give you any details, you're crazy."

"You mean there are details? Hot damn! Wait until I tell Cindy."

Nick got up and walked around the desk. "Hold it. I don't want you to tell anybody anything, because there is nothing to tell."

Larry looked deflated. "I thought you and Cari…well, I thought there was something between you two. When you guys stopped by to borrow the beach house, I thought I saw something going on between you. C'mon, man, the woman is gorgeous."

Nick knew just how beautiful Cari was, inside and out. "It just wouldn't work, Lar."

"How much of a chance did you give it? C'mon, friend, not every woman out there is like Tory. From what I've seen of Cari with Danny, they're crazy about each other." Larry stared him in the eye. "I think you're crazy about her, too."

Nick *was* crazy about Cari. In fact, if he would admit

it, he was halfway in love with her. "Like I said, it just wouldn't work."

"Why? Because you're worried about Danny's future?"

Nick glared at his friend, ready to deny his comment, but in truth, that was part of it. He let out a sigh and tossed his pen on the desk. "That's only one of the reasons, friend. The big one is Cari deserves more out of life."

Larry shrugged. "So does Cindy, but that didn't stop me from marrying a woman I love and adore. I've seen Cari look at you, Nick. You could have warts and I don't think it would matter."

Nick felt his heart race. God! If it was only that simple.

"Okay," Larry began as he sat on the edge of the desk. "Why don't you two take it slow? Just date casually."

Nick remained silent, then finally spoke. "Cari isn't someone I can just date. And you know I'm not looking for a permanent relationship."

Larry shook his head as he got up and walked toward the door. "You are crazy, Nick, if you let a woman like Cari slip away."

Nick watched as his friend pulled the door closed. The drumming of the machinery in the background hadn't blotted out Larry's words. He shut his eyes and drew a long, tired breath, remembering his past failures at relationships.

Victoria Elizabeth Harper had been the love of his life since his junior year in college. Even though he didn't want to get involved in a serious relationship until school was finished, Tory had other ideas. They compromised, waiting until a month after graduation to be married.

What with his father's illness and the challenge of keeping the family business going, Nick didn't need a demanding bride to add to his problems. But Tory wouldn't be denied. She wouldn't take second place to anything or anybody, including his ill father and the struggling business. So when Tory decided she wanted a baby, Nick had been shocked.

He never got to find out if she would have made a good mother, because she wasn't given the chance. Danny was born with his heart problem. And from the doctor's first diagnosis, Tory let Nick know that he was responsible for their imperfect child. Then, when Danny was still a baby, she told him she couldn't handle their son's illness and left him.

He wouldn't go through that hell again. Although he knew Cari wasn't shallow like Tori—she wouldn't run out on a sick child—he couldn't give her what she needed. He had a fatal flaw that he'd never saddle another woman with. Especially a woman like Cari, who was meant to be a mother, to have babies of her own. Healthy babies. How could he ask her to pour her love into a child when the possibility of that child being snatched from her was so great. She had already suffered such a loss once before. He couldn't put her through that again. He wouldn't.

Chapter Ten

Nick climbed out of his car, grabbed his briefcase from the back seat and headed to the house. He was exhausted tonight. But he decided he was going to make it home for dinner if it killed him. Besides, he looked forward to spending time with Danny. They had had such a great time together at the plant last week that he'd decided to make it a regular outing, if time permitted. He couldn't help but get excited, wondering how Cari would feel about it.

Cari. His pulse raced just thinking about her being inside waiting for him. He discovered he looked forward to coming home evenings, and it wasn't just for Danny. It hadn't been easy living in the same house with her, having her sleeping across the hall and not being able to touch her…to make love to her.

He couldn't deny it anymore. He thought about Cari all the time. Day or night, it didn't make any difference. He wanted her with a need that was more than just physical.

He opened the front door and walked in the entry, placing his briefcase on the table.

"I'm home." He called out his usual greeting, then smiled as he heard the familiar footsteps.

"Daddy!" his son yelled from the top of the stairs, then started the long climb down. "Look, Daddy. I got a haircut."

Nick's smile slowly faded as his son's nearly shaved head came into view. His jaw tightened as he examined the barber's close work. He looked up and saw Cari coming down the stairs. "Did my barber do this?"

"No, Dad," Danny volunteered. "We went to the park today and my new friend Jason had a haircut like this and I wanted one. So Cari took me to the barber."

"Danny," Cari said, "you left out a big part of the story, don't you think?"

"Oh, yeah." The boy's face paled. "I kinda tried to cut it myself." He raised his large brown eyes to meet his father's. "I didn't do it very good. So Cari took me to the barber."

Nick hunched down in front of his son. "I thought you knew you weren't supposed to play with scissors. They're dangerous."

"That's what Cari said. I'm sorry, Daddy." His lower lip jutted out. "I won't do it again. Promise."

Nick looked up at Cari. She was trying to keep from smiling. "What kind of punishment should we give him?" He surprised himself by asking her.

"I think a week without going to the park should do it."

Danny gasped. "But I want to show Jason my hair."

Nick was going to find out who this Jason character was. "Well, your friend is going to have to wait awhile. And you're going to have to promise to keep your hands off the scissors."

"I promise only to use mine," he vowed.

"And no more cutting your hair," Nick said, studying the black stubble on his son's head.

"And I won't cut my hair anymore," he repeated as he shook his head vigorously. "I love you, Daddy." The child threw his arms around his father's neck.

Nick swallowed hard. "I love you, too, son," he murmured, knowing he hadn't told him that nearly often enough. He hugged his little boy tightly. "No matter what you do, Danny, I'll always love you."

Danny pulled back, and his dark eyes stared into his father's. "That's what Cari said. Parents always love their kids, even when they do dumb stuff." The boy lowered his gaze. "Does that mean that my mother still loves me?"

Nick felt as if he'd been punched in the gut. Again he found himself glancing up at Cari for help. She looked just as shocked as he was. "Danny, who could not love you. Your mother has been gone a long time…"

"I know. But can we call her?"

Nick tried hard not to show his panic. He wasn't prepared for this. How was he supposed to explain to a four-year-old that his mother didn't love him enough to stick around? "I don't think that would be a good idea."

His son looked more confused than ever. "But why?"

Cari walked over and knelt down on the floor beside them. "Danny. Sometimes people can't be with us," she began. "And sometimes it's not anybody's fault."

"Like when your little girl died?" Danny asked.

It tore at Nick to watch the pain on Cari's face as she stroked Danny's back. "Yes, like when Angel died," she said. "It's not your fault that your mother isn't here. You have a lot of people who care about you—your dad, your grandmother and Marion."

Danny smiled. "And you?"

Cari smiled back. "And me."

He giggled. "And you have me, and you have Dad, too. So you won't be alone, either." Danny hugged them, drawing them all in a close circle, then he proceeded to share his kisses. "Now, Daddy, you kiss Cari."

Nick bit back a groan. Oh, God! He wasn't going to survive, he thought as he leaned forward and placed a soft kiss on her cheek. Before he pulled away, he could hear her sharp intake of breath. Then his gaze locked with hers, and he couldn't seem to move. His hands itched to pull her into his arms and hold her sweet body against his.

"I'm hungry," Danny cried.

That broke the mood and Nick stood. "Yeah, so am I. Let's go see about dinner."

The child's face lit up. "There isn't any."

Nick frowned at Cari. "Is Marion not feeling well?" The housekeeper had rarely missed cooking a meal.

"No, she went to her sister's," Cari said. "Your mother is also out for the evening."

"My mother went out?" Nick knew she hadn't ventured out of the house since she'd been in a wheelchair, only for doctor visits and to get her hair styled.

"She went to her friend, Mildred Shaffer's. She's filling in at bridge club."

"Mother's playing bridge?" He was in shock. He'd tried for months to get her out of the house.

"Grandma can hold cards now, 'cause Cari's been practicin' with her."

"I didn't do that much," Cari denied as she looked at Nick. "A few weeks ago I found out about your mother's love for bridge, but because of her arthritis she couldn't play anymore. I told her about an arthritic patient at St. M's whose husband made a metal clip with a handle to help her hold her cards. Your mother sounded interested, so I talked to John. He's so handy around the house and garage, I hoped he'd be able to put something together." Cari looked embarrassed. "I know the logical thing was to come to you, since you have a whole design department, but your mother didn't want anyone to know about it. Just in case it didn't work.''

Nick didn't say anything.

"Well, I drew John a rough sketch of what I needed, and the next day he had welded a holder together.''

"We wanted to surprise you, Dad,'' Danny said.

"You sure did, son.''

"Now, your mother still has to be able to insert the cards into the fan, then pull them out,'' Cari added. "I talked to her doctor and he gave me some exercises for Eleanor to help improve her range of movement. One she should have been doing all along but didn't see much reason to. Now that she has incentive, she's been doing them twice a day. And we've all been playing cards with her.''

"And Grandma plays Go Fish with me, too.''

Nick had no clue about what was going on in his own home. Ever since Cari had been in the house, things had been changing—for the good. Maybe it was time he did, too. "So tonight is her debut?''

Cari nodded. "John will bring her home about nine-thirty.''

"So that leaves us to fend for ourselves. Well, first thing is dinner.''

"I can fix us something,'' Cari suggested.

Danny jumped up and down. "Pizza.''

"I think everyone can use a break tonight. How about we go out for pizza?''

Cari knew she should turn them down and let father and son go together. But she was going to be selfish tonight. She needed to spend time with the two people she cared about the most. "That sounds like a great idea.''

"Okay, Danny. You go get washed up and put on a baseball cap so your head won't freeze.''

Danny giggled. "It's too warm to freeze, silly.''

Nick tickled his son, then sent him off to his room to get ready. He turned back to Cari. "Thank you.''

Cari had trouble swallowing. "For what? The barber repaired the damage."

"I'm not talking about the haircut. I'm talking about Danny's mother. Damn! I hate to even call her that. Tory was never around. I was surprised Danny asked about her."

"Nick, your son is getting older. He sees kids with their mothers. It's only natural he's curious." So was Cari. "Is there any chance that he could see her?"

"No! Never!" Nick said adamantly. "Tory's too selfish to do more than walk in, then leave again when the going gets rough. I refuse to put Danny through that again." A smile spread across his face. "You've been more of a mother to my son than Tory ever was."

She felt herself blush. "I care about Danny."

Nick reached out and cupped her chin, making her look at him. "I know you do. And he cares about you. We all do."

Cari couldn't seem to draw a breath, seeing the fire smoldering in his silver eyes. Slowly his head lowered and she knew he was going to kiss her. She closed her eyes as the warmth of his breath caressed her face. Suddenly Danny's voice rang out and she opened her eyes to find Nick smiling.

"I need to talk to my son about his lousy timing."

Cari walked quickly down the hospital corridor on her evening shift. Usually the nights were quiet, but she had spent the first four hours at Riverhaven in emergency. The long Thanksgiving weekend approached and it seemed that several motorists had been celebrating early. Luckily everyone had survived, but two of the crash victims had to be rushed to surgery. She congratulated herself on her composure during the entire crisis.

Now, back on the fourth floor in pediatric cardiology, her patients were sound asleep. All except for Billy Wolfe,

Matt Landers's newest patient. The seven-year-old was frightened about his upcoming surgery. Cari had planned to sit with him after his parents left, but she had been called down to emergency.

She came into his room and saw his light on. "Billy, you should be asleep." She walked across to his bed. "Tomorrow is a big day."

The black-haired boy looked up at her with his midnight eyes. His native American heritage was prominent in his bone structure and dark skin. "I woke up and was scared," he said.

Cari quickly sat down on the bed and hugged the small child to her. "I know, Billy, but Dr. Matt is the best doctor around. He's not going to let anything happen to you."

"What if he can't fix my heart? My grandfather told me to be brave, but…"

She drew back and looked down at the child. "Billy, you have to believe that everything is going to be okay." Cari knew that any heart surgery was risky, but Matt Landers was the best cardiac surgeon on the West Coast. "Now, you need some sleep so your body can be strong for the surgery."

She eased him down on the bed and began rubbing his back, hoping to relax him enough to sleep. It worked. Within ten minutes Billy was sound asleep. Cari covered him with a blanket and headed for the door. Then she discovered Nick in the hall.

"What are you doing here?" she questioned as her heart pounded. "Is Danny okay?"

He shook his head. "Danny is fine. He's home with Marion. I needed to talk to you."

Cari had no idea what Nick could possibly need to discuss with her. "Let me tell the desk I'm going on a break."

They walked to the fourth floor break room and Cari directed him to the table while she went to the coffeemaker. She grabbed two cups as Audrey Michaels got up from the other table and poured her remaining coffee in the sink.

The forty-year-old scrub nurse had been a good friend to Cari since she moved to Riverhaven. "Girl, you got to tell me how you do it."

Cari looked at her confused. "Do what?"

"Find the best-looking men." The nurse winked and left the room.

Cari glanced over her shoulder at Nick. He was dressed in jeans and an oxford shirt, and with the cool November temperature, he wore a camel-colored leather jacket. Audrey wasn't telling her anything she didn't already know.

Lord help her, she was weakening, she thought as she carried the cups to the table.

"Thank you," he said. He took a few sips, then finally pushed the cup aside. "I was watching you with the kid. You were good with him."

Cari shrugged. "Billy was scared. And once the sedative took hold, he fell asleep." She took a sip of her coffee, not really tasting it. Her attention was on the man sitting across from her.

"You probably wonder what I'm doing here."

Cari smiled, but he didn't smile back.

"I came to ask if you would come with me to the Riverhaven Hospital charity dinner."

Her mouth opened, but no words came out. Nick Malone was asking her out? "I thought you—we decided that it wasn't a good idea," she stammered.

"It's only a simple dinner party, in a nice restaurant down at the beach."

Cari fought her panic, remembering what had happened at the beach house. The past few weeks she'd worked hard to keep her distance from the man. And now he'd come down to her work and asked her out on a date.

"I thought we decided not to get involved."

"I told you, Cari, it's not a date." He combed his hand through his hair and stood up. "Dammit! I knew this was a mistake."

Cari saw his frustration.

"It's a charity function for the hospital," he explained. "Larry and Cindy, Matt Landers and even Bess will be there. I wouldn't even be going except Larry talked me into it—correction, Cindy bullied me until I gave in and bought the tickets."

"I've met Cindy Keaton." Cari crossed her arms. She had liked her. "She's tiny, petite—it's hard to believe she bullied you into going to a dinner."

"You haven't seen her when she's put in charge of a charity function. She becomes a barracuda. Please, Cari, you've got to help me out."

Cari wanted nothing more than to be with Nick, but she doubted she would fit in with these people. She had been raised by her single mother in a housing project in Seattle. After her death, the foster homes Cari had been placed in hadn't exactly taken the time to teach her which fork to use. Nick had had money all his life. His friends, Larry and Cindy, were nice, but she still wasn't sure.

"Isn't there someone else you would rather take?"

He swung around and glared at her. "I don't want to go with anyone else." His face softened, as did his voice. "Just you."

She felt a shiver rush down her spine. He made her a believer.

"I don't have a dress that would be appropriate."

"I don't care what you wear. But if it bothers you, just go buy something and charge it to me."

"No!" she said, trying to control her sudden anger. She wasn't taking any handouts. "I can buy my own clothes."

He came across to her and sat down again. "All I meant to say was that you'll be beautiful whatever you wear."

"Thank you."

"I don't want your thanks, Cari. Just say you'll go with me."

"I'll go," she said, relenting.

A week later Nick stood in front of his dresser mirror. "Dammit!" He jerked loose the crooked bow on his black tie. This wasn't working, he thought as he blew the third attempt at making a decent bow. How could he with his hands shaking and his stomach churning? He hated these functions, but he knew the hospital needed the money, especially the cardiac wing. It was the only reason he was attending tonight.

He worked the tie again, but soon discovered he'd done another lousy job. "Damn! Damn!"

"Oh, Daddy, you said a bad word," Danny said as he came into the room. "Marion's gonna put hot sauce on your tongue."

"I guess I'm just frustrated 'cause I can't tie my tie." He looked down at the boy. "Think you can help me?"

Danny shook his head. "Cari's only teaching me to tie my shoes, but I can't do it yet. I'll go get her."

Before Nick could stop him, Danny was gone. But not for long. When he returned, he was pulling Cari by the hand and into his bedroom.

"Cari can do it, Dad." Danny released her hand and smiled at them.

Nick wasn't paying attention to his son. He was too busy eyeing Cari. She looked beautiful. She was dressed in a strapless black evening gown. The top was fitted, showing off her delicate shoulders and full breasts. His gaze lowered to her small, trim waistline. The gathered skirt draped nearly to the floor, but a small slit up the side allowed a peek at her shapely legs, encased in sheer black stockings, and her feet in slim high-heeled sandals.

"Danny said you were having trouble with your tie."

"Huh? Yeah." Nick shook his head and his eyes met

hers. Her blond hair was pulled back from her face and lay in soft curls around her shoulders. There were pearls adorning her ears, and a delicate strand around her neck. "You're beautiful."

She beamed. "Thank you. Cindy took me shopping at this wonderful outlet in San Jose." Her hands went to her throat. "Your mother loaned me these pearls."

They both stood there, just staring. Finally Cari said, "You look very nice, too."

"I might look a little better if I could get this tie right. Usually Mother would rescue me, but..." He cocked an eyebrow. "You wouldn't happen to know how one of these works?"

"It just so happens I do. Herb and Alice Phillips were my foster parents when I was about thirteen. Herb play the tenor saxophone in a dance band, and every Saturday night I used to help him with his tie because Alice had arthritis."

Nervous, Cari walked across the room, very aware Nick was watching her closely. He looked so gorgeous in his dark tuxedo pants and pleated shirt. The black studs blinked at her as she examined his broad chest. She tried to hide her trembling hands as she reached up and grabbed hold of the stubborn tie. Luckily Nick had to lift his head so she could do her job without his silvery gaze on her.

"Did you like the Phillipses?"

Cari shrugged. "They were nice people." Somehow she managed to tie the bow in just one try. She made sure it was straight and stepped back.

"There. Now you're perfect."

Danny jumped up and down. "Cari, you did it. You made a bow."

After glancing in the mirror, Nick grinned at her. "Thank you."

"You're welcome." Cari watched as he pulled a hand-kerchief from the drawer and dropped change into his pockets. He walked to the closet, pulled his jacket off the hanger and slipped it on, then put his wallet in the inside pocket. It all seemed so intimate. "I'll just wait downstairs," she murmured.

"No, we'll go together," he said, then turned to his son. "Go down and tell Grandma we're coming so she can see how nice we look."

Danny took off and Nick winked. "Just give me a second." He stepped into the bathroom, then in less than a minute returned. "I'm ready," he announced. "How about you?" He came up beside her and she caught his familiar scent, a mixture of soap and woodsy cologne. Her insides did a somersault.

"I just need to get my wrap and purse—" He took her by the arm and she forgot what else she was going to say.

He walked her by her room and waited while she retrieved her things off the bed. Once again he took her arm and they started down the stairs. Suddenly cheers broke out from everyone gathered at the bottom.

"Oh, Cari, you look so lovely," Eleanor gushed from her wheelchair, and Marion agreed.

"Thank you, Eleanor. Especially for letting me borrow the pearls. I'll take good care of them." Cari knew this was her Cinderella night. When the clock struck twelve, she had to come back to being plain old Cari.

Eleanor waved her hand. "Just both of you have a good time."

"Mother, this is a charity function," Nick said. "They're after my money." He leaned down and kissed Eleanor.

"More the reason to enjoy yourself," she said. "And don't worry about coming home early. Danny's staying downstairs with me tonight."

"Grandma said I can stay up as late as I want."

Nick bent down and kissed his son. "Oh, she did, did she? Well, just remember to behave yourself."

Danny gave Cari a kiss, too. "Have fun."

Nick helped Cari with her cape and whispered, "I think they're up to something. Let's get out of here before we find out what it is."

Cari didn't care what anyone was up to, as long as no one woke her from her fairy-tale dream, she thought as Nick took her hand and escorted her out the door.

Cari had never had such a special night. She had never been to a prom when she was in school, so dressing up and going out to a formal dinner with Nick Malone was like a dream come true.

The minute they walked in the front door at the restaurant, it seemed that every woman in the room turned to look at him. Cari knew Nick was by far the most handsome man there.

Where she was shy, Nick was comfortable with the whole group of wealthy contributors. He pitched the importance of the cardiac unit and the research. By the end of the dinner, he had lured thousands of dollars from these generous people, all in the name of charity.

Finally the dinner was over and Cari expected her special night to come to an end. It was a surprise when Nick accepted Larry and Cindy's invitation to stay for the dancing.

"Unless you want to go home?" Nick asked her.

"No. Your mother is watching Danny," Cari said. "We can stay for a little while." Her eyes met his. "If you want to."

Nick smiled and leaned toward her. "I have to warn you it's been a while and my dancing is a little rusty."

Just then the band began to play, and already Cindy and Larry were on their feet, along with several other couples. "C'mon, you two." Cindy waved to them. "Before the floor gets crowded."

Nick took Cari's hand. It had been years since he had last danced. Usually he sat through these functions, then quickly disappeared before dessert was served. Tonight, he thoroughly enjoyed introducing Cari to everyone. She had charmed the men with her beauty and intelligence, and the women with her honest caring for the children.

Finding an open spot on the crowded floor, Nick drew her into his arms. He placed a hand on the small of her back and held her as close as he dared. He laid his chin against her soft hair and breathed in her sweet fragrance.

The band's female singer drifted from one throaty ballad to another. And before long, Nick's body was all too aware of the lovely woman in his arms.

"It's been a nice evening." Cari raised her head and looked at him, her blue eyes sparkling.

"You made it wonderful, Cari," Nick said as he pulled her back into his arms.

This time he tightened his hold and shifted his leg between hers, immediately creating a hot friction. When she didn't resist, he placed her hands on his chest and wrapped both arms around her. Before long her fingers were linked behind his neck. Their dance steps had slowed to a slight shifting back and forth, his body sizzling from the intense heat her touch generated. Lord help him. He couldn't take any more. He needed her. He knew he shouldn't, but there was so much more than just a physical lust that he craved from her.

He pulled back and Cari tilted her face upward, her eyes filled with longing. Without saying a word, he knew she wanted the same thing. They were crazy to think they could stay away from each other. "Do you want to leave?" he asked, unable to keep the tremble out of his voice.

She nodded, and he grabbed her hand, and without saying any goodbyes, he headed for the nearest exit. They were outside waiting for the valet to get his BMW before anyone noticed they were gone. Once inside the car, Nick turned to Cari, eyeing her tempting mouth, but decided against kissing her, knowing he wouldn't be able to stop.

"God, woman! You're making me crazy," he growled.

"Just take me home," she whispered.

"I'm on my way." He threw the BMW into drive and shot out of the parking lot.

It took nineteen minutes to reach the front door. Nick pulled out his key and helped Cari from the car. Once inside the entry, he couldn't wait any longer and his mouth came down on hers as he pushed her against the closed door. One kiss led to another, then another, until Nick grabbed her by the hand and led her upstairs into his dimly lit bedroom.

After the door was closed, he continued to kiss her. "Oh God, Cari!" He stripped off his jacket and tossed it on the chair. "Tell me you want me as much as I want you." He helped her with her cape.

"Oh, yes," she breathed before his mouth came down on hers.

Cari wasn't going to fight it anymore. Loving Nick Malone was a fact of life. She jerked off his tie, then went to work on his shirt studs. After a few minutes of frustration, he stood before her bare-chested. Placing random kisses along her neck and shoulders, Nick turned her around and then went to work on eliminating her dress.

"I'll be careful," he whispered against her ear. But the last thing on Cari's mind was his treatment of her clothing as his lips caressed her neck and shoulders. Once the zipper gave way, she stepped out of the gown. He placed it carefully on the chair, then turned back to her.

Cari felt a warm shiver as Nick's eyes raked over her nearly nude body. Her dress hadn't needed a bra and she'd opted for black stockings and a garter belt.

"If I'd known what you had on under your dress, we would have come home hours ago." He grasped her against him and the blood surged through her body. "Black is definitely my favorite color."

She smiled nervously. "I'm glad."

He leaned in close and placed a long, hungry kiss on her lips.

"Let's see if I can make you more than just glad." His hands shifted from her bare back to her lace-clad hips. She gasped as he rubbed the evidence of his arousal against the cradle of her thighs.

"You smell so sweet," he said, almost to himself, as he dropped kisses down her cheek to her neck, then finally to the top of her breasts. His hands cupped their full weight in his palms. "And you're so soft."

Cari moaned and held his head in her hands, feeling a stab of desire as his mouth closed over her nipple. The gentle sucking motion caused the bud to harden and that seemed to excite him more. He eagerly gave the same attention to the other breast.

Nick willed himself to be patient, but the hunger in him was almost violent. He wanted Cari. As much as he tried to stay away, he knew he'd been foolish to think he could deny his feelings for her.

He pulled her with him across the room to his bed. Once he threw back the blankets, he laid her down against the ivory sheets and quickly stripped off the rest of his clothes. After tossing them aside, he began removing Cari's stockings. His hands shook, but he managed to complete the task and climb in next to her.

He leaned over her and whispered, "You're all I've dreamed about for the past three weeks." He shut his eyes as he pressed against her. "I thought I'd go crazy from wanting you."

Cari couldn't speak, afraid she might blurt out her feelings. "Just no regrets, Nick." She couldn't stand his rejection again.

"Never." His hands moved over her body, caressing

every inch of her, her breasts, her stomach, then into the triangle of hair between her legs, letting him discover she was ready for him.

"Please, Nick," she begged, and raised herself up to meet his touch.

"Soon," he promised, willing himself to hold back. He wanted her, but he wanted more than just her body. He drew deeply on her nipple and felt her heart pounding under his mouth. His lips skimmed lower, somewhere around her navel and she sucked in her breath and whispered his name. He reversed his direction and took her mouth in a kiss that nearly took them over the edge.

Cari pulled her mouth away and stayed his hand. "No! I want you inside me." She reached between them and began stroking him.

Nick sucked in a long breath. The muscles bunched in his shoulders beneath her searing touch. His hard chest beaded with sweat as he fought for control. But once he saw the desire in her eyes, he was lost.

"Now! I want you now," she cried as she rotated against him.

He reached into the nightstand drawer and took out a condom, tore open the foil wrapper and put it on. Rolling back to her, he spread her legs further apart and, for what seemed an eternity, held her gaze as he slowly pushed into her. Whispering her name, their bodies meshed and the pace had to quicken or he'd go crazy. He found her breasts, laving them, then drawing them into his mouth when she arched her back. When she cried out her joy, it was like sweet music, accompanied by the driving beat of his pulse.

"I've dreamed of this, Cari," he breathed. "Being this close to you, being inside you." He nearly withdrew, but before she could voice a complaint, he thrust back inside her as far as he could go.

Cari gasped as the sensation nearly drove her off the bed. "Oh—" She bit her lip, wondering if she could die from such pleasure. She clung to him, her mouth desperate on his, her body straining toward each shattering stroke.

Nick lifted himself up and stared deep into her eyes, twining one of his hands with hers. His other slipped under her hips, tilting her so he could penetrate more deeply. He moved in a slow, deliberate rhythm that had her womb tightening.

"Don't fight it," he told her.

Helplessly, she was unable to stop what was happening to her. Nick's eyes held hers as he repeatedly moved inside her, building pressure that had her climbing to heights she never knew existed. He reached between them and rubbed his thumb over her swollen nub, caressing her as she murmured his name.

"Let go, Cari," he ordered.

Suddenly a spasm burst through her and she exploded into a million pieces. Just as she came out of her haze, she heard Nick cry out and he collapsed on top of her. Cari pulled him tight against her and tears filled her eyes.

"I love you," she whispered, not even realizing that she had spoken out loud until she felt the man in her arms stiffen.

For an endless, timeless moment no one moved, then finally Nick rolled off her, got out of bed and went into the bathroom. He returned shortly, wearing a robe. He sat on the edge of the bed with his back to her.

"Nick, what's wrong?"

He combed his hand through his hair. "I can't give you what you want, Cari."

"I think you did a pretty good job," she tried to joke as she covered her nakedness with the sheet. But she knew he was talking about her earlier confession.

"Good sex isn't what you want. You want a husband and a family." He turned to her, no emotion showing on his face. "I can't give you that."

"I didn't think I was asking," she denied.

"Then you should be." He stood abruptly. "And if things were different, I'd..." His words died. "But I can't."

Cari sat up, wrapped in the sheet. "Why, Nick? Why can't you love? Is it me? Because I'm from a different social class?"

He gripped her arms and gave her a little shake. "Dammit, Cari. That has nothing to do with it. I don't care where the hell you came from."

"Then tell me, Nick." She fought the tears that threatened.

"I can't give you marriage and children." There was pain etched in his eyes. "Dammit! I carried the flawed gene that caused Danny's birth defect. And I can't take the chance of passing it on to another child." He started to walk away, but Cari grabbed his arm.

"How do you know?"

He shrugged. "It's true. My father had heart disease for years until he died five years ago. And I passed it on to my son."

Shocked, Cari gaped at him. "Nick, babies are born with defects every day and they're not necessarily caused by their parents. Have you discussed this with Matt?"

"It doesn't matter. I can't risk it."

She couldn't believe it. "So you're just going to live in a vacuum of guilt and self-pity?" Cari tugged angrily at the sheet she wore. "How dare you? How dare you do this to us—to Danny. Don't you think he deserves a life?"

"If it weren't for me, he'd have a life."

Cari closed her eyes. *No! Danny has a good life, thanks to Angel,* she cried silently. But he wasn't going to listen to what she had to say. Not now. Maybe not ever.

"Maybe you're right, Nick. It's not a life when you're kept locked away." She caught his gray eyes. "You're the one I feel sorry for, not Danny. At least he wants to live." With a cold look, Cari tossed her hair off her shoulder and strolled out of the room. So much for their promise of no regrets.

Chapter Eleven

Nick sat at his office desk and jabbed at the buttons on the keyboard, but nothing was happening. Dammit! He didn't need this. He'd had no sleep last night and had consumed enough coffee this morning to float away. And to top it off, his password didn't access the file he needed. Another attempt went awry, until finally he managed to get into the system. But the screen was one big blur. His thoughts were on last night and Cari.

The image of her gloriously naked, lying on his bed, was enough to drive a man crazy. When she had offered him more, her love, he'd had to turn her away. A tremor racked his body at the sudden realization of his feelings. Leaning back in his chair, he rubbed his hand over his face, thinking back to when he had fallen in love with Cari. He couldn't remember a time that she hadn't been on his mind, when he hadn't wanted her. But he could never give her what she longed for. What she deserved.

If only that logic would stop the unbearable ache that

drove him from his bed at four this morning, the same bed he had shared only hours before with Cari. But he could never have her again. He had no right.

Suddenly the intercom buzzed and he reached to answer it. "Yes, Peg."

"Dr. Landers is here to see you."

Matt Landers? Here? "Send him in." Nick got up and came around the desk when the door opened.

The doctor entered with a bright smile. Nick would bet his secretary was wearing one, too. "Matt, this is a surprise. Didn't your department get enough donations last night?"

The surgeon was dressed casually in a polo shirt and a pair of tan slacks. "We did pretty well, Nick. Thanks to you. Looks like we might be able to staff the research department after the first of the year."

Nick sat down on the edge of his desk and directed Matt into a chair. "Glad to hear it. So, what's the reason for this visit?"

Slowly the doctor's smile faded. "I talked to Cari this morning. She's concerned about you."

"Hell." Nick stood and walked to the window. He glanced down from the third-floor office that had once been his father's. Nick had always liked it here. When he was a kid, in the summers, his dad had let him spend time at Malone Industries. He sighed. How he wished for those simpler days.

"I was wondering where you got your medical degree," Matt said as he came up behind him. "It took me nearly ten years to get through med school and residency to become a pediatric cardiothoracic surgeon."

"Okay, Matt. Get to the point."

"Cari said you had this notion that you're responsible for Danny's heart problem."

Nick glanced away. He'd held the guilt to himself for

nearly five years. This was the first time anyone had ever questioned him about it.

Matt cocked an eyebrow. "Who told you this? A doctor?"

"No." He shook his head. "Tory told me it was my fault because of my father."

"And did a doctor tell her?"

"Hell, I don't know, but I figured that's where she got the information."

"You ever think that your wife might be afraid, and she needed to blame someone?"

Nick's heart seemed to stop. He couldn't believe that even Tory could be that hateful.

"Look, Nick," Matt began again. "Since I didn't come in on Danny's case until his heart transplant, I never met your wife—"

"Ex-wife," he clarified.

"Ex-wife," Matt repeated. "Like I said, I wasn't there the first two years of Danny's life, but I know for a fact that dilated cardiomyopathy is a congenital birth defect. It isn't necessarily passed on through genes. It could have been caused by many things. Something that happened during pregnancy, a virus maybe. We don't really know. We doctors call it an act of God." Matt walked across the room. "I called Dr. Carlton and we discussed your medical history, Nick. There's nothing from your last check up that shows any abnormalities in your heart. You're as healthy as a horse."

Nick was confused. "But my father had a heart condition all his life."

Matt waved a hand in the air. "Your father's heart problems were caused by stress, bad eating habits and smoking too many cigars. His doctor had warned him for years to lose weight and take better care of himself. He didn't heed those warnings. Now, as a doctor, I'm here to warn you that you work too hard." A smile appeared on his face.

"My prescription is that you take a day off occasionally and play a little golf."

"Are you saying I wasn't the cause of Danny's heart problem?"

Matt shrugged. "There isn't any family history of genetic heart trouble. So I'd say you're capable of having healthy children...."

Nick wasn't listening anymore. He was busy taking the news in. All these years he'd thought... The sudden rush of emotions was so overwhelming tears welled in his eyes. He wasn't responsible for Danny's heart condition. The words were the most beautiful he'd ever heard. He leaned against the window ledge for support as the guilt of the last five years seemed to vanish.

Tory. He clenched his hands into fists. But his anger quickly faded into joy. It was a waste of time to hate her. Besides, she couldn't hurt him or Danny anymore.

He looked at Matt. "Thank you. You have no idea how good that is to hear."

"My pleasure. But you owe Cari all the thanks."

"Cari! I've got to talk to her." He hurried to the desk and picked up the phone.

"Wait, Nick," Matt said, stopping him. "Cari's been through a lot. If anyone deserves another chance at happiness, she does. If you're not going to offer her that, then I suggest you back off and let her have that chance with someone else."

Matt's sudden protectiveness surprised Nick. It was obvious Matt was interested in Cari. Well, too bad. "Forget it, Doc. I have no intention of backing off." He put the receiver to his ear. "Peg, cancel my appointments for today, and tell Larry I need him to cover for me. I'll call him later." He hung up, turned off his computer and headed for the door.

"Does this mean you won't be free for golf anytime soon?" Matt said with a knowing grin.

Nick paused. "I guess not." He studied the brilliant surgeon who had performed the heart transplant that saved his son's life. Now he had helped him find happiness with Cari. "Thank's, Matt."

The doctor nodded. "I only wish you had come to me sooner."

"I guess I was afraid to know for sure," Nick confessed, then smiled. "I owe you."

Matt shook his head. "Just give me the name of the guy who made your clubs."

"You got it," Nick said, and then he was out the door.

A quick stop at his personal physician's, Dr. Carlton, office verified Matt's finding. He was in perfect health. Nick thanked the doctor and couldn't get home fast enough. He rushed in the front door, and without stopping, he was up the stairs. Once in the suite he didn't slow down until he found Cari in Danny's bedroom. He paused at the door, taking in the sweet picture of the two of them. Cari in a rocker, with Danny seated on her lap. She was reading him a story. His son had already fallen asleep, but that didn't stop her from rocking and cradling the child in her arms.

Cari raised her head and found Nick standing in the doorway. Her heart pounded in her chest. What was he doing home in the middle of the day? Was he going to ask her to leave? Was she going to have to give up Danny? Her hold tightened on the child.

"I think you've lost your audience." Nick leaned over, picked up his son and carried him to bed. After covering Danny with a blanket, he asked Cari to come with him.

She fought her panic but did as he asked. Once in the living room, Nick didn't hesitate. "Matt Landers came to my office this morning."

Her eyes widened, but she didn't say a word.

"Out of the blue, he showed up at my office about an

hour ago, giving me a clean bill of health. He also informed me that I wasn't responsible for Danny's heart condition." He gave her a smile that sent her pulse racing. "Thank you."

"There's no need to..." she began, when he stepped closer and took her hand. "It was unfair for you to go on thinking—"

He pulled her into his arms. "Thinking what, Cari?"

"That you're responsible. Now you can go on with your life." She tried to pull away, but he refused to let her go.

"I want to, Cari. More than anything."

"It's not good to dwell on the past," she agreed. "I came here to get on with my life." And she'd found so much more. Was Nick going to take all that away? Her eyes searched his, hoping to see into his thoughts.

The back of his hand stroked her cheek. "You've changed my life as much as Danny's."

"I'm sorry. I didn't mean to—"

He placed his finger across her lips. "I want you to know what you said to me last night when we were making love...it meant a lot to me. But I'm not sure if I'm able to handle it right now."

She swallowed hard, unable to speak and afraid of the consequences of her confession of love. She nodded.

Nick let out a breath and wrapped his arms around her. She felt him tremble as he held her tight. "Oh, Cari. You make me want things, things I haven't wanted for a very long time," he said huskily.

She closed her eyes, knowing she couldn't stop herself. "Maybe it's time you start."

He pulled back. His gray eyes were like silver lightning. "Will you promise to be there with me?"

Cari's hand trembled as she reached up to touch his jaw. "If you want me to be." She needed the words, too.

"Oh, lady, I want you all right. More than you'll ever know." He lowered his head to meet her mouth in a heated kiss. She moaned as his tongue slipped inside, stroking until they were both breathless. He drew back and rested his forehead against hers. "If I'm dreaming, don't wake me up."

The last thing she wanted to do was break the spell, but she knew that she had to tell Nick about Angel before they went any further.

He nibbled on her ear. "How long do you think Danny will nap?"

Cari bit her lip. "Should be a least an hour."

"Good." He tugged her toward his bedroom. Once inside, he closed the door, then reached behind her and turned the lock as his mouth came down on hers, driving away her doubts. He pressed his hard body against hers, and his thigh found its way between her legs.

"I'd like to take the rest of the day to show you what you mean to me," he began, "but maybe I can give you a little sample to tide you over until later." He picked her up and carried her toward the bed.

"We need to talk, Nick." She still had to tell him about Angel. Cari made a weak attempt to stop him, but she knew that making love with Nick was all she wanted right now.

"Later." He unbuttoned her blouse and pressed his lips against the top of her breasts, and Cari lost all thought of resistance.

"The end." Cari closed the storybook. "Now it's bedtime," she told Danny.

"But I want you to read another one."

"Danny, we've already gone through half your library."

"But..."

"Daniel Malone, Cari said it's time for bed."

The child looked up at his dad. "Yeah, but she didn't read me my rabbit book yet." Tears started to build up in his eyes.

"Then we'll save it for tomorrow."

Nick took the book, placed it on the shelf, then kissed his son good-night. He thought about giving a kiss to Cari but resisted, knowing he'd get too many questions from Danny. And he wanted his son in bed—asleep. He didn't want any interference with his plans tonight.

"Now go to sleep," he said, and took Cari's hand to make sure Danny wasn't going to keep her in his room any longer.

"'Night, Daddy. 'Night, Cari."

"Good night, Danny," she said. "Sweet dreams."

Nick pulled her from the room and shut the door. Now it was their time. He kissed her surprised mouth and walked her into the living room. After their sweet lovemaking this afternoon, he knew how distracting she was. And they needed to sit down and talk.

"Now, what is this important thing you have to tell me?"

Cari felt herself tense at his question. She knew they could never have a relationship without honesty. He deserved to know the truth. "I need to tell you about Angel."

He nodded, as if expecting this talk. "Okay." He drew her into his arms and rested her head against his shoulder. Cari couldn't remember ever feeling so safe.

"I wish I could have been there for you." He hugged her closer, his lips caressed her hair. "I hate to think of you handling it all alone."

Tears welled in her eyes, tears she had refused to give in to until now, as she remembered Tim's lifeless body on the table and the doctor just shaking his head, telling her how sorry he was that they couldn't save him. Then everyone's attention was on trying to stabilize Angel as they pushed Cari out the door into the waiting area.

"At first I was hopeful," Cari began. "Then, after sitting by my daughter's bed, I knew, even before the tests came back, that she would never open her eyes again. I'd never get to see her smile again." A tear fell from her eyes and she wiped it away. "She was starting to talk in sentences. You should have seen her, Nick, even at two and a half, she was so independent. Danny reminds me a lot of Angel."

She looked up at Nick. She laid her head back on his shoulder, borrowing his strength to continue. "The morning the test results came back, I had been up all night, holding Angel's hand. In between talking to her, I prayed nonstop, asking God for a miracle. I mean, I was a nurse, I'd seen people come out of comas and walk out of the hospital. But the doctor just shook his head, telling me that they had exhausted every test, and the result showed that she was brain-dead."

Nick linked his fingers with hers and squeezed tightly, but it didn't stop her from reliving the pain all over again. "Even though I was expecting it, it was as if someone kicked me in the stomach. I couldn't breathe. I wanted to die."

"Oh God, Cari. I'm so sorry."

She sniffed and wiped the tears off her cheeks. "Marge Brunner, a hospital counselor, was with me when I got the news. She stayed and helped me make some hard decisions." Cari's eyes met Nick's. "I had to sign to have Angel taken off the respirator."

Her tears blurred her vision as she looked up at Nick. "There's something else I need to tell you, too."

Nick froze, afraid of the worst, wanting to stop her because of the pain it was causing her to live through this again. "If you're going to tell me that you loved your husband more—"

She put her trembling fingers over his mouth. "No. Tim will always have a special place in my heart because of our daughter, but I never loved him the way a wife should love her husband." *Not the way I love you,* she cried silently.

Nick felt his heart was going to burst. "Oh, Cari." He leaned forward to kiss her, but she stopped him.

"Please, Nick. I need to finish...."

He saw the pleading look in her eyes and knew there was more. He raised her hand to his lips. "Okay."

"Like I said, Marge helped me make some hard decisions." Cari's gaze held his. "She helped me make the decision to harvest Angel's organs."

Nick couldn't hide his shock. Ever since Danny's life had been saved by a donor heart, he'd had nothing but admiration for the families who did such a selfless thing. "Why didn't you tell me?"

"Marge was the only one who knew. Then I told Matt after I started helping out at the parent support group meetings. That was one of the reasons I left St. M's and came to Santa Cruz. After two years, the memories were still too strong, too sad. Everything reminded me of the family I had lost. I had to get away from Seattle. I figured as a nurse I could go almost anywhere and start over. Marge called her friend Bess Lindley. She got me the information about the openings in the new wing at Riverhaven."

"I hate the reason, but I am so glad you came here."

Her blue eyes locked with his. "The job wasn't the only reason I came to Santa Cruz." She swallowed. "Ever since Angel's death, it was as if I'd been drawn to the Bay Area."

Nick was confused.

"The night they took Angel's organs, I overheard the doctors say that her heart would be sent to a San Francisco hospital where a child was already being prepped for transplant surgery. That was two years ago last June. June 25."

My God, Cari's daughter had died the same day Danny's life began, Nick thought.

"That day in Matt's office when he asked me to assist on Danny's biopsy, I had to read his file, Nick. I discovered that your son's transplant was done in the same San Francisco hospital they flew Angel's heart to.''

Nick's eyebrows drew together. What was she trying to say? "You can't possibly think that Danny is the recipient of your daughter's heart."

Cari nodded. "I saw the records, Nick. Danny's surgery was done at 2:00 a.m. the morning of June 26, less than six hours after Angel died. They have the same blood type—O positive. There are so many other similarities. Yes, I believe that Danny has Angel's heart."

Nick got up off the sofa. He was numb. The whole idea was crazy. What was worse was thinking that Cari was only here because she thought that Danny... "Wait! Wait! Are you telling me that you set out to get involved in my son's life?"

Cari got up, too. "Nick, I know this is a shock. And with the confidentiality clause in the transplant program, it should have been kept a secret. But you've got to believe me, it was an accident that I found out that Danny was the recipient."

Nick wasn't listening anymore. All he could focus on was the realization that Cari had used him. Worse, she had used an innocent child.

"So all this is a lie? You and I? You only cared about replacing your daughter?"

"No. No, Nick, it wasn't like that. I love Danny. I love you."

Nick turned away, unable to look at her. She had lied to him. They had spent months together, and she had had every chance to tell him the truth. He combed his hand through his hair. Had she ever truly loved him, or were her feelings clouded because she felt a connection to his son? "How can I believe you—" he swung around "—when all you've done is lie."

"I didn't lie."

"No. You just omitted a few very important facts. You

used me, and worse, you used my son.'' Damn! It hurt.
He'd thought she was different. That he had finally found
someone who loved him, not his name or his money. He
glared at her. Or his son.

''No, please, Nick, just listen.'' She reached for him but
he stepped back.

''I'm through listening, Cari.'' He could see the pain in
her eyes, but it didn't compare with his own agony. He
had to get the hell out of there. ''I'm going out for a
while.''

''Nick, please, don't go. I love you.''

''No! Don't say that. If you loved me, you wouldn't
have done this.'' He grabbed a jacket and walked out, the
sound of her sobs echoing in his ears.

It had been two days since Nick had been home. He'd
talked to Danny on the phone and had his secretary relay
messages to his mother, but he didn't want to speak with
Cari. He didn't know if he ever could again. He'd thought
that Tory had hurt him when she walked out three years
ago. That was nothing compared to what he felt now. The
pain of knowing Cari had lied, that she had never cared
about him.

The intercom interrupted his thoughts. He pressed the
button. ''I told you, Peg, I don't want to be disturbed.''

''I'm sorry, Mr. Malone, but your mother—Mrs. Malone
is here.''

''My mother? Send her in.'' He jumped up and went to
open the door to find Eleanor maneuvering her wheelchair
toward him.

''Mother? What's wrong?''

''Plenty,'' she said as she drove past him. She stopped
her chair in front of his desk and looked over her shoulder.
''I suggest you close your mouth and the door before the
entire world hears what I'm about to say.''

Nick did as he was told. ''Is there a problem at home?''

"Yes, as a matter of fact there is, but I believe the biggest problem is right here in this office."

Nick released a long breath. He didn't need a lecture. "Mother, don't talk in circles."

"Why haven't you been home?"

"I've been busy."

"That's convenient," she said wryly. "Then explain to me what's going on between you and Cari."

He glanced away. "Nothing."

"You're a lousy liar, son." She folded her arms across her chest. "So you might as well tell me, because I'm not leaving here until you do. And don't try to say that you and Cari don't care about each other. I may be in a wheelchair, but there's nothing wrong with my vision."

Nick sank down into his chair. "It's a long story."

"I'm not going anywhere, son."

Nick began to explain about Cari's deception. Why she had relocated to Santa Cruz. How she'd harvested her daughter's organs. The connection to Danny and why she came to work for Nick.

For a long time, Eleanor sat in silence. Occasionally she raised her gaze to her son across the desk, but didn't give any indication how she felt about the situation.

"Well, aren't you going to say something?"

"You're not going to like it," she warned.

Nick's jaw dropped. "You're condoning what she did?"

"What *did* she do?" Eleanor asked. "Take wonderful care of Danny? Help make you realize your son needs a normal life? Add a little spice to your life?"

He stood. Hell, he didn't want to hear all the things Cari had done. "But she lied, Mother. Who knows how far she would have gone?"

"To what—find love?" his mother countered. "Try to be a part of a family? C'mon, Nick. You had Cari checked out before you hired her. You know she has no one. The only family she had died two years ago in an automobile wreck.''

Nick remembered Cari's file. How could he forget it? From the time her mother had died when she was eight years old, Cari had been in a dozen foster homes. The only listing under her next of kin was her friend in Seattle, Marge Brunner. As far as Nick knew, Cari was all alone in the world.

His mother's voice broke into his thoughts.

''It wasn't enough that Cari had to live through her own personal tragedy of losing her husband and child. She unselfishly donated her daughter's organs so another child might have a chance at life. Cari is a brave and generous woman.'' There was a tremble in his mother's voice as she spoke. ''How can you take another child away from her?''

Nick felt the tightness in his chest. He couldn't seem to breathe.

''She lied to me, Mother.''

''I think I'd do more than just omit the truth if I were in the same situation. Besides, I don't remember Cari asking to work for you. She had a job at the hospital. You went out of your way to ask her to take care of Danny. And speaking of your son, think of what this is going to do to him. He loves Cari.''

''Danny's not even the same child he was a few months ago. Cari had a big hand in that. And if you weren't so stubborn you'd realize you aren't the same, either. Love can do that to a person, Nick.'' She stared at him. ''Think how empty your life was before Cari came into it.''

Nick had been lonely. So lonely he thought he'd die from it. His work had been his only refuge, but since Cari had come, he couldn't wait to get home...to her.

Suddenly, it didn't matter why Cari came into his life. He needed her and he'd do anything to get her to stay with him.

''I've got to get home.'' He jumped up from his chair.

"Well, hallelujah!" Eleanor raised her hands in the air. "It's about time."

Nick came around the desk and kissed her on the cheek. "Is Cari at the house?"

"Yes, but you better hurry, she was packing."

Nick felt panic surge through him. "She's leaving?"

Eleanor nodded. "She thought it was best for everyone."

"I've got to stop her."

"I think it's going to take a lot of convincing."

"I'll get down on my knees if I have to," he promised as he turned back to his mother. "Mother, do you have a ride?"

She waved her hand. "Don't worry about me. You just make sure you get Cari to stay."

"How come you hafta go?" Danny asked as Cari put her bags in the back of her car.

"It's just better if I do." Cari was trying to fight off the tears as she looked at the little boy she'd come to love with all her heart. "Pretty soon you'll be starting school."

"But who will take me to the park, and the beach?" Danny ran to her and threw his arms about Cari. "Please! Don't leave me, Cari. I'll be good, I promise. I won't cut my hair anymore and I'll take my nap every day. I love you." He began to sob and Cari was lost. She looked at Marion standing in the walkway. She, too, was wiping her eyes.

"Oh, Danny. I'm not leaving because of you." She made him look at her, swiping at the tears on his face. "You are the best boy in the whole world. And if I had a little boy, I'd want him to be you. I love you."

His chin trembled. "Then stay and be my mom."

Cari couldn't stand it. She'd known this would happen one day, but she didn't think it would hurt so much. "I can't—"

Just then the familiar BMW came racing up the road and with squealing tires turned into the driveway. Cari's heart pounded in her chest as she watched Nick jump out of the car and rush to her.

"Daddy! Daddy!" Danny hugged his father. "Don't let Cari go away."

Nick ignored his son, his eyes on Cari. "You're just running out on us?" he asked. "Not even a goodbye?"

Cari couldn't breathe as her hungry gaze traveled over him. It had been two days since he'd left the house. He looked tired, but wonderful.

"It's just better for all concerned."

Nick took his son's hand and walked to her. He was going to use whatever he could to get her to stay. "It's not better for us, Cari. We need you." He saw the glint of hope in her eyes and prayed it wasn't too late. "I was angry and said things that I didn't mean."

"I thought that you wanted me to leave." A tear rolled down her face. And Nick swore it would be the last he'd ever cause her. He let go of Danny's hand and gripped her by the arms. "I went a little crazy, Cari. I'm sorry. If you leave, I don't think I can live without you." He glanced down at Danny. "We need you."

Her gaze darted away for a second. "I should have told you what I discovered."

Nick felt a glimmer of hope. "We can work through this, Cari," he promised, not caring if the whole world was watching him confess his feelings. "If you care about us, Cari. You do love us, don't you?"

Her mouth dropped open.

"Say yes, Cari." Danny jumped up and down. "Say you love us."

Nick smiled at his son's enthusiasm and drew her into his arms, relieved when she didn't resist. "Say yes, Cari," he whispered in her ear.

"Yes...." she finally answered.

"You won't be sorry," he promised before his mouth covered hers.

"Oh boy, they're kissing." Nick barely heard his son's voice as the woman he loved melted against him. His mouth devoured hers. When he broke off the kiss, he managed to say the words, "God, Cari, I love you." His hands cupped her jaw. "I'm so sorry about what I said the other day."

Cari shook her head and bit her bottom lip. "It's okay."

"No, it's not." He knew he still had more to tell her. "There is something else we need to discuss." He took her hand and led her into the house. Marion had corralled Danny and said something about feeding him lunch. Nick thanked her and asked not to be disturbed as he took Cari into his office.

He shut the door and kissed her long and hard. When he tore his mouth away, they were barely able to catch their breath. "Damn, but you're tempting." He smiled and she smiled back. "C'mon and sit down. I have something to tell you." He pulled her toward the chair and sat her down, then he leaned against the edge of his desk. "I think there have been too many secrets between us. If we're to have a future, we need to have everything out in the open."

He watched as she toyed with her hair, then nodded. "I want you in my life, Cari." He gave her a wry smile. "I never thought I'd ever say that to another woman."

Cari stood and put her arms around Nick's neck. She couldn't believe how happy she was. "I want to be in your life and Danny's. I love you both so much. And not just because he has Angel's heart."

She felt him tense and he avoided her eyes. "What's wrong?"

He rubbed his hand over his face. Suddenly he looked worried and much older than his thirty-three years. "Cari, Danny's surgery was done at the same San Francisco hospital they flew Angel's heart to.'' He paused. ''Danny didn't receive her heart.''

She froze. Nick was wrong. Danny was the recipient. ''But he has to be.''

He moved away from her. ''As you know, the majority of the time, the donors are kept secret. I was lucky enough to get to meet Danny's donor parents.'' He sighed. ''Cari, I know for certain that my son doesn't have Angel's heart.''

''No! That's not true. It can't be.''

''There were two surgeries on June 26. It was very unusual, but it happened.''

Cari sank into the chair. She suddenly felt weak, as if the life were draining out of her. All this time she thought she could hold on to a part of her daughter if only…

''I'm sorry, Cari.''

She used the back of her hand to erase the tears from her face and forced a smile. ''It's all right. I never really thought I'd find her.'' Another tear fell. ''But in the back of my mind I thought my prayers were answered and I'd been given a chance—'' She choked on a sob. ''I only had her for two years.''

''Oh, Cari.'' Nick pulled her into his arms and held her. They both cried. For the child she'd lost, the child she'd never hold again or watch grow up. And for the child out there whose life had been saved by her daughter, and who Cari would never know.

For the first time in a long time Cari had someone to comfort her, and, more important, someone who loved her. For so long she'd been alone. Now she had Nick, and she had Danny.

But there were still questions, and she needed answers before she could go on.

Chapter Twelve

"I need to ask you a favor," Cari said as she walked into Matt Landers's office.

"Another?" The much-too-good-looking doctor grinned. "Between you and Nick, the IOUs are piling up."

Cari smiled, but her heart wasn't in it. "First, Eleanor Malone instructed me to extend an invitation to you for dinner tomorrow night."

"Wow! A home-cooked meal. Tell her I'll be there. And I'm planning on a game of gin rummy. Nick said she's been quite busy socially these days. Word's out that, thanks to you, Mrs. Malone's regained her card shark status."

She shrugged. "I only passed on some information."

"Whatever you did, Cari, it worked. Eleanor Malone is a new person these days." He motioned to a chair as he took a seat behind the desk. "Now, what brings you into the hospital on your day off?"

Cari ignored his offer. She was too nervous to sit and

decided to walk around the room. "I need to ask you a few questions about the donor program."

At first he looked perplexed, then nodded. "Ask away."

She drew a long breath and tried to get up her nerve. She guessed the best way was to blurt out what she wanted to say. "I need to find out who the recipient of my daughter's heart was."

Matt blinked in surprise. "Cari, you know that's kept confidential."

She stopped her pacing. "I know. But sometimes there are exceptions." She thought about Nick knowing Danny's donor parents. "What if they want to meet me?"

Matt leaned his elbows on the desk. "And maybe they don't."

"How do you know that?"

The doctor closed his eyes momentarily. "Cari...don't do this to yourself."

"Matt, just listen," she insisted. "I've thought about this long and hard. I never realized I wanted to know, but I discovered after meeting Danny, I need to know who received Angel's heart. Not to hang on to my child who's gone, but to get closure." Tears welled in her eyes but she fought them. "My baby was only two years old when she was taken from me. You're not a parent yet, Matt, but God, I hope that's something you never have to live through." Cari turned away and tried to compose herself, then swung back around.

"I can understand and accept it if the parents don't want to meet me." She reached into her jacket pocket and pulled out an envelope. Last night she had spent hours pouring out her heart onto the six pages. How she felt and everything she wanted to ask about her daughter's recipient. She hoped the parents would be caring enough to understand her plight.

"All I want is for you to get this to them." She knew he had access to the records. "It's something that I need to do, Matt. If I'm going to move on with my life, I need closure." She swallowed. "I need to say goodbye."

Matt studied the envelope for a long time, then finally he looked up at her. "I can't make you any promises." He got up and came around the desk.

Her eyes widened. "I don't expect any. I just need you to try."

He smiled. "Okay."

"Oh, Matt. Thank you." She threw herself into his arms, nearly knocking him off balance.

"Whoa, Cari. Nothing has happened yet."

She leaned back and looked at him. "I know, but at least it's out of my hands now. It was important for me to put how I felt down on paper."

He frowned. "So if nothing comes of this, if the parents refuse to see or talk to you, you'll be satisfied to let it go?"

"I'll never forget my daughter, but maybe I can allow myself to be happy again."

"If anyone deserves it, you do," he told her. "Nick's a lucky guy. I hope he knows that."

"He knows that very well," a familiar voice said, breaking the couple apart.

"Nick—" Cari walked over to him "—Matt has agreed to help me."

Nick gave a wry smile as he placed a protective arm around her. "He did look pretty agreeable a few minutes ago."

"Your lady can be pretty convincing."

Nick hugged her close to his side. "Oh yeah? Well, I hope she's convinced you that she belongs to me."

The waves crashed against the shore and the wind rustled Cari's hair. Nick wrapped his jacket around her and they continued to walk along the sand in front of the Keatons' beach house. The sun was setting, throwing a golden orange glow over the water.

Nick needed to spend some time alone with Cari before he took her home to the family and the questions. She'd had a rough night, and asking Matt about the recipient parents hadn't been easy on her.

All he could do was be there for her. Hold her when she needed holding, talk when she needed someone to talk to. The loving part was easy. And somehow he was going to convince her that he was never going to stop that. He drew her close to his side as they walked silently along the wet sand.

"It's beautiful here," she said as she laid her head on his shoulder. "Thanks for bringing me."

"I thought we both could use some time alone. If you like, we could spend the night. I asked Larry and he said it was okay."

Cari raised her head and glared at him. "What would your mother think if we didn't show up at the house until the morning?"

"I stopped asking my mother's permission a long time ago." He hugged Cari close again. "Danny is a different story. I don't want to have to face his questions."

"He asks enough as it is," Cari said.

Nick stopped and turned to her. "Speaking of questions, I have a few of my own."

Cari touched her finger to his lips. "Nick, I can't answer them now," she admitted. "I'm going to need some time."

He nodded. "I can wait for a while. Just as long as you never stop loving me."

She smiled at him through watery eyes. "I could do that about as easily as I can stop breathing." She rose up on her toes and pressed her mouth against his. She gasped as his tongue slipped inside, doing an erotic dance with hers. Finally he broke off the kiss and looked at her. Her sparkling blue eyes revealed her desire, and his body suddenly stirred. "God, woman! You turn me inside out." He moved his hips against hers. "I need you so much."

"I need you, too, Nick," she whispered.

Her words were enough to convince him. They had agreed to keep things normal at the house. She'd sleep in her room and he in his. But that didn't mean they couldn't steal time together away from prying eyes and well-meaning family.

"How do you feel about borrowing Larry and Cindy's fireplace for a few hours? We can still be home in time to tuck Danny into bed."

She kissed him. "I think you're reading my mind." She placed her head on his shoulder and they walked toward the house. And for the next few hours, all they worried about was loving each other.

It was only two weeks until Christmas, and with Danny to remind them, no one in the Malone house would be able to forget it. Cari stayed busy working at the hospital, and Bess Linley had asked her to take charge of a children's Christmas party.

For the past two years Cari hadn't even bothered celebrating the holidays. Since she had no family, she usually offered to work. But this year she found herself agreeing to Bess's request, telling herself that with Nick and Danny it was going to be a wonderful Christmas.

Excited about her new task, Cari had already lined up an oversize orderly from the second floor to play Santa. Along with Cindy Keaton, they managed to get toy donations and volunteers to help with the wrapping and decorations. But most important, Cari had convinced Nick to allow Danny to attend the party.

Nick was into the holiday spirit, too. Instead of using catalogs and his faithful secretary, Peg, he was doing his own shopping this year. With a lot of coaxing from Danny and his mother, he'd gone to the attic and dragged down every Christmas decoration the Malone family had ever bought. Cari took charge of supervising the hanging of the outside lights, and by the time she finished, the colorful sparkling bulbs could be seen from a mile down the road.

On Saturday they had gone to look for a tree, and Danny immediately decided on the biggest one. Without argument Nick agreed and had it delivered to the house. And once it got there, he had been the one most eager to start the decorating.

They were a family, Cari thought. She hadn't been this happy in years. Nick was home every night, and when she worked at the hospital, he waited up for her, if only to rub her tired feet or talk about the day. The only problem was, they usually ended up in each other's arms on the sofa.

Tonight Cari broke off the kiss and gasped for breath. "I thought we were trying to avoid this." She gave him a questioning look as she tugged her uniform top together, covering her exposed breasts.

Nick grinned and scooted further down on the sofa, pulling her on top of him. "Can I help it if you're so tempting?"

"So is that what you're going to say to your son when he wanders out here and finds his dad in a…compromising position?"

"I guess I won't have to give him the big sex talk when he gets older, then." He grinned and Cari's heart did funny things.

"C'mon, Nick. I don't want to answer a whole new set of questions."

Nick felt Cari stiffen. She pulled out of his hold and sat up. He hated it when she withdrew from him. It wasn't the physical part that bothered him as much as the emotional. How could he help her if she kept shutting him out? And it seemed to happen every time he brought up the subject of their future.

He understood she was going through a rough time. He couldn't help but wonder if it made a difference that Danny hadn't been her daughter's recipient.

Nick sat up, too. "Cari, what's wrong?"

She looked at him. "Nothing. I'm just tired. I know I've only worked two days a week, but those twelve-hour shifts are killers." She rested her stocking feet on the coffee table.

He reached for one of her dainty feet and began rubbing it. "Why didn't you just ask me for a foot massage?"

She gave him a sideways glance. "I think I was distracted."

Nick smiled, remembering how much he'd missed her tonight. The minute she walked in the door he had scooped her up in his arms and carried her to the sofa. "You could have stopped me anytime."

She turned to him, her eyes dark with desire. "I didn't want to."

He groaned and reached for her, his mouth covering hers in another heated kiss. When he broke it off, he had her practically purring. "I want you, Cari."

"I want you, too," she breathed. "But we decided that it's best to wait."

"You decided," he amended. "I'd have you moved in with me right now, if you—"

"No!" she stopped his words. "I can't…not yet."

He took hold of her hand and kissed it. "Is it because of Danny?"

Cari looked confused.

"Because he doesn't have Angel's heart?"

This time she looked shocked and hurt. "Oh, Nick. How could you think that? I love Danny."

Suddenly he felt such relief. "I'm sorry, Cari. It's just that so much has happened between us. And I want you to be mine."

"I *am* yours, Nick." Her hand touched his face. "I've never felt this way about anyone."

His heart pounded like crazy. They'd never talked about their past lives. His marriage had been so troubling, but he'd just taken it for granted that she had been happy with her husband. "But you were married."

"I loved Tim, but it was nothing compared to how I feel about you." Her vivid blue eyes met his, revealing such love that he shook from the impact.

He pulled her in his arms and cradled her head against his chest. "Oh, Cari. We'll get through this, I promise you. We'll be together."

"Boys and girls, I think I hear Santa," Cari announced, causing the room to grow silent and drawing every child's attention to her as the sound of jingling bells erupted. She went to the door of the meeting room where the hospital Christmas party was being held and glanced down the hall. She smiled. Santa had arrived. She opened the doors, and the large orderly, Rob Brown, dressed in the red suit and white beard, came into the room of cheering kids.

"Ho, ho, ho, Merry Christmas, boys and girls," he called in a big booming voice. He flipped his bag over his shoulder and walked to the large tree at the front of the room.

Cari sighed in relief as her Santa chatted with the youngsters, then reached into his bag and began handing out gifts to each child.

"You did a wonderful job with the party, Cari."

Cari turned upon hearing Bess's voice. The personnel director was playing one of Santa's elves, dressed in a red sweater with a stocking cap cocked on her head.

"I had a lot of help," Cari said. "It was Cindy Keaton who made sure that all the kids got gifts. And the hospital volunteers did the decorations."

Bess raised an eyebrow. "And you didn't work here

until midnight helping to get things ready?" The older woman glanced at the row of stockings on the wall. "And just who stuffed all the stockings?"

"Nick helped, too."

Yes, Cari had done a lot of work. But she had loved doing it. She had loved every late night, every piece of candy and each little toy she and Nick dropped into a child's stocking. How many pieces had they stolen for themselves? It had been so long since she'd felt like celebrating the holidays. "It was fun."

"Good. I'll put you on the volunteer list for next year."

Next year. Cari couldn't help but wonder what the following year would bring. The answers she needed? The answers she was afraid to get? Would she be able to move on with her life?

She turned to the front of the room and smiled at Nick, who was walking toward her. He looked so handsome in his gray slacks and burgundy sweater over an open-collared shirt.

"It's going great, honey," he said, and bent down and kissed her on the lips.

"I'm so glad." Cari felt herself blush at his public display of affection. It was no use hiding the fact they were involved; everyone in the hospital already knew they were a couple. She glanced at Bess and got a you-lucky-duck look. But Cari already knew how lucky she was to have Nick and Danny.

She glanced around. "Where's Danny?"

Nick grinned as he pointed. "Having a little talk with Santa."

Cari looked up to find the little boy sitting on Santa's lap, chatting up a storm. "Looks like your son has a pretty long list."

"I know. I hope he leaves me some money for my old age."

"If not, I'll take care of you," Cari said.

Nick's arm came around her. "Good. I like the sound of that. But all I need is you."

She had never seen such tenderness in his eyes. "And all I need is you," she whispered back.

"I wish I had you alone." He leaned forward and whispered in her ear what he'd like to do to her. Cari felt her face redden.

Nick straightened and mouthed the word, "Later." Then he walked off toward the front of the room and Danny, leaving Cari aching to follow him.

The next week flew by quickly with all the preparations for the holidays. Like most kids, Danny was anxious for Christmas. Cari was anxious to hear news about her letter, but other than camping outside Matt's office, all she could do was wait, hope and do a lot of praying.

"That's the biggest and prettiest tree I've ever seen," Cari said in amazement. She bent down and placed her presents under the large decorated green spruce standing next to the stone fireplace in the Malones' living room. The entire family had helped with the trimming last week, but no one had been allowed to put any presents under it until Christmas Eve.

Dressed up in a pair of dark slacks and hunter green sweater for the Malone Christmas Eve party, Danny was jumping up and down. "I can't wait," he cried.

"Well, you can't open any presents until tomorrow," Nick announced. "Besides, the Keatons and Dr. Matt aren't here yet."

"Can I open one?" The boy stuck up his finger.

"Just the exchange gifts tonight. So go upstairs and bring our presents down."

Smiling, Danny took off out of the room just as Eleanor was coming in. "That child has entirely too much energy. Where's he going in such a hurry?"

"Just upstairs," Nick said, and leaned down to kiss his mother. "You look wonderful tonight."

Eleanor smiled down at her ivory crepe dress. Her hair was done up and small diamonds graced her ears. "Why, thank you, son. I wanted to look nice for the party. It's been so long since—" She directed her attention to Cari. "Oh my, you look lovely, dear."

Nick took Cari's hand and drew her close to his side. She was wearing a royal blue dress with a fitted bodice and flared skirt that reached the middle of her calf. It had cost more than she wanted to spend, but she had decided it was her Christmas present to herself. And seeing the look on Nick's face, she knew the dress was worth every penny.

"She looks beautiful," Nick announced, his eyes shining with such raw need that it made her blush.

"My son may be slightly prejudiced," Eleanor said. "But it does bring out your eyes."

"Thank you."

Eleanor moved closer and took Cari's hand. "No, child, thank *you*. It's been a long time since this house has been this joyous, and I'm not just talking about the holidays. You've brought love and laughter back to these old walls and I'll be forever grateful."

Cari blinked back tears before the woman who'd come to mean so much to her. "You've given me a lot, too." She kissed Eleanor's cheek. "Thank you."

Just then the doorbell rang and Danny raced down the hall to answer it. "I guess we better head him off at the pass," Eleanor said as she started for the entry. Cari tried to follow but Nick stopped her.

"Things are going to get pretty busy later, and before all the activities start, I want to wish you a Merry Christmas." He drew her into his arms and his mouth covered hers. The kiss was all-consuming, wiping out any coherent thought except for the wicked effect he had on her senses.

Never in Cari's life had she experienced such raw, primitive need for a man. She was suddenly trembling, realizing it had been more than two weeks since they'd made love.

Someone cleared his throat. "Excuse us for interrupting, but I believe there's supposed to be a party here."

Nick and Cari broke apart and found Larry and Cindy Keaton standing in the doorway.

Nick grinned. "We're warming up the mistletoe."

"I hate to tell you, buddy, but you're a little off the mark. The mistletoe is over here," he said, pointing to the green sprig hanging overhead.

Holding on to her husband's arm, Cindy was smiling approvingly at them. She was wearing a deep red dress with a matching ribbon in her hair.

"Minor detail," Nick said.

"You're right." Larry took the direct hint, pulled his wife in his arms and placed a long, hard kiss on her mouth.

Nick leaned his head against Cari's. "I think we started something."

"I guess so," Cari said dreamily.

"I'd like to finish this celebration later." He raised an eyebrow and waited for her response.

Cari hesitated, but it didn't take much to realize how badly she wanted to be with Nick, especially tonight. She nodded.

He gave her a smile that sent the blood surging through her. "I'll meet you in my room after the party and everybody is tucked in."

"Until later." She gave him a quick kiss, then walked toward the guests coming in the door.

The first guest she greeted was Dr. Landers. "Merry Christmas, Matt." She kissed his cheek.

"Merry Christmas," he returned. He handed her several presents to put under the tree. "Thanks for inviting me."

"We're glad you could come," Cari said. "I didn't think you had any family in the area."

"I don't. But my family is gone anyway."

"I'm sorry, Matt."

He shrugged matter-of-factly. "It's been a long time."

Cari had spent a lot of years alone. There was a sadness in Matt's eyes that Cari recognized immediately. He spent so many hours at the hospital, she doubted he had time for a social life, even though the single nurses all wished the handsome heart surgeon would give them the time of day.

"So I bet you've volunteered to work the day shift tomorrow at the hospital."

He didn't say anything.

"Okay, Matt. After your shift, come here for dinner."

"Oh no, Cari. I can't intrude on family."

Cari raised her hand. "How can you say that? You've been such a good friend to all of us. You've been there when we've needed you." Cari knew Matt had pulled some strings to try to help her send her letter. "Besides, Eleanor adores you. You're good-looking, and you let her beat you at cards. Danny will love to have someone to show off all the loot he's going to get. So how about it? Say around four o'clock?"

He nodded. "You're a hard woman to turn down."

Cari smiled. "Good, I'm glad you realized that. It makes things so much easier." She slipped her hand through his arm and they walked toward the other guests.

Four hours later, the house quiet, Nick placed his arm around Cari and together they stared at the glittering Christmas tree. All the presents had been wrapped and placed underneath, stockings filled, a new two-wheeler put together, complete with a bell and a big bow on the handlebars.

"Do you think Danny is ready? I mean, he's only four."

Cari stared at the bright red bike with training wheels. She couldn't believe she had talked Nick into buying it.

"He'll be five in two months," she said. "Besides, he'll

be riding it here at the house. It's not like we're sending him out into a busy street.''

"I guess you're right." He sighed. "It's just that I still worry about him."

Cari's arms circled his waist. "All parents worry. It's part of the job."

He kissed the top of her head. "I guess you're right." Together they walked out of the living room, stopping at the doorway and turning off the lights. It was nearly midnight and Danny had been tucked into bed and all of Santa's gifts placed under the tree.

"Now it's our time," Nick said as he walked her upstairs and straight into his bedroom. "I want you to spend the night with me. The entire night."

At Cari's nod, he opened the door to his bedroom and she gasped.

There were numerous candles displayed around the room. All different sizes and shapes lined the dresser and the headboard and windowsill. The soft sparkles of light were like diamonds. Glancing around, Cari noticed several vases of red roses, their erotic scent wafting through the air.

"Oh, Nick." So this was where he had disappeared to for so long when she was bringing down some presents. She wandered around the room and touched one of the perfect rosebuds. "It's beautiful." All the time he must have spent making everything so special.

"I wanted to put you in the holiday spirit." He touched her hair and she turned to look at him. "But," he began, scanning the room, "none of this compares to your beauty."

Words clogged Cari's throat as she went into his arms. He lowered his head and found her lips. His mouth was warm and searching. She pressed closer, melting into the hard length of him, moaning softly when she felt his body respond to hers. He half lifted her against him as his mouth became more demanding. This was what she needed.

He broke off the kiss. "Sorry, Cari, I wanted to go slow and gentle tonight."

"How about next time?" she suggested, urging her hips against his as the masculine scent of his aftershave teased her nostrils.

He pulled away with a pained smile. "Later," he promised, and he took her hand and led her to the turned-down bed, scattered with rose petals. "First I have something for you." He reached into the nightstand for a small velvet box.

Cari swallowed hard. Thrilled and afraid at the same time, she accepted the box but didn't open it. "Oh, Nick. I thought you weren't… Shouldn't we wait?"

"Wait for what?" he stressed. "What difference is it going to make if we commit now or wait until the call comes in—if it ever does?"

She glanced away, feeling the tears flood her eyes. He touched her chin and drew her back to face him.

"I love you, Cari. It's not going to make any difference. I'm still going to love you and you're still going to love me. But there's a little boy across the hall who we also have to think about. He loves you, too."

Her heart raced, hearing the previous words. "And I love you both," she said.

"Then what are you waiting for?"

"It's just that I can't—"

Nick placed his finger across her lips. "Yes, you can, Cari. We can handle anything, you and I, as long as we're together. Is it going to make any difference between us when you find out about Angel's recipient? Or if you don't?"

Cari's chest felt tight at his honest appraisal. She shook her head.

His gray eyes darkened with desire. "Cari, I can't live

without you. I want you to be my wife. I want you to be Danny's mother, too.''

She couldn't take a breath as he opened the box and removed a gorgeous diamond solitaire. He held it up. ''Will you marry me?''

Cari looked at Nick. She had never thought she could love someone as much as she loved this wonderful man. There was no doubt in her mind that he'd always be there for her. He'd already given her so much. Love. A chance to have a home and a family again. Now all he was asking was that she be there for him, and for Danny.

''Oh, Nick. Yes, I'll marry you,'' she cried, and went into his arms.

''Oh, Cari, I love you.'' Nick nuzzled her cheek before finding her willing mouth. He nibbled tormentingly along her soft lips, then slipped his tongue inside, dancing wildly with hers.

He finally broke off the kiss and slid the ring onto her finger. She was surprised to find it fit perfectly. ''I want a short engagement. I'll go crazy with you across the hall.''

She slipped her arms around his neck. ''My, my, aren't we anxious.''

Nick proved it as he quickly undressed her and eased her down on the mattress, then Cari watched, unashamed, as he removed his clothes. He was a beautifully built man. Broad chested, dark hair swirled across his flat stomach. Her gaze moved to his narrow hips and powerful legs. She'd never get tired of looking at him.

''Enjoying yourself?'' he asked as he took the place next to her on the bed.

''Just like unwrapping my Christmas present.'' She placed her arms around him and pulled him down on top of her. His hands cupped her breasts and he circled her nipple with his tongue, feeling it bead under his mouth. She made a purring sound and rotated her hips against his.

''Easy, Cari. I want to take things slow.''

"If it's my present, can't I decide how I want it?" she asked teasingly. She began placing kisses against his chest, her fingers finding the flat nipple, her mouth swiftly working it into a hard bud. He groaned and pulled away. His eyes slid down her body and back up again, desire kindling in their gray depths.

Nick had never fought so hard for control, and Cari wasn't making it easy. She wiggled her sexy little body down and positioned herself under him. He stilled and watched her incredible blue eyes as she spread her legs and whispered, "Make love to me." He lost it, and without hesitation, he pushed himself inside her.

Cari gasped as her hands pulled at him to go deeper. He smiled and bent down to cover her mouth with his. There had never been a time when he felt so virile, and her soft moans and her body were begging him for more. He shut his eyes and moved to the ageless rhythm that brought them as close as possible to heaven. As much as he tried to prolong this aching pleasure, he felt her tense, then heard her cries of release. He watched joyously as she reached for the stars and he continued to coax her through her climax. Then he let go himself, groaned her name and collapsed on top of her.

Cari hugged Nick tight as she tried to catch her breath. She never wanted to let go. He raised his head and smiled down at her. "You okay?"

"I'm wonderful."

"You're telling me," he said, and rolled off her, pulling her with him. Nick cradled her next to him. "That was incredible," he breathed, then kissed her on the forehead.

"It was better than incredible," Cari said as he covered them with a blanket and she snuggled closer. Off in the distance she heard the church bells chiming in Christmas.

"Merry Christmas, Cari."

She placed her hand on his chest, feeling the steady rhythm of his heart. "Merry Christmas, Nick."

But her mind quickly went to the child that would be forever in her heart. Cari closed her eyes and saw the face of Angel. Like every other night, her last conscious thoughts were of her daughter. Tonight they were a little sweeter, maybe because she had faith that one day she was going to get to meet her daughter's heart recipient.

"Merry Christmas, Angel," she whispered.

Chapter Thirteen

Cari felt someone nuzzling her cheek, creating a rush of warm shivers down her arm. She rolled over and opened her eyes to find Nick smiling down at her.

"Good morning," he said, then placed a soft kiss on her lips.

"Good morning to you." Her arms snaked around his neck and pulled him against her as she gave him a greeting he soon wouldn't forget. When he drew back, they were both having trouble catching their breath.

"Whoa, sweetheart. As much as I'd like to spend all morning making love to you, I think we're going to be summoned downstairs in a few minutes to see what Santa has brought."

Cari's eyes widened as her brain started working. "Oh my gosh, it's Christmas!" Just as she spoke the words, Danny's voice rang out just outside the bedroom door.

"Daddy! Daddy! Hurry up, it's time to open presents."

"Give us a minute, son," Nick called back. He picked up Cari's left hand, now displaying the engagement ring he had given her last night, and kissed it. "There are going to be a lot of questions this morning. Are you ready?"

She touched his face, wondering how she had ever gotten so lucky. "I think I'll handle them better if I have some clothes on." She tugged at the sheet.

"Your wish is my command." Nick climbed out of bed and Cari watched as he walked naked to the closet. He reached for a pair of jeans and slipped them on. He tossed her a knowing grin that caused another rush of shivers as he worked at buttoning the fly.

"Keep looking at me like that and Danny will have to wait a long time to open his gifts." He pulled a robe from the hanger and brought it back to the bed. "Here, this might get you across the hall."

Cari got out of bed and put on the robe, but not before Nick eyed her closely, then groaned and pulled her into his arms. She gasped as his mouth found hers in a hungry kiss.

He released her. "That'll have to hold me awhile," he said, and pushed her toward the door.

Ten minutes later Cari was dressed and went downstairs to find everyone waiting for her. Nick took her hand and together they went into the living room.

"Oh, wow!" Danny cried as he ran to his new bike next to the tree. "It's just what I wanted. It's what I told Santa."

"Well, you're not to ride it until we can go together," his father announced. "And you have to wear a helmet."

Danny nodded, then attacked his other presents. He got some new video games, some clothes and building toys. Cari had bought him some books that she knew he wanted and was thrilled at his excitement.

Next Nick handed her a small present. She looked at him curiously. "But you already gave me something."

He leaned close to kiss her. "It's only the beginning. I plan to buy my wife a lot of presents."

Cari blushed and looked around to see if anyone heard. But Danny and Eleanor were busy opening their gifts.

She tore off the paper and opened the jewelry box to find a pair of diamond earrings sparkling up at her. "Oh, Nick, these are beautiful, but you didn't need to—"

"I wanted to." He bent forward and whispered, "Later tonight you can model them for me."

"Daddy, here," Danny said, and held out a gift wrapped in Santa paper. "It's from me," he said proudly. "Cari helped me make it."

Nick tore off the paper and opened the box to find a small three-ring binder with the words Danny's Book printed in bold letters across the cover. He took it out and opened it to discover Danny's baby picture on the front page.

"That's me," the boy said excitedly.

Nick looked at his son and smiled. "I know." How could he forget standing outside the nursery window, staring at his son in awe. He turned to the next page. Another picture when Danny was a year old.

"I was sick then," Danny began, "but Cari said when you make a book you have to have every year."

Nick nodded, almost overwhelmed by his emotions as he turned another page to find his two-year-old son smiling back at him. He turned the page again to find pictures of an active three-year-old.

"See, I was better." Danny pointed to the pictures. "This is after I got my new heart."

"It sure is," Nick said. "And you've been healthy ever since."

He turned another page, to find a recent picture of his

four-year-old son. "This is a new one. Cari took me to a store so we could surprise you."

"Well, you sure did." Nick couldn't take his eyes off the boy in the photo. He was losing his baby features. All along Eleanor had said that Danny looked like him, and except for Tory's dark eyes, he did. That pleased Nick— a lot. "This is a great book. Thanks, son."

"Wait, Dad. There's more." Danny turned another page to show the blank spot for a five-year-old and his first day of school.

"When I go to school, you can put my picture here. And there's a whole bunch more pages—" he flipped through the rest of the book to show him "—for when I grow up real big. Cari said there is plenty of room for my whole life." The child stood back and beamed. "Do you like it, Dad?"

Nick glanced at Cari. She was smiling. He had never loved her more than he did at that moment for what she was trying to do for him. He pulled his son into his arms. Why had it taken so long for him to realize what a precious gift he had with his child? "I love it, son. And I love you, too."

"I love you too, Dad." Danny hugged him back, then squirmed out of his father's arms. He went back to the tree and picked up another gift and took it to Cari. "This is for you."

Cari was surprised, wondering when Danny had had the time to shop for her. She stole a glance to find Nick smiling. She opened the box and carefully took out the framed picture. It was a simple child's crayon drawing of a house and four people standing in front of it. "Oh, Danny, this is so nice."

"That's our house," he pointed out. "See, Daddy helped me spell the names on the bottom. There's Grandma, Dad and Mom and me. I asked Santa to give me you as my mom." The boy shook his head from side to side. "But he said he couldn't give people for Christmas. I had to ask you myself." His brown eyes were wide and hopeful. "Will you be my mom, Cari?"

Cari's eyes filled with tears as she looked at this beautiful child. "Oh, Danny, I would love to be your mother." She hugged him in her arms. "I always wanted a little boy like you."

Nick was at her side, she could feel his arms around her. "You're going to have to share, son, because Cari said she'd be my wife."

Eleanor gasped. "Oh, Nick, that's wonderful."

Danny jumped up and down. "Oh, boy. This is the best Christmas in the whole world."

Nick kissed Cari. "I think I'm going to have to agree with my son. You've made this the best Christmas ever."

The phone rang and Nick got up to answer it. "Malone residence."

"Hello, Nick. It's Matt."

"Well, Merry Christmas, Matt." And Nick meant it, too.

"I'm sorry to bother you so early, but when I came into my office this morning, I found a message on my machine. It was from the Lowells."

Nick's smile faded. "The Lowells?"

"Their child was Angel Hallen's recipient."

Nick's eyes closed in prayer, hoping that Matt was going to give him some good news. He couldn't stand to see Cari disappointed again. "Matt, just tell me one thing. Have they agreed to see Cari?"

"Yes. Can you bring Cari to my office tomorrow around one o'clock?"

Nick released a long sigh. "Sure, we'll be there. And, Matt, thanks."

"You're welcome, Nick. You and Cari have a merry Christmas."

"I hope we'll be seeing you later. We have an announcement to make," Nick said proudly.

"I have a feeling I already know what it is." There was hearty laughter on the other end of the line. "So you finally wised up and asked the lady to marry you."

"You got that right. And she accepted."

"Congratulations, Nick. Give Cari my best wishes and explain to her I won't be able to be there for dinner. I have a patient I'm monitoring closely and I may have to do surgery."

Nick's heart sank as his thoughts went to the parents, knowing too well what they were going through. He glanced at Danny next to the tree and thanked God for his blessings.

"Cari will understand, Matt. We'll look forward to seeing you and the Lowells tomorrow." He hung up the phone and went back to the festivities. He sat back down next to Cari.

"I have another present for you," he announced.

"Please , I don't need any more."

He raised his hand. "I can't take credit for this one. That was Matt on the phone. He wants us in his office tomorrow at one o'clock."

She gripped his hand. "You mean the parents...they want to meet me?"

He nodded. "You got your wish, Cari."

She hugged him. "Oh, Nick, thank you."

"It's Matt you should thank."

She smiled. "And I plan on it."

Danny walked over and handed his dad a large present. "This one is from Cari." The boy grinned and exchanged a look with Cari.

Nick took the present, wondering what the two were up

to. He quickly opened it to find a camera. A Polaroid camera.

"You can take my picture, Dad. Anytime. So you won't miss me being a little boy when I'm all grown up. And we got you a lot of film." He dug into the bottom of the box to show him.

Nick turned to Cari. He didn't know what to say. He knew he had been amiss not keeping a record of Danny's development. His mother had been the one to insist on the few photographs taken of her grandchild.

Maybe he'd been afraid to build too many memories, only to lose... He took a long breath as he studied the love shown on Cari's face. In the past few months, she'd given him the strength to realize that there was always hope, especially when you had love.

"Thank you." He took her hand.

"I just didn't want you to miss out on tomorrow's memories."

He leaned forward and kissed her. "I don't plan on it."

"Dad! Take my picture with my new bike," Danny called, posing beside the two-wheeler with a big smile.

"All right." Nick stood, and with a quick once-over, he figured out the mechanics of the camera and held it up to his eye. "Okay, son. Say merry Christmas."

"Merry Christmas." The camera flashed and Danny giggled.

Nick turned to Cari. "Now, your turn."

"No!" she argued. "I'm a mess."

"You look pretty, Cari," Danny said as he came up to her. "I'm going to have the prettiest mom in the whole world."

"Oh, Danny." She reached for the boy and hugged him. "What a sweet thing to say."

"Okay, you two, smile," Nick instructed. They did and the camera flashed. They waited patiently for the developing to be completed. Finally the picture came into view to Danny's cheers.

"Can I have the picture for my room."

"Okay, son," Nick said. "But stand next to Cari again. I want one for my office." He pressed the button, then pulled the photo out. "This is going next to my computer right here at the house—where I'm going to be spending most of my time." He looked at Cari. "We have wedding plans to make."

"Maybe we should wait," Cari hedged, "until after the holiday. At least until after I meet the parents. I need this closure first."

He wouldn't allow it. "No, we've waited too long. Whatever happens tomorrow isn't going to change anything." Nick prayed silently, hoping what he said was true.

Cari brushed at the imaginary wrinkles on her suit skirt. "Do I look okay?" she asked Nick as they got onto the elevator.

He punched the fourth-floor button. "You look great. I like you in skirts. I get the chance to see your legs."

"Oh, is it too short?"

Nick took her hand. "Honey, calm down. The Lowells aren't going to care what you're wearing."

Cari nodded. "You're right. I guess I'm a little nervous."

"That's understandable. You've wanted this for a long time." When the elevator doors opened, they stepped off and walked toward Matt's office. All the time Cari's heart was hammering with excitement. She'd waited so long.

Nick stopped at the door. "Ready?"

Cari took a deep breath and released it. She nodded and Nick knocked, then turned the knob and ushered her inside.

Matt got up from his chair behind the desk and smiled.

"Cari, Nick. I'm glad to see you." He glanced toward the young couple seated on the sofa. They stood as Cari searched the room. Her heart sank in disappointment. They didn't bring the child.

"I'd like you both to meet Jane and Bob Lowell. They're from Portland, Oregon. Jane and Bob, this is Cari Hallen and Nick Malone."

In a daze, Cari shook their hands as anxiety seized her. Why didn't they bring their child? she wondered. Maybe they thought this meeting would be too emotional for a four-year-old.

Jane Lowell stepped forward. She was about thirty, slightly built and with sandy-colored hair. "Cari, I want to thank you so much for the letter you sent us. For so long we've wondered about our Nora's donor."

"You have a little girl?" Cari's hopes lifted. "Please, tell me about her."

Jane glanced at her husband and nodded. They were seated, the two women together on the sofa and the men in chairs close by. Jane took a picture from her purse and handed it to Cari. Cari looked down at the small dark-haired girl with big brown eyes and an infectious smile. "She's cute."

Cari pulled out a photo of her daughter and gave it to the Lowells.

"Oh, look, Bob, she does look like a little angel."

"That's what her daddy used to call her. Tim, my husband, died in the same accident." Cari didn't want to talk about the past. She had questions she needed to ask. "Was Nora healthy?"

Jane nodded. "She came through the transplant great, and she did very well her first year. Of course, we took all the precautions, but we also didn't want our daughter to feel she was any different than the other children. So when I needed to go back to work, with the doctor's okay, of course, Nora went into day care. And she loved it. Loved being with the other children. We think it was good for us, too.''

Cari hoped that Nick was listening to this. Maybe he'd feel better about sending Danny off to school. ''My Angel loved to be with other people, too. To her, no one was a stranger. It always used to worry me that she would wander off with just anyone....'' Cari felt her emotions stirring at the memories. Her daughter's smiling face, her chubby little hand waving bye to her when she had to go off to work.

''I know, Nora did the same thing. She would wave and smile at everyone.'' Jane Lowell laughed as she reached for her husband's hand. ''And if you didn't return the gesture, she'd just keep doing it until you acknowledged her.''

''Sounds like our daughters are a lot alike,'' Cari said, aching to ask if she could meet Nora sometime. ''I bet Nora's excited about starting school.''

The Lowells exchanged a quick glance and Cari noticed tears in Jane's eyes. ''What's the matter?'' Cari asked. She felt Nick's hand against her back, but it didn't prevent the horrible feelings coming over her. Her hands trembled as her gaze darted between the two Lowells. ''Please. Tell me.''

It was Bob who finally spoke. ''About a year ago, Nora started having complications.''

Cari's hand covered her mouth. She wanted desperately to cover her ears so she wouldn't hear what he was about to tell her.

''The doctors tried different medications, but it didn't stop the rejection. They wanted to do another transplant, but nothing came available in time.''

Jane dashed a tear from her face. ''Our daughter died last May.''

''Oh, God!'' Cari said, unable to stop her own tears.

Nick gripped her shoulders, trying to give her support. But she didn't want comfort now. It didn't help, anyway. Nothing could stop the unbearable pain that tore through her. Then suddenly she looked at Jane and saw the same pain mirrored in her eyes.

"I'm so sorry." Cari put her arms around her. All she could do was comfort the other mother, share the grief she knew so much about. For the next few minutes, they hung on to each other and cried for the two beautiful children they had lost.

Finally Cari pulled back, and they both managed to compose themselves. Jane spoke first. "Cari," she began, "I don't ever want you to be sorry. Because of your unselfishness, we had our Nora with us almost two years. Two years that we would never have had if it weren't for Angel. There is no way I can ever repay you for your gift." She forced a smile. "We were thrilled to get your letter. We've wanted to meet you for so long and thank you. But we hesitated because of losing our daughter. It was Dr. Landers who explained to us how much you needed to know about your daughter's recipient."

Cari looked over at Matt sitting at the desk and gave him a watery smile. "Matt Landers is an exceptional doctor and special friend."

She felt Jane grip her hand. "And you're an exceptional woman to give us such a wonderful gift." Jane's eyes showed wonder. "Your Angel was a part of our Nora." Her voice was choked with emotion. "I felt her strong heart beating in my daughter's chest for nearly two years. She kept her alive. We will always have a connection, Cari."

"I've always felt that way. Maybe that was the reason I needed to meet you, or maybe it was just to assure myself that I did the right thing two years ago."

Nick had never felt so helpless. His own fears surfaced

about Danny's vulnerability. No! He pushed the thought aside. He couldn't think negatively anymore. His son was healthy, and he was going to make sure that he stayed that way. He and Danny had spent too many years in a shell—it was time to come out and live life.

"We need to move on with our lives," Jane said, breaking into Nick's thoughts. She glanced down at the engagement ring he'd given Cari last night. "I hear from Dr. Landers that you and Nick are planning on getting married."

"What?" Cari blinked. "Oh, yes."

"When is the big day?"

"We're not sure."

Nick tried not to let Cari's indecisiveness bother him. "It's going to be soon," he volunteered, slipping his arm around Cari.

"Well, Bob and I have some good news, too." Jane smiled. "We're expecting another baby in the summer."

"Oh, that's wonderful."

Nick shook Bob's hand. "Congratulations."

"Thank you." Lowell hugged his wife.

Nick felt a sharp pang of jealousy as an intimate glance was exchanged between the couple. He looked at Cari, remembering that last night in their heated passion, they hadn't used any birth control. Maybe he had wanted Cari to get pregnant with his baby. Their baby.

"Well, we better be getting back," Bob said as he stood. "Our flight leaves in a few hours."

"We could drive you to the airport," Nick offered.

"Thank you, but we rented a car," Bob told him.

The two women stood, but only looked at each other. It was as if neither one of them was ready for the inevitable.

Cari took Jane's hand and squeezed it. Suddenly she was afraid to let her go. The Lowells were her last connection to Angel. "I wish I could have known your Nora."

Jane smiled sweetly, tears lingering in her eyes. But they weren't sad anymore. "I think you've always known her. She was much like your own daughter, Angel. Sweet and loving." Jane hugged Cari and whispered, "I like to think our girls are together now." She pulled away. "If you need to talk, call me anytime. Dr. Landers has our number. Bye, Cari. Bye, Nick." They turned and headed for the door.

Cari could only watch as the couple walked away. She wanted to call them back, but knew she couldn't. It was time to put the past away.

But could she?

Nick drove along the scenic Pacific Coast Highway. The late afternoon was cold and overcast, fitting Cari's mood. She was still numb, thinking about what had transpired only an hour ago in Matt's office. Angel's recipient had died. She had never dreamed... Squeezing her eyes shut, Cari refused to let any more tears fall.

Nick's hand reached for hers. "You okay?"

She wished she could lie and tell him yes. "I may never be."

Nick pulled the car into the driveway at the Keatons' beach house. He knew he couldn't take Cari home. She needed to deal with these feelings before she totally withdrew from him and their future together.

"C'mon, Cari. Let's go inside and talk."

She sighed and pulled her hand away from his. "I really don't feel much like talking, Nick." She opened the door and climbed out of the car, then headed down the steps to the beach.

"Cari, it's too cold out here," he called to her. "Let's go inside."

She continued toward the beach.

"Damn." He slammed the car door and took off after

her. He caught her easily. "Cari, you don't even have a coat on."

"I don't need one." She kicked off her high heels and her nylon-clad feet sank into the sand. "I just want to walk awhile. I need to think."

Nick stripped off his dark sport jacket and wrapped it around her shoulders, then discarded his own shoes and socks. "Well, you're going to have to think with me along because I'm not leaving you alone," he said as he caught up with her.

Nick followed Cari's wishes. For the next twenty minutes they walked along the shore and never exchanged a word. But he was going to be there if she needed him. God! He prayed she needed him.

He knew Cari had been alone most of her life, and he was going to make sure that was never going to happen again. He wanted to make her forget all the loneliness. First, he was going to give her all the love she could stand, and the family she longed for. She had been there for him, for Danny and his mother.... Everyone always came first, before Cari.

Finally when the mist turned heavy, then to rain, he managed to steer her toward the house. By the time they got back, they were both soaked and Cari was shivering from the cold.

Nick unlocked the front door and ushered her inside. He quickly started a fire, went upstairs and brought down blankets. He managed to help Cari out of her clothes. He didn't like how despondent she'd become by the time he wrapped her chilled body in the warm blanket.

He removed his own clothes and joined Cari in front of the roaring fire. He pulled her into his arms and placed a kiss on top of her head. "Cari, please, tell me what I can do to help you."

It was as if a dam had burst. She broke down and began

to sob, heart-wrenching sobs. He held her, cradled her head against his chest as he, too, shed his own tears, knowing how hard she was hurting. He'd never felt so helpless. Cari must feel as if she'd lost her daughter all over again. And all he could do was hold her and love her....

Slowly her tears stopped, and he handed her a tissue. Cari wiped her eyes and raised her head. Their gazes locked, and her deep blue eyes were filled with need. Silently, she reached her hand to touch his face and stroke his jaw.

He lowered his mouth to meet hers in a soft kiss that quickly turned fervent as he coaxed her lips apart and his tongue moved inside, hungry to taste her. She moaned and meshed her body with his. He felt her nipples bead up against his chest.

She tore her mouth away. "I need you, Nick. Make love to me." There was desperation in her voice as she moved over him.

"Ah, Cari. I need you, too," he breathed. She continued to torture him with her hands and mouth. Damn! But he was only human.

"Now, Nick," she said only inches from his mouth. "I need you...now."

He had no trouble understanding what she wanted. He pushed her on her back and in one swift stroke was inside her. He closed his eyes, trying to get a grip on reality, but Cari had other ideas. Breathing hard, she raised her hips as her hands grabbed him and pulled him deeper.

Sweat broke out on his forehead as they moved in unison. Cari's beautiful body alone fueled his desire, but her desperate need stoked those hot embers into an all-consuming flame. The air in his lungs burned, then he heard the throaty catch in her voice. Her body suddenly convulsed and she cried out. He, too, groaned as his release came just as quickly and everything shattered around him.

He collapsed on her, then rolled over, pulling her with him. With her head against his chest, he closed his eyes and let sleep overtake them.

Thirty minutes later, Cari woke with a start. She glanced around the nearly dark room. There was only a soft glow from the dying fire. She looked up and found Nick staring at her.

"Hi," he said. "How are you feeling?"

Suddenly shy after her out-of-control behavior, she sat up and pulled the blanket around her, but not before she saw his gloriously naked body. She glanced away.

"We should get dressed."

He grabbed her arm. "Our clothes aren't dry yet."

"Then maybe we could borrow some things from Cindy and Larry. We need to get home."

"Not yet, Cari. We need to talk. I know today was rough on you."

She looked away. "I don't want to talk about it."

"Does that go for our future, too?"

Cari froze. She wasn't sure how to answer him. Right now, all she knew was that she was afraid...afraid to give anymore. She always lost. "Maybe it's better if—"

"No. Don't tell me we have no future, when for months you've been convincing me just the opposite."

"Maybe I was wrong." She'd discovered that loving hurt too much.

He shook his head. "No, Cari. You weren't wrong." He took a deep breath. "I'm sorry about today. I know how much you wanted to keep a part of Angel alive. But it's time to let go."

Cari bit down on her lip to fight back the tears. "It hurts too much, Nick." She stood and walked across the room. "It was like losing her all over again."

He followed her. "So don't walk away from everyone who wants to help you...love you. Let us help."

"I don't know if—". She fought the tears.

"Yes, you can, Cari. I know you won't be able to forget about me, about Danny...and about the baby you may be carrying."

Cari jerked her head up. Her heart was pounding like crazy. "What are you talking about?"

Nick stepped closer. "Cari, when we made love less than an hour ago, I didn't use any protection. I didn't use anything Christmas Eve, either."

Cari thought he looked a little too proud of himself.

"I guess we got so wrapped up in each other we didn't think about it...or maybe we wanted to forget."

Cari's trembling hand went to her stomach. "A baby...."

Nick smiled as his hand covered hers. "Our baby, Cari. You can't imagine how hard I'm praying I made you pregnant."

She began to tremble, afraid to hope. "But I thought you didn't want to chance—"

Nick pulled her against him. "You made me want it, Cari. Your love taught me not to be afraid anymore. Remember yesterday when you gave me the camera?"

She nodded. "Yes."

"You said it was for tomorrow's memories. I believed you, Cari. I know you had your daughter for only a short time, but you'll always cherish her memory. She will be kept alive in your heart. Let me share those memories with you, Cari." His eyes held hers pleadingly. He was not going to lose her. "And we'll make more memories...with Danny and any other children we're lucky enough to be blessed with."

She started to pull away, but Nick refused to let her go. "No, Cari. I won't let you give up on us. I love you too much."

"But what if—"

Nick placed his finger over her lips. "There will always be what ifs. But I'll be there for you. We can get through anything together as long as we love each other. Tell me you believe that."

Did she trust Nick enough to believe in what he was saying? Cari stared at him in confusion, then slowly it began to sink in. He was promising to be there for her...to love her no matter what. To share her joy, her sorrow. Suddenly it was all she needed. Nick's love. That alone made her believe that anything was possible.

"I believe," she whispered as her arms circled his neck. "Oh, Nick, I believe you."

"Thank God!" His mouth closed over hers in a kiss that left no traces of doubt.

Never in Cari's life had she had the luxury of someone to depend on, a pair of strong shoulders to lean on.

Now she even had a heart to share.

Epilogue

Cari stared down at her six-week-old son, Matthew Thorton Malone, as he nursed contentedly in her arms. "You're so beautiful," she whispered.

"Boys aren't supposed to be beautiful."

Cari looked up to find Nick at the nursery door. Smiling, he walked across the plush blue carpet. He bent down and kissed his wife on the lips, then placed a gentle kiss on his new son's head. "The little guy is pretty handsome, though." His gaze returned to her. "But it's his mother who takes my breath away."

"Sure." She looked doubtful. "I'm still ten pounds overweight and I need my hair trimmed." She swung her ponytail back and forth to prove the lack of attention. "My face hasn't seen makeup since I went into labor."

"You don't need makeup." His hand cupped one of her full breasts and Cari felt a shiver run down her spine. "I think these are responsible for the extra weight."

Nick crouched down beside his wife, who was seated in the rocker. "Matt here is greedy enough to need it all. My boy is a hardy eater." He glanced at his wife. "And you were beautiful when you were pregnant." His eyes darkened with desire. "Thank you."

Cari didn't have to ask what her husband was thanking her for, she already knew. "Well, we've been married less than three years, and I've been in this condition twice," she said complainingly, but in all honesty she had loved being pregnant. Their two-and-a-half-year-old daughter had been conceived that special Christmas Eve. Kristin Eleanor had arrived on September 24, healthy and happy. Their son Matt was also born perfect. "You've hardly known me any other way."

"Well, we do make beautiful babies." Nick beamed at his wife. "But it's going to be nice not to have anything between us when we make love." He raised an eyebrow. "Speaking of which, when is your doctor's appointment?"

"I went this morning while you were at the office." She glanced away shyly. She'd planned to surprise him later.

"Why didn't you tell me?" He looked hurt. "I would have gone with you."

"You had a meeting, and it felt good to get out by myself."

"Are you saying I'm crowding you?"

She wiggled her eyebrows. "Wait until tonight, and I'll show you crowding." She leaned forward and kissed him, but it was cut short when Matt started to squirm in her arms. "Tonight," she promised as she put the baby against her shoulder and patted his back.

Suddenly a familiar shrieking erupted from the other room. Then the sound of little feet coming down the hall.

"Mommy! Daddy!" Their little daughter raced into the room. "Danny's gonna skin me 'live."

Krissy's blond ponytail was already cockeyed and missing her ribbon and it was only one o'clock in the afternoon. She had light coloring and large blue eyes like her sister, Angel, and sometimes Cari was amazed at the resemblance. Then at other times her daughter would get a stubborn set to her jaw and she looked just like her dad and brother.

"Danny isn't going to touch you." Nick picked up Krissy.

Cari knew better than to believe her daughter's accusations until talking with Danny. Just then he came into the room.

"Where is that little rat?" Danny glared at his sister, who was cuddled protectively in his father's arms.

"Danny, you leave your sister alone," Nick ordered. "She's just a baby."

Krissy raised her head from her father's shoulder. "Not a baby anymore." She pointed to her new brother. "Matt is a baby."

"That's fine, Krissy. But Danny shouldn't call you names."

Big brother was still fuming. Danny was almost eight years old, and his two front teeth had finally come in, turning him from a cute little boy into a handsome young man. Most fortunate had been the fact that for the past three years he'd been relatively healthy. A year ago, Danny had had some problems with rejection, but Matt Landers had changed his medication and he'd been fine. And since starting kindergarten in the private school that Nick had selected in the area, their son had only missed a handful of school days.

"Dad, you've got to keep Krissy out of my room. I caught her playing with my computer."

"Krissy, you know better."

The little girl batted her eyelashes and produced a few tears. "I'm sorry, Daddy."

Cari had to bite her lower lip to keep from smiling.

What amazed her was that her husband and Danny fell for this ploy.

"But, Dad. She erased the project Jason and I have been working on and she even wiped out that new program you made me."

Nick had never been able to discipline his little girl, but Cari had warned him that things would soon become out of control if he didn't take the upper hand. "Okay, young lady, I think you should go to your room and sit there for the next hour." He set her down.

She looked up at him with soulful eyes. "In the corner?"

Nick nodded, hoping she wouldn't start crying. He couldn't stand it when she cried.

"'Kay," Krissy said as she started out of the room. She turned around. "Do I hafta stay by myself?"

Nick nodded again and glanced at his wife rocking the baby. She was expecting him to give in. He folded his arms over his chest. Well, he wasn't going to this time.

"But I get scared all alone." Krissy's lips trembled.

"Okay, you can leave the door open." Nick knew he was spoiling her, but seeing the smile on his little girl's face, he didn't care.

Krissy walked out, her ponytail swinging back and forth as if she knew she was the queen of the Malone household.

"Dad," Danny began, "that's not a punishment. She'll be back in my room tomorrow."

"Well, maybe it's time to get her a computer of her own. Yeah, I'll do that. I'll make her some simple programs and games. Then she won't want to mess with yours, son."

Danny didn't look convinced, but Nick knew how much he loved his sister and would go along with the plan. "Why don't you go and tell her?"

"I can't. I'm going to Jason's house. It's the last day of summer vacation."

Cari got up. "That's right, Danny. School starts tomorrow. Aren't you excited?'' She put a sleeping Matt in the crib.

Danny shrugged. "It's no big deal."

"Well, I'll make sure to be ready on time to take you."

"Oh, that's okay, Mom. You just had a baby." He looked away. "Maybe I could go by myself."

Cari felt a piercing in her heart. Last year, Tory had agreed to let Cari adopt Danny. But she had become more than his legal mother; she truly loved the boy as if she had given birth to him. She remembered how excited she had been at Danny's first day of kindergarten, when he had gone around introducing her as his new mom. Now he didn't need her to take him to the first day of school.

"Well, if you think that would be best."

Danny nodded. "I'm in second grade now. Jason and I want to go to our class together."

Second grade wasn't that old. "If that's what you want."

"Cool, gotta go." He gave her a kiss and a hug. "Bye, Mom, Dad. Jason's mom will bring me home in time for dinner." He ran out of the room.

Cari bit back her tears as she felt her husband's arm come around her. "It's okay, Cari. He hasn't stop loving you. He's just striving for his independence." He kissed her.

"It still hurts."

"I believe we argued for the firsts two months of our relationship because I wouldn't stop overprotecting my son."

"I liked taking him to school on his first day. I'm very proud of him." A tear fell.

"There will be other firsts with our son, Cari. His first baseball game...his first fight...first love...."

Cari looked up at the husband she loved so dearly. For the past three years, she had been trying to convince him to take each day as a gift and treasure it. Nick had. He had gone back to the support meetings. She knew how hard it had been for him to open up to the other parents, but he did, and he confessed his fears and hopes for his child. But he also realized that to love was to let go. And he let go so Danny could have a normal life.

Cari turned to the baby pictures lining the nursery wall. Angel's photo was in the first spot. It had taken Cari a long time to let go and to say goodbye to her daughter. But Nick helped her, just being there for her. And with Matt's assistance, they had located another one of Angel's organ recipients. A little girl was now living a normal, healthy life, thanks to a liver transplant. Cari had thanked her kind, loving husband for understanding her need.

Nick in turn had thanked her for the precious gifts she had given him and also promised her that Angel would never be forgotten. That every child God blessed them with would know about their special older sister. So would everyone else. The new research section of the cardiac wing at Riverhaven had been dedicated in the name of Angel Hallen and was now affectionately known as Angel's Wing.

Cari rose up on her toes and placed a kiss on his mouth. "I love you, Mr. Malone."

"I love you, too, Mrs. Malone." Gathering her in his arms, he bent his head and kissed her, making it obvious what he wanted from her. He tore his mouth away and rested his forehead against hers. "Since Matt is sleeping so peacefully and Krissy is about to spend her punishment downstairs with her grandma, how about I show you just how much?"

Cari's heart raced at the thought of making love to her husband. "That's a tall order." She moved against him. "Think you're up to it?"

His silver eyes danced with mischief. "Give me a lifetime, Cari. And I promise we'll make some unforgettable memories...together."

* * * * *

COMING NEXT MONTH

THE 200% WIFE Jennifer Greene

That Special Woman!

Abby Stanford always gave everything she did 200%—particularly her job. But now she wanted the love of a good man, too. Where could she find one of those?

MAIL-ORDER MATTY Emilie Richards

Matty Stewart had a champagne celebration on her birthday and she ended up winging her way off to the Bahamas to get married and become a mother! Better still, her new husband was none other than Damon Quinn, the subject of more than one midnight fantasy!

THE EIGHT SECOND WEDDING Anne McAllister

Channing Richardson couldn't believe that his mother had found him a wife! Even the proposed bride thought it was ridiculous. So certain were they, that they agreed to spend the summer together...

A HERO'S CHILD Diana Whitney

Parenthood

Rae Hooper's love had marched off to glory a decade ago, never to return. But at ten, their child had found herself a father figure—a mysterious drifter who drew Rae just as much as he affected her daughter. *Could it be...?*

MOTHER NATURE'S HIDDEN AGENDA Kate Freiman

Lily Davis didn't plan on falling in love with a rugged single father. But Blake Sommers *was* irresistibly sexy.

SEVEN REASONS WHY Neesa Hart

She had seven reasons to accept Zack Adriano's marriage proposal; her foster sons' futures were at stake. But exactly *why* had the cynical, too-smooth lawyer asked her to marry him?